PROJECT ARMA

MASON

NYSSA KATHRYN

MASON
Copyright © 2020 Nyssa Kathryn Sitarenos

All rights reserved.

Cover by Dar Albert at Wicked Smart Designs
Edited by Kelli Collins
Proofread by Beth Attwood

❀ Created with Vellum

Falling for each other was never part of the plan...

Doctor Sage Porter has moved to Marble Falls to be the private physician for a group of men unlike any the world has ever known. But she has a second, secret reason for moving to the small town. A reason she can't share with another living soul...

Especially not the men under her care.

Mason Ross is a born guardian. Protecting his team and their families comes naturally, and he'll do anything to keep them safe —but what if the peril is less than obvious? Like the gorgeous doctor who's caught his attention. She's hiding something. And Mason is more than aware that secrets can be deadly, and sometimes the least likely threat poses the greatest danger.

Getting close is a risk; both Mason and Sage have a lot to lose... including each other, if they can't work together to survive the coming menace.

ACKNOWLEDGMENTS

Thank you to my editor, Kelli Collins, for your guidance and helping me grow as an author.

Thank you to my daughter, Sophia, for filling my days with endless love.

Thank you to my husband. You are an inspiration.

CHAPTER 1

I need you to break into Marble Protection and do something for me.

Sage Porter read and reread the text message. Indecision clawed at her insides.

Had the message come from any other person, the decision would have been easy.

No. A hundred times over, no.

Sage was not a criminal. Far from it. She was a doctor. She spent her days helping others. Not breaking into businesses.

But this message wasn't from just anyone. It was from *him*. The best friend she hadn't seen in three years. Her twin brother.

Jason.

Scrubbing her hands over her face, Sage had no idea what she was going to do. Her feet felt like they were glued to the floor. If she moved, she'd have to choose—say no to her brother or break the law.

But she couldn't choose. So there she stood, in the living room of her one-bedroom apartment, frozen in time.

It was a Tuesday evening. She'd only just returned from the labs where she'd been studying a blood sample from a very special baby. Baby Fletcher. He was special because he was differ-ent. He had different DNA from the average person.

That was what Sage should be thinking about. At this very moment she should be curled up on the couch in her baggy track pants, going over her notes.

Not considering breaking into Marble Protection, the local security and self-defense business.

Letting out a deep sigh, Sage knew she needed to make a deci-sion. And that decision had to be no. She *could not* break into Marble Protection, or anywhere for that matter.

Her fingers hovered over the keys, ready to type those exact words. But she hesitated.

Jason had never asked her for anything. It had been three years since he began working the new job and two years since he'd gone into hiding.

She missed him. Like going-to-go-crazy-if-she-didn't-see-him-soon missed him. And right now, he needed her. She couldn't say no. She physically couldn't.

Making a split-second decision, Sage slid the phone into her back pocket and moved to the bedroom. Opening the top drawer of the dresser, she reached toward the back until her fingers wrapped around a key.

It was a key she shouldn't have. It didn't belong to her and no one knew she had it. But she did. Because she'd taken it.

A week ago, Sage had visited her patient and friend, Lexie Harper. Lexie was the mother of baby Fletcher. During the visit, the other woman had left the room for a moment. The key had been sitting right there on the nightstand.

Something in her had pushed her to take it. So she had. Slipped it into her pocket like a thief.

It had been a moment of madness. And she'd sworn to herself that she would return it the next chance she got. But she hadn't.

Christ, she was a terrible friend.

Pocketing the key, Sage left the apartment and headed down

to her car before her sanity returned.

Climbing behind the wheel, she flicked her gaze from the apartment building to the road as she drove away. She'd only been living in the apartment for a week. Before that, she'd been staying at the local inn. Although if things didn't pan out well tonight, she just might be finding herself in need of another inn room. But this time, somewhere far away.

Her stay in Marble Falls was only supposed to be temporary. To take care of Lexie during the pregnancy. But after Fletcher was born, Lexie had urged her to stay. Remain Fletcher's doctor. Lexie's doctor. As well as the guys' doctor. Lexie had even offered her old apartment, which was where Sage was now living.

It hadn't taken much to convince her. She had her own reasons to stay close to the guys.

Sage tried to calm her thundering heart at the thought of them. She feared it might actually beat through her chest. The men who ran Marble Protection were former Navy SEALs.

But they were really so much more than that.

The men were genetically altered. That meant that they could move faster, hear things from incredible distances, and heal quicker than almost any species on Earth. And they were strong. Stronger than humanly possible.

So basically, if Sage was caught, she was screwed.

She had spent the last two years of her life studying their DNA. It was utterly fascinating. Like nothing else on the planet.

The eight men had been part of a government-funded training program designed to improve their physical performance and decrease recovery time.

Or so they'd thought.

In reality, Project Arma had been testing experimental drugs on the men, ultimately turning them into deadly weapons.

The entire team was fierce. Lethal. And there was no way she wanted any of them to turn against her.

There was one man in particular Sage didn't want to upset. A man whose piercing blue eyes and midnight-black hair consumed her thoughts way too often.

Mason.

A shiver coursed down her spine thinking about the sexy, six-foot-five former SEAL. There was no way she wanted to do anything to cause those heated glances he threw her way to turn into anything else.

Like anger. Disappointment.

Pulling into a parking space around the back of the building, Sage switched off the car and sat there. Her hands were ice cold and trembling as the reality of what she was here to do set in.

Grabbing the rearview mirror, Sage turned it so she could see her reflection. Yep, she looked like she felt, as frightened as a person on death row.

Calm down, Sage, you'll be fine. It will be a quick in and out.

Although, she didn't actually know if it would be a quick in and out, because she didn't know what Jason needed. She'd never asked. She had just driven down here like a crazy lady, desperate to do anything that would help her brother.

Pulling out her phone, Sage sent a quick message to Jason. It took her trembling fingers several goes to hit the right keys.

What do you need me to do at Marble Protection?

Her eyes were glued to the phone screen. Whenever she sent a message to her twin brother, she couldn't tear her gaze away. She was desperate for his responses. For any communication with him.

He didn't take long.

I need something from the office.

The office. As in, the place the guys keep all their business stuff. Likely, their private and confidential stuff.

Crap.

Shutting her eyes, Sage blew out a long breath. *Quick in and out.* Maybe if she repeated it enough times, she would start to believe it.

Climbing out of the car, Sage moved to the back door of the building. Every step sounded loud in the eerie quiet.

Slotting the key into the back door, Sage paused.

What if there was an alarm? Jeepers, she hadn't considered that possibility.

If there was an alarm, she wouldn't have the first idea how to switch it off.

Darn it. Maybe she should turn around? Surely there was another way she could help Jason. Bring him home.

Sage pulled out her phone.

I don't think I can break in, Jase. There must be another way to help you.

The response took a few seconds to come through.

Sage, I need you to do this for me.

He needed her to do this. He *needed* her. Oh, darn it to hell.

Sage looked up at the sky and said a silent prayer. A prayer for no loud beeping alarm to sound, no flashing lights, and no former SEALs running in with guns trained at her.

She didn't think that was too much to ask. Surely.

Releasing a shaky breath, Sage lowered her gaze back to the door and turned the key. Pushing the door open, she scrunched her eyes shut and waited.

Ten seconds passed, and nothing. No deafening siren, no flashing light. Just heart-pounding silence and darkness.

Good. This was good. Maybe she would actually be able to get in and out without being noticed.

Stepping inside, Sage quickly shut the door behind her. The only light came from her phone. Turning the flashlight function on, she used it to lead the way down the hall.

She'd been to Marble Protection a few times. Rooms led off from the hall that she knew were used for meetings, small group classes, and individual self-defense sessions. At the end of the hall, her gaze scanned the front desk and then the large area to the right covered in mats.

It was strange to see the place under the cloak of darkness. The few times she'd visited, there'd been noise. The hustle and bustle of the men running sessions, of people moving around. Because this wasn't just their place of work, it was the little sanctuary that they'd created.

And Sage was breaking into that sanctuary.

Pushing down the guilt, she turned to the office and moved inside. On autopilot, she reached for the light switch, only to pull her hand back.

No. The dark felt safer.

Sage quickly sent a message to Jason, letting him know she was in and again asking what he needed.

As she waited for a response, her eyes scanned the room. On the shelf to her left, she noticed a framed picture. Out of curiosity, she slowly walked over to it and lifted the frame. She shone the flashlight onto the picture and eight deadly men stared back at her. The owners of Marble Protection.

Her gaze moved over each person. When she reached the last man, her gaze held.

Mason.

Beautiful. Beautiful and rugged and powerful. He was the perfect mixture of all three. The guys called him Eagle. She assumed it was because he watched out for people. Because he was a protector. Although, she'd never been told the story behind the name.

You only had to take one look at the man to know he was a protector. He observed what went on around him, then he acted. Always looking for a threat.

At the flash of a text message on her phone, Sage started so badly that the picture slipped from her fingers. The sound of shattering glass pierced the silence.

Cursing herself for being so clumsy, she ignored the broken glass for a moment to read the message from Jason.

I need you to gather any information on the child that was born.

EIGHTEEN.

That's how many people were in AJ's Bar. Eighteen people. And Mason could hear the heartbeat of every single one of them.

Most days, he blocked it out. Most days there was too much noise and not enough silence. But tonight, he listened. Because he was on edge, and a person's heart rate told you a great deal about them. Whether they were relaxed. Happy. Scared. It gave away a lot. Almost everything.

"You look tense, Eagle."

Mason pulled his attention from the crowd to look at Kye. Better known to his team as Cage. Next to him sat their teammate Wyatt. The team called him Jobs because he was a damn genius with technology.

Both men were his business partners but felt more like brothers. Both men were as dangerous as him.

"I *am* tense."

There was no point in lying. They could spot a lie as easily as him.

Wyatt set down his beer. "It wouldn't be because of a certain blue-eyed doctor, would it?"

The reason he was tense had a *lot* to do with her. But then, there had rarely been a time in the last few months that she wasn't affecting him in some way. "Sage always has me tense."

Tonight, he wasn't just tense because he couldn't get her delectable curves out of his mind. No. Tonight, it was because less than fifteen minutes ago, the curvy doctor had received a message on her phone. A message from her brother asking her to break into Marble Protection, the business owned by him and his team.

And the only reason Mason had seen the message was because about a month ago, he'd inserted a device into her phone that forwarded to him every message she sent or received. Sage knew nothing about that, though.

Was it ethical? No. Hell no. But he didn't feel guilty about it, either. Not when the pretty doctor was keeping things from his team. Things that could be dangerous to her or them.

He'd known she was hiding something because just a few months ago, Mason, Asher, and Bodie had searched her room at the inn. They'd found a bag that she had hidden inside a cushion cover. Within the bag had been a gun, cash, a burner phone, and a photo of Sage with her twin brother, Jason.

"Damn, he's going to be the next one to get snapped up," Kye laughed.

Wyatt nodded as he lifted the beer to his lips. "That will be half the team down."

Mason continued to cradle his beer but had yet to take a drink. He wanted to have his wits about him if he needed to move. "She's our doctor. We're keeping a close eye on her. That's it."

That was it for *now*. The guys didn't need to know that every time he was in the woman's presence, it took every ounce of his willpower not to reach for her and run his hands down her body.

Christ, he was getting hard just thinking about her.

Glancing back down at his phone, Mason noticed that Sage had yet to confirm whether she was going to do as Jason asked. He honestly had no idea what she would do. He didn't think Sage was the kind of person to break and enter. What he'd learned about her so far was that she was a good person.

But Mason knew that when it came to protecting family, all bets were off.

"You still tracking her phone messages?"

Mason looked up at Kye's question. The guy had caught him checking his phone. Both men had. They'd probably caught him the last ten times he'd checked.

"I am."

The disapproving look he received wasn't new. Far from it. The whole team disagreed with Mason's actions. They wanted a more direct approach.

But Mason believed that if Sage wanted a direct approach, she would have brought up the go bag and her mysterious brother herself. There was a reason she hadn't come to them. And the last thing he wanted to do was scare the doctor out of town.

Kye's gaze didn't leave Mason's. "I still don't think that was the right decision, Eagle. It's an invasion of the woman's privacy."

"Not to mention the whole reason she moved to Marble Falls was to help us. Lexie in particular," Wyatt added.

Sage may have moved to town to help with Lexie's pregnancy, but that didn't mean there wasn't more to the story.

Mason shrugged. "I get that. But her go bag told us that there's a danger in her life. She hasn't volunteered any information to us, even though she knows we'd be able to help her. If we ask her, she could skip town. Who knows? We certainly don't know her well enough."

Kye leaned forward. "If we don't trust her, should we really be keeping her on as our doctor? As Fletcher's doctor? I mean, she's studying his DNA. If that got into the wrong hands…"

Wyatt shook his head. "We need her. At least while Fletcher's so young. The woman's a genius, and she's spent the last two years familiarizing herself with our DNA."

"And I don't think she'd do anything to hurt us. Not intentionally." Mason was almost certain of it. "She's done nothing to make us think she's our enemy."

Kye's brows pulled together. "Still no idea on the location of her brother?"

Mason's expression didn't change at the mention of Jason. He hadn't told the guys about this evening's messages between Sage and her twin. And he didn't intend to. Not yet anyway.

Wyatt shook his head, looking frustrated. "Nothing new. He

graduated from MIT, top of his class in Pharmaceutical Science, then disappeared."

Except, people don't just disappear.

Kye ran his hands through his hair. "You said Jason did a stint in the military, didn't you?"

Wyatt nodded. "In the Army. From the reports of his superiors, he was good. But he left five years in, to go to college."

And right there was the biggest red flag of all. A man with a military background, trained in pharmaceutical science, would be an asset to an organization like Project Arma.

And tonight, his message to Sage had all but confirmed he was connected in some way.

Project Arma had been uncovered and raided two years ago. Since then, very little progress had been made in locating those who worked for the corrupt program. Mason and his brothers had been hunting, but the underground organization was good at remaining hidden.

"I think she would have told us if she had a brother connected to Arma." Wyatt directed his words at Mason. Knowing exactly what he was thinking.

Mason wasn't so sure about that. Secrets lurked behind Sage's blue eyes. Secrets and fear. It was the fear that he wanted to extinguish and the secrets he wanted disclosure on.

"We don't even know if the person she's messaging is in fact her brother," Kye said. "You said yourself that the number changes regularly, all from untraceable burner phones. It could be anyone."

"It could," Mason agreed. "But Sage thinks it's him and she's smart. He must have said something to convince her of his identity at some point."

Mason's phone finally lit up from its place on the table. His gaze darted over the words.

Ah hell.

Sage had just asked Jason what he needed her to do. That had to mean she was considering doing as he asked.

Scrubbing a hand over his face, Mason waited for Jason's response.

He didn't need to wait long. Less than a minute later, the message came through.

He wanted her to do something in the office. The office where they kept not just their Marble Protection files, but a lot of the information they had on Project Arma.

Mason now blocked out the guys across from him completely. His sole focus was on the text exchange in front of him.

Both relief and regret hit Mason when Sage confirmed she wasn't going to do it. On one hand, it meant Mason wasn't going to find out what Jason wanted in the office. Not tonight at least. But it also meant Sage had made the right decision.

About to pocket the phone, he looked down when another text came through. This one had Mason pushing to his feet.

Sage, I need you to do this for me.

He couldn't see her saying no to that. He'd read the previous messages she'd sent to her brother. There was a desperation in her words. A desperation to find him. *Help* him.

"Sick of us already?" Kye asked.

Mason opened his mouth to respond but was cut off by Wyatt also jumping to his feet. "Someone just tripped the silent alarm at Marble Protection."

Kye visibly tensed. His smile dropping immediately.

"I know who it is," Mason said quickly. Both sets of eyes swung to him. "I'll handle it."

Without offering any further explanation, he turned and left the bar.

Climbing behind the wheel, he had just begun driving when the last message from Jason came through.

I need you to gather any information on the child that was born.

CHAPTER 2

$\mathcal{F}$ive minutes had passed. Or maybe ten. Sage wasn't sure. She'd spent all of those minutes just standing there. Letting the words Jason had written roll around in her mind. Sink in.

He hadn't told her why he needed the information. And it didn't seem like he planned to.

She'd asked. Once she'd gotten over the shock, her fingers had flown over her cell. She hadn't been able to ask quick enough. But, so far, nothing. No message. No words of explanation. Sage was left standing there, in a place she wasn't meant to be, reading a message asking her to do something she couldn't.

Dropping her head into her hand, Sage let out a long sigh. What the heck was she doing? She should have said no to Jason the moment his first text came through.

If Jason needed her, she would help him, but next time, she would be drawing the line at anything that went against her ethics. Or any action that could land her in a jail cell.

Her attention drew back to the shattered glass. Before she left, she needed to tidy the mess and pray that she could sneak out without leaving a trace. She would take the frame and have it fixed. Cross her fingers that no one noticed it missing in the meantime.

Turning, Sage was about to search for a dustpan when her flashlight landed on shoes.

Large shoes, connected to legs standing close.

When her muddled brain caught up to the fact that there was a living, breathing human standing directly in front of her, she let out a loud gasp before taking a hurried step back. The crunch of glass beneath her shoes had her attempting to lift her feet too quickly and losing balance.

The phone dropped from her fingers, throwing the room into darkness. She would have toppled over and fallen directly on the glass had she not been saved by hands on her upper arms.

They immediately pulled her upright so that her body was pressed to his. The hands were firm and strong, but gentle.

She held her breath, almost too scared to breathe for the way her breasts pressed against his big chest. Heat radiated off him. And he smelled good. Really good. Musky and woodsy.

Slowly, big hands trailed from her upper arms to her waist. His hands were so large, they seemed to encompass her entire middle.

She should be scared. But she didn't feel any fear. She felt something else. Something she couldn't quite define.

Her hands went to his chest. But instead of pushing him away, like any normal person would do, Sage glided her fingers over muscular ridges.

Like they had a mind of their own, her hands kept exploring. Rising to his shoulders, where she felt their thickness. He was hard all over.

Slowly, her hands slid to his biceps. They were huge. But then, everything about the man felt huge.

Just then, the hand on her waist tightened. At the same time, she felt a thumb shift to the underside of her shirt, touching her bare skin.

That was enough to pull her out of the trance. He could be anyone. And he was touching her. His body was pressed firmly against hers.

Fear replaced any desire that had begun to build. Her heart sped up.

As if sensing her fear, the stranger immediately dropped his hands from her body. He took a step back, giving her the space she needed.

Only, once she had that space, she didn't know whether she felt relieved or bereft.

Suddenly, the lights in the room flicked on, and for a moment she was blinded by the brightness.

Holy hell, it felt like she was looking directly at the sun.

Scrunching her eyes shut, Sage had to blink a few times before she could make out the large blurry figure by the switch.

He'd moved fast. One second he'd been touching her, the next he was across the room. And he hadn't made a sound. Not that it should surprise her. She hadn't heard the guy enter the building and walk right behind her.

Slowly, the fuzziness began to fade, and she realized the man wasn't a stranger at all. She'd recognize those piercing blue eyes anywhere.

Mason. The man who sent hot flashes through her system and made her heart thunder whenever he was close.

She said the first thing that popped into her head. "What are you doing here?"

She'd spoken the words quietly, but in the silence of the night, they sounded loud. Deafeningly so.

Mason took a step forward. "This is my business, Sage. Why don't you tell me what *you're* doing here?"

His voice was hard and carried an edge of danger.

A shiver coursed down Sage's spine.

For the third time tonight, she found herself at a loss on what to do. She hadn't told Mason about Jason. She hadn't told anyone about her brother. Not only because Jason had asked her to keep their communication a secret, but also because she feared the day Mason or his team found out who her brother had worked for.

Mason continued to watch her. Panic began to build in her chest.

Think, Sage, think.

She needed a plausible reason as to why she was here, and she needed it fast. Preferably, a reason that didn't end with her being locked in a jail cell. Or worse.

Mason took another step forward, shrinking the space between them. "I can see the wheels turning behind those pretty blue eyes. Just tell me the truth."

The truth? That she'd blindly followed a request from her long-lost twin before she'd come to her senses? That just for a moment she'd considered stealing?

No. Sage would not be sharing that. She didn't know Mason well enough to share any of it with him. And even if she did know him, she still wasn't sure she'd tell him.

"I wanted to read over some of the Project Arma files you have. I just got home from the labs. I was studying Fletcher's bloodwork. It got me curious as to whether any of your info on Arma would tell me something I didn't know."

Something flashed across Mason's face. Disappointment maybe? Before she could question it, it was gone. "Is that the truth?"

He took more steps forward. She had to tip her head back to look the big man in the eye. She was sure that if she stretched her arm out, she would be touching him.

This close, his size was emphasized. His height, his width, everything about him was huge. And all hard muscle.

"Yes."

As soon as she saw the flash of disappointment reappear on his face, a wave of remorse washed over her. She wanted to tell Mason the truth. Let him help Jason with her.

But fear rendered her silent. She just couldn't risk Jason's life. Not for anyone.

Mason stretched out his arm. Unsure of his intention, Sage held her breath. His finger brushed her skin as he pushed a loose strand of hair behind her ear. "You're not wearing your glasses."

That was not what she had expected Mason to say. Although, she didn't know the man well enough to presume to know *anything* he would say.

And his touch was making her skin break out in goosebumps. It was not helping her already sluggish thought process.

"They're reading glasses. I only use them when I'm working." The moment the statement left her lips, she realized her mistake. If she was here to look over files, she would have brought her glasses. "I mean, I forgot to grab them."

Jeez, the guy was going to have her cuffed and in a cell within the hour.

Rather than appear angry, Mason trailed his fingers down her face, then her arm. "You must have been in a rush."

Swallowing, she tried to ignore the heat that began to build inside her at his touch. "I was."

Was it her, or was Mason closer to her again?

"You strike me as a methodical person." Mason's hand touched her waist, just like before. Only now that she knew it was him, she felt ten times more turned on by it. Heat transferred from his hand right through her clothing to her skin. "How did you get in?"

"I have a key." The words slipped out of her mouth. Her brain was too muddled to censor them.

"Who gave you a key?"

No one. But Mason would already know that.

Sage needed to get out. Before she said something she shouldn't. She'd already said more than she'd wanted to.

The ability to think was diminishing with every passing

moment. With every touch. There was no way she could stand here and not let more secrets slip.

Eyeing the door, Sage weighed her chances of escape.

"No chance."

So, not only was the man sexy as hell, he was also a mind reader.

His head lowered until his mouth hovered just over her left ear. "Who gave you the key, Sage?"

Mason's breath brushed against her sensitive skin. She opened her mouth to respond but it took a few goes before she produced words. "No one. I took it."

Sage expected some sort of backlash. Or at least for Mason to step away. Instead, his other hand lifted and pressed to Sage's back.

"You stole Lexie's key."

It wasn't a question, rather a statement. Yep, it was confirmed. The man was a mind reader.

"How did you—"

"She lost it not long ago."

Sage scrambled to come up with a plausible reason for taking the key. But there was none. At least none that she could think of with his hands on her. "I just saw it one day and took it."

Another truth in the long line that she was spewing.

She lifted her hands to Mason's chest. She had no idea where any of this would lead. She should have listened to her gut that told her—no, screamed at her—to stay home tonight. If she had, she wouldn't currently be breathing in Mason's intoxicating scent, wondering whether he was going to turn her over to the police or push her against the desk and kiss her.

Thoughts of the latter made her heart speed up.

"You don't look like you feel very guilty about what you've done."

"I'm finding it hard to think about anything other than your body pressed up against mine right now."

A knowing smile pulled at his lips. He looked happy with her response. Then his head lowered. His mouth hovered over hers.

Oh crap, if his lips touched hers, she was a goner.

"Do you know how long I've wanted to taste you?"

Taste her? "No."

"Too long."

Every limb of her body was oversensitive. She couldn't remember when this conversation had shifted from being an interrogation to a seduction. Or at least feeling like a seduction.

All she was sure of was that she didn't want him to take his hands off her.

Sage could count on one hand the number of men she'd kissed in her life. But somehow, she knew that none of those kisses would come close to one from Mason.

A moment of courage hit Sage. Or maybe it was stupidity, she wasn't sure. "Do it."

Holy jam on a cracker. Had she really just said that?

Mason's eyes immediately heated. He paused, and it was almost like he was giving her time to back out. Move away. But her body remained still. Waiting.

Finally, his lips touched hers.

The outside world faded, and the room went oddly quiet.

At first the kiss was soft. Gentle. The lightest of touches. Mason was exploring Sage.

Then his tongue slipped inside her mouth. It was intoxicating. A moan of pleasure released from her lips.

Mason's arms lifted her body against him. Immediately, her legs wrapped around his waist. Her hands lifted to his head.

She ran her fingers through his hair. It was cropped short and soft to the touch.

As they continued to taste each other, a desperate yearning filled Sage. A yearning that she hadn't felt before. That she didn't know existed.

Every inch of her front was pressed to his. Still, she tightened her legs, attempting to bring their bodies closer together.

Suddenly, Mason began to withdraw. His lips pulled away from hers as his head lifted.

A small gasp of protest escaped her lips. There was no part of her that wanted to separate from him.

"Sage..." Mason ground out her name. His voice raw. Guttural. "We need to stop."

Breathing deeply, Sage gave her galloping heart a moment to slow.

Nobody had ever kissed her like that before. Not a single person.

She had been right. A kiss from him made all other kisses fade into insignificance.

"I knew you'd taste sweet. Like strawberries," Mason murmured.

Her eyes reluctantly fluttered open and reality began to creep back in. Glancing down, she was reminded of the fact that she was currently wrapped up in Mason's arms, his hands firmly on her backside.

And she had just been kissing him. Kissing the heck out of him. Mason. A man she barely knew.

Averting her eyes, Sage felt heat fill her cheeks. But this time for a different reason than earlier.

She was mortified.

"I need to go."

Sage attempted to push against his big chest. But the man didn't let her go.

Forcing her eyes up, she saw Mason studying her. Searching. For what exactly, she wasn't sure. Did he see embarrassment in her expression? Because that was all she felt.

Eventually, Mason lowered Sage to the floor. "Okay."

She almost thought she'd heard wrong. "Okay?"

Already turning to the door, Mason spoke over his shoulder. "I'll walk you to your car."

He was just going to let her go? Just like that?

Sage's moment of confusion rendered her still. It wasn't until Mason had disappeared into the hallway that her feet were moving. Chasing after him, it took her a moment to catch up to his long strides. "You're just going to let me go? After I broke in?"

"Yes."

One word. That was all Sage got.

Mason pushed outside, then proceeded to hold the door open for her. She squeezed through, not wanting to touch him. Not after the way her body had reacted to him moments ago.

He remained beside her as they walked to her car. Unlocking the door, Sage was about to climb in but suddenly turned. "I'm sorry."

"Apology accepted."

Okay. Sage was confused. Beyond confused. She felt like she was in a twilight zone. He was acting like what she'd done was no big deal. And like they hadn't just kissed with her entire body pressed against his.

Reaching into her back pocket, she pulled out the key and handed it to him. "I know I have no right to ask this, but if you could keep this from Lexie, I would really appreciate it."

"Done." Then he took the key and dropped it into his own pocket.

Sage opened and closed her mouth before deciding a nod would suffice. She doubted there were any words she could say that would gain her the clarity she was after.

Climbing into her car, she was pulling the door shut when it suddenly stopped moving.

Mason lowered his head so he was eye level with her. "Stay safe."

Then he closed the door and walked away.

CHAPTER 3

*M*ason turned the key over in his hand. The key that Sage had used to get in last night.

Damn, even thinking about what happened in this room had Mason feeling hot and bothered. Her silky-smooth curves and soft moans were etched into his memory and he couldn't get them out.

Not that he wanted to.

"So her brother wanted information on Fletcher?" Wyatt asked, pulling Mason's attention back to the present.

Wyatt was seated across the table from him while Asher sat next to Wyatt, looking stiff as a board. Bodie sat beside Mason. All three sets of eyes were trained on him, looking for answers.

"He did."

A moment of silence followed before Bodie broke it. "What did you say to her when you caught her here?"

Mason couldn't help but shift his gaze to the spot in the room where he'd kissed her. Not just kissed; he'd been moments away from stripping her bare and making love to her right there and then. And he had a feeling he wouldn't have regretted it.

"I asked her what she was doing here. She told me she wanted to read any information we keep on Project Arma and compare it to her notes on Fletcher. She didn't volunteer any information about her brother or the messages. I didn't let her know what I knew. Then she went home."

That was the very short and condensed version of the story. The only version the guys were getting.

"You just let her go?" Asher asked, clearly agitated. "After she broke in with the intention of taking information?"

Asher's eyes were spitting fire. Mason didn't blame him. This involved his family, and he didn't mess around when it came to Lexie or Fletcher. None of them did.

"Sage already has all the information on Fletcher. Hell, she's his doctor, she gave the information to *us*. Besides that, I have a feeling she followed her brother's request on impulse but regretted it once she got here. Regardless of what he asked her to do, I think she was going to leave. I don't think she would have done anything to hurt us or our company."

Mason was almost a hundred percent certain of that. Besides the fact that he saw nothing but kindness in her, she was also very careful about what she told her brother. She wrote to him about her work without telling him about Fletcher.

Which raised the question of how Jason even knew about Asher's son.

Asher didn't appear so convinced. It was a complete three-sixty from any other time he'd spoken about Sage. The man was usually her biggest advocate. She'd cared for Lexie throughout her pregnancy, and then both Lexie and Fletcher after the birth.

"Sage isn't the problem," Mason continued. "Jason is. Before last night, they'd never messaged about Project Arma or Fletcher. There is the possibility they'd spoken about one or both before I started watching their exchanges, but it would be strange that it hadn't come up again. It's more likely that he's working with them."

Wyatt began tapping his pen on the table, a habit he did when he was thinking. "Has there been communication between Sage and Jason today?"

Mason had been watching his phone closely all morning. "They've been back and forth messaging. Sage keeps asking why he needs the files, while Jason wants to know if she got them. Neither of them has answered the other's question."

"We need to work out where the hell this guy is," Asher ground out, scrubbing his face.

"We could ask her?" Wyatt suggested.

"I don't think she knows." Mason wasn't a hundred percent certain, but nothing in their exchanges eluding to her knowing his location. "From what I've picked up, he gives her very little information about himself, while she tells him a lot."

Bodie leaned forward. "But she doesn't tell him about us?"

"Not in so many words. She never mentions our names or what we can do but she talks about her job in a general way."

Wyatt frowned. "Maybe it's time we watch her a bit closer. You never know when this brother might pop up in person, if it's even him who's messaging her. We can put someone on her. Watch her movement. I can put together a schedule."

Mason tensed at the idea of any guy watching her other than him. He knew he had no claim over her, but hell, he wanted to. Every time he saw the woman, he wanted her more. Last night, having her in his arms, had confirmed it.

He shook his head. "No need for a schedule. I've got it."

Wyatt didn't argue. "Okay. And maybe have a chat with her. You don't need to mention her brother. Just have a conversation and ask her if everything is okay."

"Done."

Any excuse to spend more time with her was fine with him.

"She's coming in today, isn't she?" Bodie asked.

Wyatt nodded. "She is. She's taking some blood from us. Comparing it to our last samples. She should be here any minute."

Asher pushed his chair back and stood. "I'm not sure I trust her anymore. If you guys are okay having her around us, then fine. But she's not going around my family, at least not until we have more information. I'll call her for an emergency as a last resort, but that's it."

Mason stood so he could look the man in the eye. "I get where you're coming from. And I understand you needing to protect your family. I maintain that Sage isn't a threat to us and that keeping her close is for the best. Even if she was a threat, there isn't much she could learn that she doesn't already know."

"Are you a hundred percent certain she's safe to us, Eagle?"

An air of danger filled the room.

Mason knew what his friend was asking. "Your family is my family. And I'm certain they're safe."

Asher studied Mason for another moment before speaking. "You need to be right on this one."

He watched Asher's retreating form. Mason *was* right on this one. He could feel it with every fiber of his being.

～

Sage sprayed some sanitizer onto her hands as she listened to the door close behind Bodie.

Turning to her phone, she saw another message from Jason pop up. A week ago she couldn't get a word out of the guy, but in the last twelve hours he wouldn't leave her alone.

Every message was the same—did she get the information? And every response from Sage was her asking why he needed it. It was like a game of Ping-Pong where the winner was the first to get an answer.

Besides the fact that she hadn't told her brother about Fletcher, she also hadn't told him that the men she was working for were part of Project Arma.

He'd been on the run for two years. Yes, he would be keeping a close eye on Project Arma to ensure he remained safe, but how would he have accessed information about Fletcher? About Marble Protection? She doubted that information was easily accessible.

They were questions only Jason could answer. But so far, he hadn't answered anything.

Ignoring the message, Sage turned back to her equipment. She had been taking blood for the last half hour and had only two men left—Asher and Mason.

When Sage had arrived at Marble Protection, she had been nervous. No, scratch that, she had been scared out of her mind. Scared that the other seven men had been told that she'd broken into their business and would come down on her hard.

That's why, the moment Sage had stepped foot inside the building, she had rushed down the hall and set up in the back room, effectively avoiding any and all eye contact. She'd probably looked like a crazy lady.

Once in the safety of an empty room, Sage had taken the few minutes alone to set up and calm herself. That was all she'd been given. Because exactly three minutes later, Luca had walked in. Only he hadn't been hostile. Or threatening or unkind. He'd just been normal Luca.

At one point, he'd even cracked a joke. The joke was in no way funny, but it had been a joke all the same.

After taking blood from a few more guys, she'd realized that not one of them was acting any differently.

Was it possible that Mason hadn't said anything? Maybe he hadn't been able to get their kiss out of his head so had forgotten to inform his team.

Ha. Yeah right. If that wasn't the most deluded, imaginative idea, Sage didn't know what was.

She was pretty sure it was just *her* who had been left breathless and unable to think of little else.

Shaking her head, Sage prepared for the next patient.

When she'd gotten home last night, she had barely remembered that she'd broken into a place of business. Mason and his soft lips had been all she could think about. The feel of his hands on her waist, his mouth on hers.

Maybe Mason would be the next patient? Her heart rate went up a notch at the thought of touching him again, even if it was for purely medical reasons.

Sage didn't have to wonder long. A moment later, the door opened. But it wasn't Mason who walked through. It was Asher. An Asher who looked far from his normal, jovial self.

Without a word, he walked straight to the seat in front of Sage and rolled up his sleeve.

No smile. No hi. Nothing.

She swallowed to try to alleviate the sudden dryness in her throat. Lifting an alcohol swab, she wiped Asher's arm. "How are you doing today, Asher?"

"Not too great, actually. Got some bad news this morning."

Her hand was midway to the trash can when his words caused her to pause. Had he found out she'd stole Lexie's key? That she'd used it to break into his business?

Rather than immediately responding, she took the blood sample from him in silence. No way could she focus on her job and him at the same time. Not if she wanted to do her job well.

She moved to store the blood, ensuring she'd done everything she needed to do before turning back to Asher.

He was stiff. And his face may as well have been carved from stone, it was so hard.

She'd never seen this side to him before and was unsure how to approach the situation.

"If that bad news had anything to do with me"—*or everything to do with me*—"I'm sorry."

Wish I had a time machine and could go back to never taking Lexie's key, sorry.

Asher studied Sage. The intensity of his glare made her want to shrink back and hide behind the closest big object. Either that or run from the room as fast as her short legs would allow her.

But she didn't. Instead, she stood there and met his gaze. Waited to hear what he said next.

"Tell me something—can we trust you?"

Can they trust her? With their medical needs? If that was what he was asking, then the answer was yes. Always yes.

"Of course."

She meant to say those two words firmly. With clarity and confidence. Instead, they sounded weak, even to her ears.

Asher pushed out of the chair and stood in front of her. He was close. As close as Mason had stood the previous night. Only, where Mason had looked at her with desire, Asher looked at her like she was an enemy. An enemy he needed to extinguish.

"There's something you should know about me, Sage. There's not a single thing I wouldn't do to protect my family."

Her skin chilled. He suddenly seemed incredibly large. All the men at Marble Protection were, but she had never felt intimidated by it. Until this moment.

Opening her mouth to speak, she stopped at the sound of the door opening.

"Striker."

Mason. Would it be childish if she ran and hid behind him? Because that was exactly what she wanted to do.

It took him less than a second to get to her. For her to feel the heat radiating off his body. It went a long way toward calming her frazzled nerves.

"You're done here, Striker."

Asher didn't immediately acknowledge Mason's words. Silence stretched as his gaze remained narrowed on her. But finally, he turned.

Air whooshed out of her lungs when his eyes released her. He moved to the door and pulled it open. But before he could step through, she finally found her voice. "I would never hurt your family, Asher. And I'm sorry if I did anything to make you think I would."

He paused, then he disappeared into the hall without saying a word.

Did he think she was a threat now? Because she'd broken into their business? Why did he think she would harm his family? Because that's where his focus had been. The safety of Lexie and Fletcher.

Mason's hand on her shoulder jolted Sage from her thoughts. There was concern in his eyes.

"You okay?" Mason's voice was gentle. Tender.

Yes. Yes, she was okay. Angry at herself for her actions the previous night. But okay.

Shaking her head to clear it, Sage took a step back, causing Mason's hand to drop from her body. "Of course. Would you like to take a seat while I get things ready?"

Turning toward her medical supplies, she got the syringe ready. Her heart was still beating too fast. But in time, it would slow.

Sucking in a few slow breaths, she turned toward Mason with syringe in hand.

His gaze was on her face. Exploring her features. She didn't want the man to see that Asher's behavior affected her.

But it had. Not just because he'd towered over her and basically threatened her, but also because it was almost like Asher knew what she had really been doing here last night.

Which was impossible. Wasn't it?

Touching Mason's arm as she searched for a vein, she let his warm skin ease the tension in her body.

Once she'd taken the sample, Sage turned to store the blood.

"I'm sorry."

Mason's words cut through the silence, jolting Sage. The vial of blood that had been in her hand slipped from her fingers.

Shutting her eyes, she waited to hear the glass shatter. But it didn't.

Her eyes flicked open to find Mason holding the vial in front of her.

Jeepers, he was quick. Sometimes she forgot just *how* quick they were.

"Thank you, I almost cost you more blood."

"You're welcome, sweetheart. And I'm sorry about Striker. He knows you took Lexie's key. I told him you didn't mean anything by last night. He's just protective of his family."

Glancing up at Mason, way up, Sage shrugged her shoulders. "I don't blame him. I shouldn't have done it. Any of it."

Mason lifted his hand and stroked from her shoulder down her arm. A trail of goose bumps followed in his path. "Your actions last night had their benefits."

Was the man flirting with her? Sage didn't know the first thing about flirting. Especially not when it involved a tall, dark, and handsome man.

"Nothing to say, Dr. Porter?"

No. Because anything she did say would likely be wrong. Or awkward. Or a combination of both.

Clearing her throat, she took a step back. "Thank you for your help, Mason. I should get these blood samples to the lab."

Turning, she began packing her equipment into a bag. Despite her dismissal, she was sure he hadn't moved an inch.

About to throw the bag over her shoulder, she found it quickly taken from her fingers.

"I'll walk you out."

Before she could argue, he was already through the door.

That was the second time he'd done that in two days.

Sage jogged through the building to catch up with him. By that stage, they were already outside by her car.

Mason stopped by the door of her Honda. "Is it okay if I pop over to your apartment tomorrow?"

Her eyes widened. "What for?"

Mason shrugged. "Just to chat."

Chat? About what? Last night?

"Sure." The word slipped from Sage's lips. What else could she say? No? She refused to have a chat with the sexy man in the privacy of her apartment where anything could happen? "I finish work at one."

"I'll be there half past."

Handing the bag to her, he gave her a lopsided smile before turning and walking back inside.

Sage stood and watched him for a moment. Even though he wore a shirt, she could see the ripple of muscle beneath the material. Pair that with his powerful legs, and the man was sexy as sin. At the very least, he was the sexiest man she'd ever laid eyes on.

Shaking her head, Sage forced her eyes back to the car.

Get a grip, Sage. One kiss does not mean he wants to jump your bones.

Sticking her hand into her bag to search for her car key, Sage paused when a beep sounded from her phone.

Huffing out a breath, she pulled out the phone and read the message. More of the same questions from Jason, and again, no answers.

Sage climbed behind the wheel. She wanted to help Jason, she really did, but there was no way she could betray the guys. She also couldn't let any of Fletcher's medical information get into the wrong hands.

The fact that Jason was asking weighed on her. The brother she knew was a good man. Was it possible he'd changed?

That thought was too painful to consider right now.

Blowing out a long breath, Sage finally responded.

I want to help you, but the guys don't have any medical files on any babies. So please stop asking.

Once the message was sent, she tucked her phone into her bag and began driving home. She didn't want to think about it anymore. She just wanted to see her brother. Hear his voice.

Two years ago, Jason had left a voice mail on her phone telling her he was leaving. That he was going into hiding from Project Arma. He planned to keep in touch with her by sending messages whenever he could, changing burner phones frequently.

Sage had saved that message and she listened to it often. Hearing her brother's familiar voice was calming. Maybe she would listen to it tonight.

It might dim the whispers in her head that kept trying to remind her that two years had passed, and a lot could happen in that time.

CHAPTER 4

*S*age turned her Honda onto her street. Her shift at the hospital had run late and then she'd gotten caught in a conversation with a coworker. It was one of those chats that you just couldn't get out of no matter how hard you tried.

Now she had exactly ten minutes until it hit half past one. Ten minutes to have the quickest shower of her life and raid her closet for something half decent to wear.

Pulling into a parking spot out front of her building, she jumped out of the car and jogged to the door. Her apartment was on the third floor and she spent the entire time cursing her short legs for slowing her down.

Not that she could place all the blame on her height, or lack thereof. There were plenty of short quick people in the world. But Sage didn't exactly make fitness a priority. She was by no means overweight, but she was soft. Curvy. Sure, having some more definition in her body would be nice, but when she wasn't working, she was reading. And that reading was usually work related.

Reaching her door, she unlocked it and rushed through to her bedroom. Hastily dropping her bag beside the bed, Sage was about to move to the bathroom when she stopped short. A light breeze catching her attention.

Shifting her gaze, Sage saw the reason immediately.

The window beside her bed was open. Not cracked open. All-the-way-to-the-top open.

The blood rushed from her head. There was no way she would have left it that way. Only a few months ago, she had returned to her room at the inn to find her window left open. It had freaked her out. So much so that she now triple-checked that all windows were closed and locked before leaving.

Without moving her feet, she scanned the room. For the first time, she noticed what she had missed in her haste.

Chaos.

Every drawer to her dresser was open and the contents were strewn across the floor. Her jewelry box had been smashed, splinters of wood covering the carpet. Even her pillows had been slashed down the middle.

Her hands became cold and clammy.

Someone had been in her apartment and they'd gone through every inch of her space.

She had to get out. Away. Be anywhere but in this room.

Taking a step back, she collided with something hard. Before Sage could turn, an arm came across her neck, cutting off her air supply.

For a few seconds, she didn't move. Shock and fear rendering her still. Then her lungs began to rebel, screaming at her for air. Grabbing the punishing arm around her neck, she dug her fingers into the skin and used all her strength to try to pull it away.

Her efforts were futile. If anything, the man's grip tightened. His strength was overwhelming.

Then her body was flung to the floor and her shoulder hit the nightstand painfully. Air whooshed into Sage's lungs and she greedily sucked it in. Moving her hand to her neck, she blinked away the cloudy vision.

Fixated on the air traveling through her starved lungs, she realized too late the man had moved over her. Grabbing her wrists, he forced them above her head before immediately transferring them to one hand. The free hand disappeared for a moment before returning with a knife.

When he pushed the knife to Sage's throat, her breathing stopped. The sharpness of the blade mixed with the coldness of the metal had her terror escalating.

Then she noticed something else. The man wasn't wearing a mask. He was letting her see every inch of his face. From his sandy-blond hair down to his sharp jawline.

People only assaulted someone without a mask for one of two reasons. Either they intended to kill their victim or take them.

A whimper escaped her throat. Neither of those options was particularly appealing.

"Where is it?" His voice was deep and raspy. His repugnant breath blew across her face.

For a few seconds, Sage couldn't speak. It wasn't until the knife pressed harder that her trembling voice produced words. "Where is what?"

The man dug the knife deeper again, this time until a sharp pain shot through her neck. "Do you know how many people I've killed in my life? More than you could possibly imagine. Killing is easy, and killing you would be child's play. So insignificant I would forget by dinner. Do you understand what I'm saying?"

That he could kill her without hesitation? She had known that long before he'd told her.

She wanted to nod but was too aware of the knife digging into her skin. "Yes."

"Good, now tell me where you store the child's medical files, or I'm going to plunge this knife so far into your neck you're going to choke on your own blood."

He wanted information on Fletcher.

Icy fear shot through her body. She was going to die.

"I—I don't have them."

The rage that flashed through the man's eyes was the only warning Sage received before he lifted the knife and sliced her upper arm.

She couldn't stop the piercing scream of pain that escaped her lungs. It was like nothing she had felt before.

"I'm going to do that every time you don't tell me what I want to know."

A SMILE PULLED at Mason's lips as he drove to Sage's apartment.

The feeling of excitement that grew inside him was almost foreign. He hadn't smiled nearly enough in the last few years. Not since the truth about Project Arma had come out.

Sure, his brothers made him happy. But the betrayal he'd experienced was always at the back of his mind. It cast a shadow on his life.

That wasn't to say that he didn't like the perks of being stronger and faster. As well as everything else he'd gained physically.

But on a deeper level, his trust had been broken. He had trusted the system. He'd consented to being injected with tried and tested recovery drugs. Not experimental drugs designed to change his DNA.

That was what had consumed his every waking thought the last couple years.

Until now. Sage had shifted his focus. When he was with her, he didn't think about the project or the betrayal. The shadow temporarily lifted.

He didn't know exactly what it was about her that had him so distracted, but he wasn't going to question it.

Climbing out of his car, Mason made his way to the apartment building. Once inside, he took the stairs two at a time.

It wasn't until he was halfway up that he heard it. The anguished cry of pain.

Sage.

"I'm going to do that every time you don't tell me what I want to know."

In an instant, his body was flying up the stairs. Moving faster than should be possible. He arrived at Sage's door within seconds. Pushing down the handle, he broke the lock easily and stepped inside.

Mason moved into the bedroom. Fury swept through him at what he saw. A man holding a knife over Sage. Blood dripped from her right arm and pain etched her features.

Something inside him snapped.

Rushing forward, he pulled the man off her, throwing him across the room. The crash of a body hitting wall sounded. Mason positioned himself between Sage and the intruder.

The impact of the hit should have rendered the man unconscious. If any normal man had been thrown, it would have. But this wasn't a normal man. Instead, he was back on his feet within seconds. And when he turned to face him, recognition hit Mason.

Alistair. A former SEAL and Project Arma drug recipient.

Mason was well familiar with the man's team. He knew they lacked morals and ethics. Which had been confirmed when they'd gone into hiding alongside the project.

"Where's your trusted leader, Carter?" Mason sneered.

Members of their team had popped up since Arma had gone underground. But usually with Carter leading the pack.

Alistair kept his features neutral. "She was a one-man job. Before you got here, that is. We've really got to stop meeting like this."

Mason's eyes narrowed. He remembered their last meeting well. And it still made him mad as hell. "If you're referring to a few weeks ago, when you tried to take Asher's woman while she was pregnant, then I agree. Stop messing with us and our families and let us kill you already. You'll die eventually. As it is, you're going to pay for what you did to Sage."

Alistair took a step forward, his eyes remaining on Mason. "On the contrary, my friend. I'll be killing the bitch once I have the files I came for. I might even let you watch."

"Not gonna happen." *Any of it.*

Mason lunged forward. He tackled him, hitting the knife out of his hand in the process. The impact of the hit threw both men to the floor. Mason immediately placed his forearm to the other man's throat. Pressing down, he applied enough pressure to cut off his air supply.

"Every time one of you threaten to hurt one of my own, you fuel my rage. That's a dangerous thing to do."

Alistair spluttered for air, his skin quickly developing a red tinge. But Mason didn't let up.

"If I killed you right now, I'd be doing you a favor by granting an easy death. You don't deserve easy."

Alistair began to buck beneath Mason. He reeked of desperation. Desperation to breathe. To live.

An elbow hit Mason in the gut, catching him off guard and giving Alistair a chance to jump to his feet. Mason stood and watched as the other man stumbled a few times, coughing as he went.

"You care about her, don't you?" Alistair choked out. "That's why you won't kill me. Not in front of her. That's what feelings do to you. They make you *weak*. That's why you'll never beat us."

Eyes narrowing, Mason took a step forward. Alistair followed and swiped a fist at Mason. The hit caught the side of Mason's face and left the metallic taste of blood in his mouth.

One hit. That was all the asshole was getting.

Drawing his arm back, Mason threw his own punch.

Alistair stumbled back, blood rushing from his nose.

Ignoring the rustle of movement behind him, Mason lunged forward again. Alistair attempted to move but wasn't quick enough. Throwing an arm around the man's throat, Mason tightened immediately.

"Caring about people doesn't make us weak," Mason whispered into Alistair's ear. "It makes us fearless and more powerful than a hundred of your men. You and every other person at Project Arma should be scared. Because every day, we get closer to ending you."

Once the last word had left him, Mason tightened his grip again, this time until Alistair was unconscious. They needed to know what he knew. And that required him remaining alive.

Dropping his limp body to the floor with a thud, Mason sent a quick message to his brothers before turning around.

What he saw made him want to turn back to Alistair and murder the fucker.

Sage had dragged herself into the corner of the room. She was holding her hand over the cut, but blood was seeping through her fingers. Her eyes were wide and red-rimmed while her skin was deathly pale.

Mason moved across the room, picking up a discarded piece of clothing on his way. Hunching down, he moved her hand away and began to wrap the wound.

"Is he dead?"

He waited until the wound was bound before raising his gaze to hers. "He's alive. The guys will be here any minute to pick him up."

He strategically moved his body so that he blocked the unconscious man from Sage's view. Sage now watched Mason but her eyes were unfocused.

"He wanted Fletcher's medical files. I didn't tell him where they were. I promise."

Raising his hand to her cheek, Mason hoped his touch would help her focus on him. "I know you didn't."

"I told him I didn't have them. But he was going to keep hurting me." Sage's words hitched at the end. Her breaths quickening.

He needed to watch Alistair. Ensure the other man didn't wake before the guys arrived. But Sage was close to spiraling. "Look at me, sweetheart. What color are my eyes?"

Sage opened her mouth but didn't speak any words.

"Come on, honey, what color are my eyes? Are they brown? Hazel?" He cocked his head to the side, a smile on his lips. "Purple?"

"Blue."

Good. Words were good. "Do you feel my hand on your cheek?"

Her eyes began to focus. "Yes."

"What does it feel like?"

"Hard and calloused. But warm."

"Good. Now what do I smell like?"

The smallest hint of a smile touched her lips. "You smell good."

A genuine chuckle sounded from Mason's chest. "So do you, sweetheart."

Just then, Sage's eyes widened in fear.

It was all the warning Mason needed.

Turning, he caught Alistair midlunge. Mason didn't think. Just acted. He snapped the man's neck in one swift move.

CHAPTER 5

S age smoothed her clammy hands over her slacks as she
walked down the hospital corridor.

Today was important. Today, she would take a step toward helping
her brother. She'd only just found out a week ago that he'd gone into
hiding. So today, there was no margin for error.

She was seeing a group of eight men. Eight former Navy SEALs who
had been the recipient of experimental drugs. The men reported that
they were healthy. Better than healthy. Apparently, they were supersol-
diers with unrivaled strength and speed.

Sage was taking a blood sample from each man. She would also do
an overall health check, as per government request.

Coming to a stop outside the first patient's door, she took a moment
to collect herself before pushing into the small room.

There, on the bed, sat a man. A shirtless man with muscles for
days.

Even sitting, he was massive. And intimidating.

Sage knew that each man on the SEAL team stood at, or close to, six
and a half feet. She'd read and reread their bios.

But seeing one of them in person was different. The sheer breadth of
his bare shoulders was easily two, maybe even three times her own

shoulder width. The man's forearms were the thickest she'd seen, and his biceps were so muscled that veins bulged from the skin.

Clearing her features, she moved forward and held out her hand. "Hi, I'm Dr. Porter, but please call me Sage."

The man's piercing blue eyes studied her as he reached out his own hand. "It's nice to meet you, Sage. I'm Mason, or Eagle to my team."

The moment his hand encompassed hers, a jolt of electricity ran through her body. Not only that, but her heart began to gallop, which, after what she'd read about his hearing, was not good.

She cleared her throat as he released her hand. "I'm going to be doing a general checkup and I'll also take a sample of your blood, if that's okay?"

He nodded but had yet to smile. Sage turned to her equipment.

"Are you a primary care doctor?"

"I'm a doctor and a biomedical scientist. I've done a lot of research on human DNA."

Sage still couldn't believe her luck that she was the doctor who was called in. It was like all the stars had aligned.

Only a week ago, her brother had left a message telling her that the project he'd been employed to work on had been shut down. That he was going into hiding and his life was in danger.

In the message, there had been no word of his location. Nothing about when he was returning.

Then, that same week, she'd received the call asking her to take this job.

She'd jumped on it. Of course she had, because she hadn't laid eyes on her brother in a year. They never gave him vacations. Or time off. And now he was running.

But she wouldn't be telling any of that to the stranger in front of her.

"You must be good for them to call you in."

Heat went to her cheeks.

Science had always come easy to her. She'd excelled in all her classes. It was no doubt why she was standing here right now.

Sage took out the blood pressure machine and began wrapping the cuff around Mason's upper arm. "I know what I'm doing, yes. You're in good hands." A moment of silence passed. "Your blood pressure is great," she confirmed seconds later as she recorded her notes.

"I'll be interested to see the results from today. Who the hell knows what they did to us."

Sage stopped at the resentment in his voice. The anger.

Looking up, she took a step forward and placed a hand on his shoulder. "I'm sorry about what happened to you. I don't know everything, just that you received drugs that you didn't consent to, but I'm sorry."

Mason's intense blue eyes held hers. They were beautiful. Everything about the man in front of her was beautiful.

"Why are you sorry? Many would consider what happened to us a gift."

That was true. But most would find it a huge invasion of bodily autonomy. "I guess it's about consent. You didn't consent to any of it. Your trust was broken."

Mason gave a small nod. "That's exactly how I feel." Then his head cocked to the side. "How do you feel about being dragged into this?"

For a moment, Sage didn't know how to respond. She didn't want to tell him the truth about what a relief it was, but she didn't want to lie. The man looked like he could pick out a lie anywhere.

"I'm good at what I do. So, I'm glad I can help."

Sage had expected someone to realize her brother had worked for Project Arma. Maybe even drag her in for questioning. But so far, nothing. It was like they didn't know. Sage didn't know how that would be possible, but she was grateful.

She wanted this job. Because she wanted to be close to the project. The closer she got, the more likely it was that she might learn something that could help Jason. Even if she just found out when everyone was caught and could tell her brother that he was safe.

"I signed a confidentiality form," Sage quickly added. "So don't worry, I'm not going to say anything to anyone."

Mason chuckled but there wasn't a lot of humor in the laugh. "Yeah, *they don't want us saying anything, either. They'll probably buy us out. Like money will fix it."*

Taking out her stethoscope, she listened to Mason's heart rate. "What are your next plans?"

For a moment, Sage hoped those plans could involve her in some way. Then she mentally shook her head.

What was she thinking? She'd just met the man. Just because she felt an undeniable pull to him didn't mean he felt the same for her.

Putting her head down, she noted his results. When Mason didn't answer her question, she looked up to find him staring at her. But something had changed in his expression. Become harder.

When he spoke, his voice dripped venom. "We're going to find every last one of the people who worked for Project Arma and kill them... starting with Jason."

At the mention of her twin's name, Sage jolted. "Wh-what did you say?"

Mason's eyes narrowed. "You didn't think we were going to let him live, did you? After he worked for them?"

She took a hurried step back. A tingly feeling entered her hands and ran up her arms. "He didn't know what was really going on when he took the job...please, don't hurt him. He'll stay hidden if that's what you want."

Mason stood. "Actually, we already found him."

No. That wasn't possible. Jason had messaged last night. He was safe.

Before Sage could respond, Mason took out his phone and placed it to his ear. "Kill him."

Lunging forward, Sage was stopped by a glass barrier. A barrier that hadn't been there moments before. Opening her mouth, she tried to scream but no sound came out.

She was powerless.

When Mason looked at her, there was no compassion in his expression. "You can't save him, Sage. It was always going to end this way."

Jolting upright, Sage gasped in air. A layer of sweat cooled on her forehead and her heart galloped.

Glancing around, Sage realized she was in a bed. In the apartment rented by Mason.

When Mason had first moved to Marble Falls, he had lived in an apartment building, in a unit across the hall from Wyatt. But while Wyatt hadn't minded living in the small space, Mason had felt claustrophobic. He'd moved, although he'd kept the apartment.

When she couldn't stomach living in Lexie's apartment, the one where a man had died right in front of her less than a week ago, he'd immediately offered this place.

She flicked her eyes to the window to see the high-security lock. There was also an alarm, which would alert the guys if it was tripped. With Wyatt directly across the hall, she should be safe.

She was under strict instructions to call one of the guys anytime she left the apartment. For security.

Closing her eyes, she tried to push the dream away.

It wasn't real. Mason doesn't know. Jason is safe.

But what if he wasn't?

Reaching over, Sage grabbed her phone and dialed Jason's number. It just rang. She tried three more times until she finally accepted he wasn't going to answer. He never did.

Instead, she listened to the voice message he'd left her two years ago. It was probably the hundredth time she'd listened, and she knew every word by heart. But hearing his voice helped calm the tidal wave of panic in her chest.

"Damn, I was hoping you'd answer. I don't have much time, so I'll try to make this quick. Sage, I'm leaving. I'm going into hiding."

He paused, his breaths heavy down the line.

"Remember my suspicions about Project Arma? Well, I was right. About all of it. And it's so much worse than I thought. I can't explain everything right now. Don't try contacting me on this number, I'm going to get rid of it and use burner phones. I'll change burners regularly and I'll probably stick to text messages, just to be safe." There was another pause.

Sage drew in a quick breath, already knowing what was coming next.

"I love you. Hopefully it's over soon and I can come home."

She closed her eyes. Hearing those words in her mind again. She wished it was over. Wished he was home.

About to put her phone down, she hesitated. The fear from the dream was still a living, breathing parasite inside her. She needed something to calm herself. Confirm the dream was just that—a dream.

Maybe if she heard Mason's voice, her brain would recognize it hadn't been real.

Before she could overthink it, Sage scrolled through and hit dial on Mason's number. The moment she heard the dial tone, she quickly canceled the call.

What was she doing? It was the middle of the night. The guy would be sleeping and she was…what, calling to hear his voice? He wasn't her boyfriend. He wasn't her anything. Even calling him a friend was a stretch.

About to put the phone back on the bedside table, she stopped when the screen lit up and Mason's name flashed in front of her.

Crap.

Dropping the phone like it was a hotplate, she sat and watched it ring and eventually stop. There was no time to feel relief though, as the phone immediately began ringing again.

Double crap. The guy would probably just keep calling until she answered.

Slowly, Sage lifted the phone to her ear. "Mason."

"Are you okay? What's wrong?"

Concern was heavy in Mason's voice. Guilt hit Sage hard.

"I'm sorry. I shouldn't have called. I just—I had a nightmare."

Biting her lip, Sage had never felt so pathetic.

There was a beat of silence before he spoke, this time in a much calmer tone. "Want to tell me about it?"

No. Definitely not. "It was nothing."

"If it was nothing, you wouldn't have called. I'm a good listener, sweetheart."

Heat rose to Sage's cheeks at the endearment. "It wasn't that much of a nightmare, I guess. It started off as a memory, actually."

"Which memory?" When she didn't respond, he spoke again. "Was I in your dream?"

He knew. Of course he did. "It was of when we first met. In the hospital."

"Ah, yes, I remember that. I was raging about Project Arma, and as I was plotting my revenge, this cute blonde comes into my room and makes me forget the bad for a few minutes."

Sage smiled to herself as she played with a thread that had escaped the blanket. "I heard the anger in your voice. What I remember most was how big and muscular you were."

His voice dropped all humor at his next words. "You know I would never use my size against you, though."

"I know."

Mason was a good guy. She'd known that from the moment she'd laid eyes on him.

"Then why did it become a nightmare? Is it because of what you saw me do?"

She knew he was referring to Alistair. How he'd snapped the man's neck right in front of her.

She didn't like to think about that. She didn't like to think about anything from that day.

Mason sighed across the line. "I'm sorry you saw me do that."

"You did what you had to do." If he hadn't killed Alistair, who knows what the guy would have done. "I think the dream was more about me anyway. I have a lot on my mind."

Like, why had a man broken into her apartment demanding Fletcher's files less than two days after Jason had asked for them?

"Was I different in the dream?"

Sage nibbled her bottom lip as she considered her response. "You didn't listen to me about something. Something important."

Another pause of silence across the line. She could almost hear his brain ticking away. "That's very cryptic. But I hope you know that the real living, breathing me would listen. Always."

Even if her brother had worked for his enemy? Sage wasn't so sure. And if she was going to tell Mason, she had to be a hundred percent certain.

"Thank you."

"How have you been since the attack?"

Sage's eyes slid to the window again. "Fine."

If *fine* meant living in a state of constant dread. Not wanting to leave the apartment for fear of returning to find a man wanting to hurt her.

The slight growl that sounded from Mason said "fine" was not a good enough answer. But it was all she had.

"How's your arm been?"

It was a daily reminder of what had happened. Just like the scar would be. "It's healing. The pain's manageable."

"Good. And Sage, they won't get you. We'll protect you."

For some reason, Mason's words made Sage feel emotional. Maybe because he was being protective of her. And the only person in her life who had previously done that was her brother.

"I should go. Thanks for calling."

"Anytime, sweetheart."

When the call ended, she swallowed the lump in her throat. Lying back down, she lifted her phone so she could see the time.

Four a.m.

She wasn't getting any more sleep. She knew that much.

MASON RAISED his hand to knock on the door. Sage's door.

He knew it was early. But he also knew she hadn't gone back to bed after being woken by her nightmare.

Well, that wasn't entirely true. He didn't know that with absolute certainty, but he had a hunch, and his hunches were rarely wrong.

Light shuffling sounded from the other side of the door before he heard Sage's voice. "Who is it?"

He was glad she hadn't just opened the door. She was being cautious. That was good. "A knight in shining armor, armed with sustenance."

There was a moment of silence. Even her breathing silenced.

Chuckling to himself, Mason waited the ten seconds it took for the door to creak open. Once he got his first glimpse of Sage, his entire body tightened.

Normally, he saw her in slacks and buttoned-up shirts. And even then, he couldn't drag his eyes from her perfect form.

This morning, she wore pink shorts with a strappy sleep top. Over her shoulders was an open silk robe paired with fluffy bunny slippers.

He wanted to say she was cute, but the word didn't do her justice. She was fucking beautiful.

Desire struck him hard.

Sage's brow furrowed. "It's six in the morning."

Yes, it was.

A smile stretched Mason's lips. "So, I'm right on time for breakfast."

Not waiting for a response, Mason walked in, enjoying the moment he brushed against her body.

Damn. He needed to get himself under control and fast. Otherwise he'd be doing more than just scaring the doctor in her dreams.

Moving to the kitchen counter, Mason set the bag down and began taking out the ingredients. He'd lived in the apartment for his first six months in Marble Falls. The kitchen was to the right of the door and open to the living/dining area. There were two bedrooms.

It was large for an apartment, plus Wyatt lived across the hall, which had been a bonus. But it wasn't large enough for Mason.

"You brought food?"

"Right again. You know, for a doctor, you state the obvious a lot."

Lifting his eyes, he saw a ghost of a smile pull at her lips. "For an upfront guy, you don't explain yourself a lot."

"Guess that makes me not very upfront."

He regretted his words immediately. The smile dropped from her lips and a guarded expression replaced it.

Switching his attention back to the bag he'd brought, he continued unpacking the food. "I wasn't sure what you felt like, so I tried to cover all my bases. Eggs and bacon, ingredients for pancake batter, strawberries, and apple strudel from Mrs. Potter's Bakehouse."

He heard her step closer but didn't raise his eyes. "Mason, that's way too much food for two people."

Maybe too much food for Sage. But Mason could eat a lot. "I like variety." When his gaze *did* return to her, he was relieved to see the tension from moments ago had lifted. "Want to help?"

She nibbled on her lip. It did nothing to calm the need that was building inside him. "I'll throw some clothes on and be back in a sec."

"Don't change on my account. I really like what you have on."

Especially the generous display of skin around the chest.

Sage shook her head. "If you had come in boxer shorts and fluffy slippers, then maybe I would have considered remaining in this. But you didn't come dressed for it." Smiling, she turned and left the room.

Well, damn. If he hadn't dressed accordingly...

A few minutes later, Sage returned wearing a T-shirt and

leggings. Even though she was showing less skin, she still set his blood pumping.

She stepped beside him. "What can I do?"

Let me plaster my lips to yours and see if you taste as sweet as last time.

He wished like hell he could say those words, but if he did, she'd likely be halfway to Australia by morning.

Indicating to the counter with his head, Mason kept his voice even as he spoke. "You're on fruit and juice duty. I'm on hot food."

Raising her brows, Sage moved toward the counter. "A man who can cook. I like it."

"I'm not just a pretty face, Doc."

The laugh that followed was lyrical. Melodic. He wanted to hear that sound again.

As they prepped breakfast, they fell into comfortable conversation. They talked about their favorite foods, favorite places in the world...she asked about Marble Protection.

"So, no one's told me, why do they call you Eagle?"

Ah, the question he was waiting for. "Are you sure you want to hear this? I come out a bit of a hero."

Mason was rewarded with another sweet laugh. "I'll be the judge of that."

He cracked some eggs into a bowl. "On one of our first missions as a team, we were sent to the Middle East. Our job was to free a group of US citizens from a hostage situation. When the mission was almost complete, and we were leaving with the hostages, I just happened to look up. I'm not even sure why. But I'm damn glad I did, because I spotted a man on top of a building with a gun trained right on us. I shot him in the head without a second thought. Red and I went up there to check on him. We found that the weapon he'd trained on us wasn't actually a gun, it was a glide bomb. It would have taken out our entire team as well as the hostages."

Sage had stopped what she was doing and was now watching him with wide eyes. "You almost died. You *all* almost died."

He could see how that would be shocking to her. She hadn't been exposed to the same world as him. The world of a Navy SEAL. "Every mission was dangerous. I was just lucky that on that day, I saw the threat. Since then, the team has called me Eagle. I guess because the Eagle sees things that most don't."

"And because you protected your team. You're a protector, Mason."

He did protect his team. But then, all the men worked to protect each other.

"When do you go back to work?" Mason asked, changing the subject.

And that quickly, her body visibly tensed. "I asked the hospital for a couple of weeks off after the break-in. To recover."

Mason knew Sage didn't just mean physically. The slice across her arm wasn't nice, but it would heal. What she really needed was time to process what had happened. The mind often took a bit longer than the body.

Unfortunately, he also knew these things took longer than a couple of weeks to recover from.

Mason put down the spatula and turned to Sage. He wanted to give her his full attention. "I'm here if you need me. Even just for some company."

Although, he'd like to be more than that.

The same thoughtful expression she often wore came over her face. "You think any harder, you might do some damage to that giant brain of yours."

She wrapped her arms around her middle in a protective stance. Mason had to clench his fists to stop from pulling her into him. "I just keep wondering if and when someone else will come for me."

Mason had no doubt someone else would come for her. And he hated that.

"I live around the corner, Wyatt lives across the hall. If the alarm is tripped, one of us will be here, no matter the time of day."

Sage studied the fruit in front of her like she was looking at a math problem that needed to be solved. "I just…"

When she didn't continue, he placed his fingers on her chin to lift her face. He wanted to see her eyes. "You just what?"

"I don't get it. I don't understand why they want information on Fletcher or why they're coming for me."

They were great questions. And questions that Mason could only hypothesize answers to. "I think the reason they want information on Fletcher is because they want to know if he's like us. If soldiers can be born, rather than created. I fear what they would do with that information."

Everyone should fear what they would do with that information.

"And in regards to 'why you'—they already went after Lexie and Fletcher, and they got beat. They know how heavily protected that kid is. So, my guess is that they've changed tack. Realized they don't actually need *him*, they just need to know what he can *do*."

Her brows pulled together. "They sound like horrible humans."

Horrible. Inhumane. Whatever you wanted to call it, they weren't good people. "They are. And we'll get them. But, until then, you're safe."

He shifted his hand so that it cupped her cheek. Whether she realized it or not, her head pressed into his palm.

When she licked her lips, his gaze immediately lowered to her mouth. God, he wanted to kiss her again. There was nothing he wanted more than to wrap her in his arms and let her sink into him.

But the sound of a ringing phone broke the silence. *Her*

ringing phone. He wanted to ignore it, but the moment was lost. She was already pulling away.

Mason went back to cooking the food, and took the moment to calm his body. At the same time, Sage went to answer the call.

"Dr. Sage Porter speaking."

"Hello, Dr. Porter, this is Agent Sinclair from the CIA. We've met a couple of times regarding Project Arma."

Mason stilled at the sound of Agent Sinclair's voice. He had met the man a few times also, and didn't think much of him.

"Yes, I remember. How can I help you, Agent?"

"We need you here in Rockdale. Today. We have a soldier who needs medical attention."

"Rockdale? Agent, that's a couple hours' drive. Could you tell me why you need me, specifically, to care for him?"

"He was a member of special forces. Only he went missing two years ago. He just escaped Project Arma."

CHAPTER 6

*S*age lugged her suitcase down the stairs. She'd never been one to pack light, even if she was only away for one night. She'd rather overpack and have everything she needed than realize too late she'd forgotten something important.

When she stepped out of the apartment building, Sage looked up and almost tripped over her own feet. There, leaning on her car, was the very man who had knocked on her door that morning with breakfast. He had changed into a tight white shirt and jeans, and holy heck did he look good. He could be posing for a Dolce & Gabbana commercial.

She shouldn't have been surprised to see him. But she was.

"Twice in one day. Is it lunch this time?"

One corner of his mouth pulled up. "Actually, I thought we'd grab lunch on the way."

Sage stopped a foot away from him, letting the meaning of his words sink in. "If you're saying what I think you're saying, then the answer is no. You are not coming with me to Rockdale. I already spoke to Wyatt, and he organized for Bodie to trail me."

She'd called the moment Mason had left. Because if Bodie was with her, then Mason wasn't. And Bodie was safe. She didn't feel the need to press her lips to his every time he was close.

"All taken care of, sweetheart. I called Red and gave him the day off. You're coming with me."

Before Sage had a chance to respond, Mason took the suitcase from her fingers, obviously taking advantage of her shock. She watched him get halfway across the road before reality caught up with her and she chased after him.

"Mason, Bodie was going to trail me in a separate car and stay outside the room while I looked over the patient. Is that what you're doing?"

"It's never any fun doing long drives alone."

She waited for him to answer the second part of the question, but he didn't. Instead, he walked to the passenger door and held it open for her.

Sage began to nervously fiddle with her fingers. "It's a two-hour drive, Mason. Then I'm staying overnight." And that was just a whole truckload of temptation that she would be having to resist.

"Yes, it is. Consider me your personal bodyguard."

She didn't move forward. Because once she got into the car, she would be with the man for hours. And she'd already spent the entire morning with him. So far, she hadn't found a single flaw.

It scared the heck out of her.

Mason didn't seem deterred by her hesitation. His voice softened as he spoke. "Think of it as a business trip. You do your medical stuff, I get information about Project Arma. And we both keep your sweet ass safe."

Heat flooded her cheeks at his words.

It was just two days. She could keep her hands to herself for two days, surely.

Finally stepping forward, she ducked into the car. But she couldn't miss the smile on his face as she did.

Ten minutes into the drive, Sage felt Mason's eyes on her again.

"If you don't keep your eyes on the road, I won't need protecting, I'll be roadkill."

Mason chuckled. "I'm an excellent driver."

She didn't doubt it. She was still waiting to find something he *wasn't* excellent at.

"Are you still mad about me crashing your trip?"

Sage's eyes fell on the man beside her. Jeez, even his hands on the steering wheel were sexy. "I was never mad." *Just nervous about falling for you, only to have the truth about Jason come out.* "You didn't mention during breakfast that you'd listened in on the phone call."

As the words came out of her mouth, she realized how silly they were. The man could hear things a street over. But she had hoped he would block out a private conversation.

"I can't help what I can hear. And I didn't mention it because *you* didn't. I'd rather talk to you about you than business."

Sage bit her lip to stop a smile. What he said was kind of sweet. "Breakfast was nice. I didn't want to take away from that."

He nodded. "That it was."

After that, they fell into a peaceful silence. Nothing but the radio and the road.

An hour in, Mason pulled into a roadside diner. "Hungry?"

Her stomach chose that exact moment to growl. Darn it, how embarrassing.

He laughed as he pushed out of the car. "Come on, Doc. Let's get some food into you."

Mason led the way inside, choosing a corner booth. He immediately took the seat against the wall. No one would know that the guy was watching. But she suspected that he saw everything.

When the waitress came to their table, Sage ordered a chicken burger while Mason ordered beef. She noticed the waitress's gaze hover over him when she thought he wasn't looking.

Sage didn't blame the woman. Mason was a heartthrob.

"Tell me about your family?"

The question from Mason startled Sage, to the point where there was no way he would have missed her flinch. When she looked at him, she relaxed slightly. She didn't know what she expected to see in his eyes. Suspicion maybe? But there was none. Or none that she could see. Instead, he leaned back in his seat, a neutral expression on his face.

"Why don't you tell me about your family first."

She expected Mason to push back. Which was why she was so surprised when instead, he did exactly as she asked.

"Sure. I grew up in California. I have one sister, Quinn, who's two years younger than me. She was always a bit of a handful, constantly getting herself into trouble. I think that's why I grew up with such a protective nature. I was always having to save her from whatever trouble she got herself into."

Sage's brows drew up. "Do you worry about her? That Arma might use her to get to you?"

"Yes. For the first year, we all hired people to watch our families from afar. We still get those people to check on them regularly. Project Arma has shown us that, for the moment at least, they're not coming after us or our families. They're building their army in other ways."

At least their families were safe. The stress of worrying about family on top of everything else would be a lot. "What's Quinn doing now?"

"She's living in New York and working as a journalist. She lives and breathes her job, and it suits the hell out of her inquisitive nature. I've visited her a few times. I don't love the fact that she lives in such a big city. But Quinn could find trouble anywhere."

Her eyes softened. "You worry about her."

"Every damn day." Mason scrubbed a hand over his face.

"She's got this tenacity about her. When there's a story, she'll stop at nothing to chase it down."

Sounded a bit similar to Mason's single-minded determination.

"What about your parents?"

A shadow fell over his face. She got a sinking feeling before he spoke.

"Mom passed away while I was at BUD/S training. Breast cancer. She didn't realize she had it until it was too late."

"Oh gosh, I'm so sorry." Reaching across the table, Sage wrapped her fingers around his.

"I wanted to move home to be there for Dad and Quinn, but they both said no. Especially Dad. A couple years later, my dad passed away. Heart attack."

Grief coated his voice. Her heart broke for him.

"I'm so sorry. Losing two parents so close together must have been hard."

Hard, painful...she couldn't imagine the heartache.

Mason turned his hand over and linked his fingers through hers. "I've become an overbearing big brother to Quinn. I mean, I always was, but now it's worse. I check on her a lot more often than she'd like. It drives her mad but keeps me sane."

"I'm sure she secretly loves it." And it reminded Sage of what her own brother used to be like. Before.

Just then, the waitress arrived at the table, holding both their meals. She had only taken one bite out of her burger when the question she'd been dreading came again.

"Will you tell me about your family?"

Sage chewed slowly. Considering what she would say.

"I have a brother and two parents. My parents live in Florida."

She knew that wouldn't satisfy his curiosity, but she gave it a go.

"Is the brother older or younger?"

Sage reached for her water and took a sip. "We're twins, actually. Although, you wouldn't know it by looking at us. I got Dad's fair features while he got Mom's olive complexion and dark hair. For our whole lives, everyone we meet is surprised when we tell them we're twins. Our parents were actually trying to conceive for years. It wasn't until they tried IVF that they conceived us."

"Do you get along with your parents?"

That question was easy for Sage. "They were both forty when they had us, so they're older. They're two of the most genuine people you will ever meet."

"You miss them." It was a statement, not a question.

"Like crazy. I don't visit them enough."

Not anymore. Mostly because she hated lying to them about Jason. But there was no way she would be telling them the truth.

"What about your brother? Being twins, you must be close."

The smile slipped slightly before she quickly recovered. "He was always my best friend. Some twins can be competitive. That was never the case for us. I was sometimes bullied for being academic. He was always right there, standing up for me. Protecting me."

"As any good brother should. Do you get to see him much?"

She moved a fry around her plate. "There hasn't been much opportunity to see each other lately."

The truth in that statement cut through her chest.

"That must be hard."

Hard. Scary. Painful. It was all those things.

Mentally shaking her head, Sage forced a smile when she looked across the table. "It's okay. It won't be forever."

Because one way or another, Sage would find Jason and bring him home.

~

MASON PULLED into the parking lot outside the hospital. Dread pooled in his stomach. He was about to meet someone who had escaped Project Arma. He would probably learn things about the program that fueled his rage.

"Are you okay?"

Mason mentally shrugged off the feeling as he turned to look at Sage.

Damn, she shouldn't have been able to see it in his expression. He was usually better than that. He needed to be more careful around her.

"Of course, sweetheart."

Giving her what he hoped was a distracting smile, he pushed out of the car and moved to her door.

Sage gave him a nervous look as he helped her out. "You know you can't actually come in when I see the patient, don't you?"

Going in with her was exactly what he intended to do. He needed to protect her, and the only way he could do that was by shadowing her movements, especially while in a room with a possibly genetically enhanced man.

Mason remained silent and placed a hand on the middle of her back as they walked toward the entrance. He caught every nervous glance his way.

As they stepped inside the hospital foyer, Mason spotted Agent Sinclair immediately. The man pushed off the wall and headed toward them.

He hadn't seen the agent for a few years, but he looked no different. He had been involved in the Project Arma raid and shutdown. But Mason had never liked the guy. He was too arrogant. Wanted respect without earning it.

"Dr. Porter, so good to see you again." Sinclair extended his arm to shake Sage's hand.

When the agent turned to Mason, his expression cooled considerably. His smile remained, but there was also something else. Frustration?

"It's been a while, Mason."

"Too long. Especially considering you're supposed to notify us when you get a lead on Project Arma. After all, it was a part of the agreement made when we got out."

Sinclair's eyes narrowed slightly. "We would have called you eventually."

That was a lie. There wasn't an ounce of truth in the statement.

"Fortunately for you, we usually end up discovering things ourselves."

The phony smile dropped from the agent's face. Good. Mason couldn't stand insincerity.

Sage cleared her throat. "Can you take us to the patient please, Agent."

Sinclair's gaze held Mason's for another beat before it eventually swung back to Sage. "Follow me."

Mason placed his hand on the middle of her back as they headed down the corridor. He made a mental note to speak to the guys about the agent's reaction to him. His team had known for a while that they weren't receiving the government's intel on Project Arma.

In the first year, the team had been given bits and pieces of information. But it was usually given too late. Once the information had become worthless. They would be given warehouse locations that had already been abandoned and the identity of Project Arma workers who were already dead.

Something needed to change, and it needed to change soon.

Sinclair came to a stop outside a closed door. Two men in suits stood guarding the door. Both were armed. It wouldn't be obvious to most. But Mason could see the outline in the men's clothing.

That meant, either the patient was dangerous enough to warrant trained, armed men at the door, or they were concerned Project Arma would come looking for their soldier. Either way, Sage wasn't getting near the guy without Mason.

"His name is Logan," Sinclair said to Sage, before he turned his attention to Mason. "You're not going in there."

"I am." Mason's hand dropped from Sage's back and he took a small step forward.

Anger darkened the agent's eyes. "You're not. And any attempt to enter the room will be deemed failure to obey lawful orders. You don't want to give me a reason to arrest you."

"Sage isn't going anywhere without me. If I don't go in, she doesn't go in."

He left no room for negotiation. Sinclair could throw his title around all he wanted but when it came to Sage's safety, there was no law he was afraid to break.

Sinclair glanced at the door guards, both of whom immediately stepped forward.

From her spot beside him, Mason heard the slight increase in Sage's heart rate before she placed a hand on his arm. "I want him with me." Her words were hurried, tinged with panic. "I don't mean to step on any toes, but if he's not allowed in there, I won't be entering the room."

Both of them or neither of them. Just as Mason had said.

The muscles in the agent's arms visibly tensed. Mason could tell he was angry. Although, he was doing his best to hide it.

The guy clearly had an ego issue.

"Fine. But you come out and report your findings to me once you're done." Without waiting for a response, the agent turned and walked back down the hall.

"Well, that was a bit childish," Sage muttered under her breath so only he could hear.

He chuckled softly. She wasn't wrong.

Sage stepped between the guards and reached for the door, only to be stopped by Mason's hand on her arm. He wanted to go in first. Ensure the guy wasn't a physical threat. *Then* she could see to him.

Stepping in front of her, he pushed the door open.

He was met with the sight of a man sitting up on a bed, positioned in the middle of the room. His head was back and his eyes were shut. But he was awake. Despite the man's position, Mason could see he was alert and ready to go.

Logan was big. His physique was similar to Mason's. To those of the men on his team.

But what he couldn't tell about the guy yet was whether he was genetically enhanced.

Sage stepped to the side but Mason kept a firm hand on her arm.

"Logan?"

Logan's eyes slid open. Brown eyes that gave nothing away. First, he studied Sage. Then his gaze shifted to Mason. Assessed him.

"I know she's the doctor, but who the hell are you and why did you fight so hard to get in here?"

Mason's brow lifted. "You heard that?"

"Like you, I have excellent hearing."

"Like me?"

Logan's expression remained blank. "I heard you laugh under your breath when she called the asshole a child. Normal people wouldn't have heard her."

That answered his question. Definitely enhanced like Mason. Next, he needed to know if he was a good guy.

Mason nodded his head. "You're right. I'm not quite normal."

"Neither am I."

Silence descended upon the room.

Sage's gaze flicked between them both. "Now that we have that out of the way..."

Again, she moved to step forward, but he pulled her back.

"Okay, now I see why you're here," Logan said quietly. "I'm not going to hurt her."

Mason studied the man in front of him, looking for any signs of deceit. But all he could detect was truth.

Untangling his fingers, he freed Sage. She moved forward and placed her medical bag on the counter. If the man was lying, Mason would be on him in a heartbeat.

Sage didn't seem to have any of the trust issues that Mason had. She smiled as she turned to Logan. "My name is Dr. Sage Porter, but I would love for you to call me Sage. I'm going to check you over today, if that's okay?"

Logan gave a small nod as he watched Sage take out her stethoscope. "Why did they call you? I was told I needed to wait for you in particular."

Sage paused, her eyes softening. "I was told you escaped Project Arma."

Logan's jaw visibly tensed. "I did."

She used her head to indicate toward where Mason was standing. "His name is Mason. He got away from the project as well. I was his doctor when he got out. I've been working with him and his team since."

Logan shifted his gaze to Mason. "If you got out, it means people already know about the project. So why the fuck is it still operating?"

Mason stepped forward. "The project was originally a government-mandated program designed to benefit Navy SEALs and other members of the military. Its purpose was to reduce injury and recovery time, as well as improve skills through tailored training programs and medical injections."

Sage got back to work as Mason spoke.

"So, what happened?"

"It was uncovered that they were actually injecting experimental drugs into people—drugs to alter a person's DNA. Make them the ultimate warriors—"

"I know all that," Logan interrupted. "Why are they still operating?"

Mason remained calm. He understood the other man's frustration. He would be just as angry. "They went into hiding. The government is searching for them, and so is my team."

As he spoke the words, he felt the weight of his failure. Failure that he hadn't stopped the project. And in the meantime, others had been taken.

"How did you get entangled in all of this?" Sage asked gently as she prepped Logan's arm to take blood.

Logan watched as she inserted the syringe. "They took me."

Mason could tell that shocked Sage, but to her credit, her hand taking the blood remained steady.

"Who took you?" Mason asked the question while already dreading the answer.

"The people behind the project. I was a member of special forces. I was home for a break in between missions. They broke into my home, drugged me, and took me. When I woke up, I was in a completely different place." Logan paused. Mason heard Sage suck in a deep breath. The silence in the room was heavy. "They forced drugs into my body and made me train. They gave me a new team with other soldiers who had also been taken. That's been my life."

A black rage coursed through Mason's body. The man had been missing for two long years. That's how long Project Arma had held him. Trained him. Drugged him.

CHAPTER 7

S age had been quiet since they'd left Logan. They'd been in the car for a good ten minutes and, as yet, no words had been spoken.

Mason didn't blame her. Hell, he didn't feel like speaking, either. To find out a man had been a prisoner for two years while having drugs forced into his body was beyond comprehension.

Logan had enlisted to fight for his country and in return had been taken, separated from his team and loved ones, held captive, and forced to become a weapon for an army he never signed up for.

"Is someone going to watch him?" Sage asked quietly, finally breaking the silence.

"Cage and Ax will come and watch from a distance. We need to keep him safe. We need to know everything that he knows."

There was no way the assholes in the CIA would let Mason's team take over Logan's protective detail. So Kye and Oliver would work in the shadows. Do what they had to, to keep the man safe.

There was also the possibility that Logan wasn't who he said he was. Mason wanted to believe Logan, but he lacked trust.

There was always the chance he could be a plant, sent by the project.

The team would need to watch him closely.

"You think the people he ran from will try to get him back?"

Yes. Hell yes. After years of training him, *medicating* him, Logan was valuable. And because he didn't have teammates to watch his back, he was also vulnerable.

"Yes."

It wasn't just the people from Project Arma who Mason suspected were a threat to Logan. There could be leaks in the CIA. It wouldn't take much for the wrong people to get their hands on him.

"Do you ever fear they'll come for you?"

Mason hadn't been expecting Sage to ask that question. But he recovered quickly.

"I don't fear it. But I do expect it. Eventually." From his peripheral vision, he could see her eyes on him. "That's why we're constantly looking over our shoulders. And we're cautious as hell. We do weekly sweeps of our homes and the business for bugs. Although we'd likely be able to tell if someone had been in our homes. We try to be armed the majority of the time. And we've just inserted tracking devices on our phones so that we can find each other."

The tracking devices had come after Asher and Lexie had been abducted. There was still a chance that, if taken, the abductors could destroy or ditch the phone. But it was better than nothing.

"It was our commander who orchestrated Project Arma," he continued. "Turning us into what we are cost him time and money. I'm sure he sees us as his property, and there's no doubt in my mind that he's working toward a plan to have us returned to him."

"That doesn't scare you?"

He was past the point of fearing them. He *wanted* them to

come for him. Welcomed it even. Because he was sick of chasing the assholes.

Just the thought of Commander Hylar had Mason clenching the steering wheel a bit tighter. "The only thing that scares me is never bringing them to justice."

That scared the absolute shit out of him.

Sage remained still and rigid. He could almost feel her nervous energy bouncing around the car.

Reaching out, he gently squeezed her leg. "Don't worry. No one is going to take any of us. Not me and definitely not you."

For a moment, she didn't react. It was almost like she hadn't heard him. Then, lifting her hand, she placed it over Mason's. Her skin was soft on his. Feminine. "They only want me because I have Fletcher's medical files. I'm not that important."

"That's why you need to stay close to me. If they can't get the paperwork or Fletcher himself, you're the next best thing. That's why you need a big, sexy protector by your side."

"So, you know where I can find one of them?"

Mason laughed out loud. Damn, it felt good to laugh. When he looked at Sage, he saw a smile on her face. "You should do that more often."

Sage tilted her head to the side. "What? Make bad jokes?"

"Smile."

Shaking her head, she turned back to the window but he could see that the smile remained.

Pulling into the hotel parking lot, Mason switched off the car and climbed out. Taking both suitcases from the trunk, he led the way inside.

A lady with brown hair pulled up into a slick bun smiled at them from behind the front desk. "How can I help you today?"

"We have a room under Mason Ross."

She nodded and turned to her computer.

"Sinclair would have booked a separate room for me," Sage said quietly.

Shaking his head, Mason spoke without looking her way. "Wyatt canceled it. We're sharing a room."

Before she could respond, the lady placed forms in front of Mason, which he began filling out. It wasn't until they were done checking in and standing inside the elevator that he realized how stiff Sage's body appeared.

Not only that, all traces of earlier humor were wiped clear from her face. Replaced by tension.

Hell, maybe he should have mentioned the room situation earlier. He'd moved them to one room because there was no way the hotel room had enough security for her to sleep on her own. But the thing was, he'd known she'd argue the point if he told her in the car. So he hadn't.

That made him a bit of a coward.

Exiting the elevator, Mason took the lead as they headed to their room. Pushing the door open, he saw a large king bed in the center of the room, with a door leading to the bathroom to the left.

He placed the bags on the floor and ran a hand through his hair.

Damn. When he'd booked, he'd asked for a room with two beds. This must be a mistake.

When he turned to look at Sage, he saw confusion and anger all over her face.

ONE BED. There was only one bed.

She didn't want to share a bed with Mason. Every time she was around the guy, one half of her wanted to jump his bones. The other wanted to run far and fast, because the closer she got to him, the greater the chance he would find out about Jason.

She turned her gaze to Mason, studying his face, hoping he would tell her this was a mistake.

"This is a mistake. I'll call reception and get this sorted."

Sage watched as he went straight to the phone to make the call. A few minutes later, she'd only heard his side of the conversation, but already knew they weren't getting another bed.

Mason hung up and took a step toward her. Frustration on his face. "There's no record on the booking that I requested two beds, and no rooms left with two. They don't even have a roll-away bed available."

Sage was already shaking her head. "I can't share a bed with you."

She tried to manage her rising anxiety, hoping he didn't notice the fear that was bouncing off her in waves. Fear of getting close to him. Fear of falling for him. Fear of the guy working out her big, gigantic secret.

Mason was studying the living area. "I'll sleep on the couch."

Sage wanted to laugh. But it wasn't funny. The couch was tiny. *She* probably wouldn't fit on that thing, let alone the six-foot-five soldier in front of her.

"Maybe I should get my own room."

Surely if he had a room right beside her, she would be safe. They could even get a room with a connecting door. That was almost the same as sharing a room, wasn't it?

"Sage, sharing a room is the easiest way for me to keep you safe. I'm sorry I didn't tell you about the single-room situation sooner. I should have. But I need you to let me look after you."

When he said it like that, she wanted to cave. Cave, then sink into him, let him shield her from the bad in the world.

And that right there was the problem. The guy was easy to like. Too easy. Combine his charming personality with his sexy-as-sin body and the man was irresistible.

"I'm sorry I've been so pushy today," Mason added, taking another step toward her. "I'm used to being a protector and making the decisions. Sometimes I get carried away. But I should be consulting you when it involves you."

Oh darn it, the man just kept getting nicer.

"I appreciate you keeping me safe." She was beyond grateful. The man was like her guardian angel. But that didn't take away the anxiety she felt. "I'll sleep on the couch. You're a million feet tall. You probably don't fit even while sitting."

Mason chuckled. "I assure you, I do. And I'll be fine on the couch. I've slept in far worse places."

She turned to eye the small couch again. Yeah, there was no way he would be able to fold his gigantic body onto that thing. She would be sleeping on it, but she'd broach the topic again when the time came.

"How about we order some dinner?"

Mason's voice sounded close. Very close.

Spinning her head back to him, she noticed he was less than a foot away. And he smelled good. Christ, he smelled better than good. Musky and masculine.

Just then, her phone alerted her to a message.

Swallowing, Sage reluctantly took a step back to see it was from a new number. That meant it was likely Jason messaging from a new burner phone.

If there was anything that could pull her out of a lust-filled moment, it was a text from her long-lost twin.

Looking back up to Mason, she noticed his expression hadn't changed. "I might have a shower if that's okay. Maybe you could order me something?"

"Sure. Anything in particular you feel like?"

Yes, you.

Internally shaking her head, Sage lifted her suitcase. "Surprise me."

Then she headed into the bathroom. She hadn't heard from her brother in a while. She'd messaged him a day after the attack in her apartment but he hadn't responded.

The moment the door was closed, she dropped the bag and clicked into the message.

Sage, I'm so sorry it's taken me so long to respond. I've had to move from one town to another. They were getting close, I could feel it. I can't believe you were attacked. I hope you're okay. I swear it had nothing to do with your messages to me. But, in case it did, in case they found a way to track that number, I ditched the burner and got a new one.

There was a second message below the first.

There are things happening that I can't tell you about. That's why I need the information. So much is going on. It might be the only thing that can save me.

Frustration hit her hard. She needed to know how he knew about Fletcher and that she was connected to him. There were so many unanswered questions. So much he wasn't telling her.

Plus, the timing of her messages to him and her attack was just so suspicious. The very day after she'd told him that Marble Protection didn't have the files, she was attacked.

But Jason would never hurt her. At least, the old Jason wouldn't.

Can't you give me some more information, Jase? Why do you need it? How do you know about the child?

His response was immediate.

Trust me. Please. It will help get me home.

At the mention of home, Sage's heart hurt. She wanted him home. There was nothing she wanted more than to see her brother again. But she couldn't betray her friends like that. She wouldn't.

And she didn't think she trusted Jason anymore. The man she was messaging sounded less and less like her brother. It was heartbreaking.

There was also the fact that there *were* no files. Not anymore. She'd destroyed them after she'd been attacked. The risk was too great that they could get into the wrong hands.

Jase, there are no files. But I'd still like to try to help you. I'm heading home from Rockdale tomorrow morning. If you want to meet somewhere, anywhere, let me know.

Sage didn't know if she *would* actually meet him. The bad feeling in her gut was getting stronger by the day.

A minute passed with no response. Then another. It wasn't until a full five minutes had passed with Sage staring at her phone that she realized he wasn't going to respond.

A knock on the bathroom door startled Sage so badly that the phone almost slid from her fingers.

"Sage, are you okay? I haven't heard the shower start."

Swallowing the lump in her throat, Sage placed the phone down on the counter. "Just getting in now. Won't be long."

Glancing at her reflection in the mirror, she saw that she looked as scared as she felt. Scared that, maybe, her brother wasn't the man he used to be anymore.

CHAPTER 8

"Nope. I refuse to believe there is anything better than a warm bath, a glass of wine, and a good book."

Sage went so far as to cross her arms just to push the point that she meant what she said.

But Mason was already shaking his head. "I just can't do it. I'm not a reader, so I just sit there staring at a wall while the water cools."

"Take your phone in there, or a laptop. Watch your favorite show."

As she said the words, she realized she couldn't actually picture the big active man opposite her relaxing in a bath.

"It'll never happen."

Mason leaned across to take her empty plate and stack it on top of his. He'd ordered them steaks for dinner from room service and she'd demolished her entire meal. It had been delicious. But now she was full and ready for bed.

At the thought of bed, a yawn escaped her mouth.

Mason stood, taking the tray of dirty dishes to the door. "I think we're just two very different people."

"We are. And I'm not sure I can be friends with a bath hater."

He chuckled from across the room. "Surely you can make an exception for me?"

Standing, Sage headed to her bag. "No can do, buddy. If I make an exception for you, I have to do the same for all the other bath haters."

Pulling out her phone, she noticed there was still no response from Jason.

"Waiting for a call?"

Stuffing the phone back inside her bag, she turned to see Mason standing beside her.

And the man was studying her a little too closely. Sometimes she forgot how much he saw, and that was a dangerous lapse.

"Nope. Just checking to see if anyone had contacted me."

Mason cocked his head to the side. "You look disappointed. Want to talk about it?"

Yes. Sage would love to open up to someone about the brother she hadn't seen in years. But she wasn't ready for that. Especially not while her nightmare involving Mason capturing Jason was so fresh in her mind.

"I'm okay. I might actually go to sleep now. I'm exhausted."

Which was the truth. Sleep sounded heavenly to her.

For a moment, Mason looked like he might say something. But then his expression cleared, and he gave a nod before grabbing his stuff and disappearing into the bathroom.

Sage had changed into her pajamas earlier, after her shower. She was thankful that she'd packed her flannel pants and top instead of something more revealing.

Going to the closet, she found an extra pillow and blanket and set herself up on the couch. She'd already switched off all the lights apart from one lamp beside the bed. That should be enough for Mason.

As her eyes slid shut, a sigh escaped her lips. It was nice to finally rest. After waking at four a.m., she had survived the day on a lot less sleep than she was used to. Mason knocking on her door with breakfast felt like days ago, rather than that morning.

Already beginning to drift to sleep, Sage snuggled farther under the blanket.

"What the hell are you doing?"

Mason's angry voice had her eyes flying open. She was about to tell him she was doing exactly what it looked like, when her mouth went dry.

Mason stood in front of her—wearing only underwear.

And holy crap, did the man look good. Like a piece of art. Never in her life had she seen something more perfect.

Every inch of him rippled with muscle. His skin was smooth and tanned.

Breaths shortening, Sage had to swallow a few times just to make her voice work.

"Sleeping." Ideally, she would have loved to say something wittier in response. But her brain was short-circuiting.

He shook his head, taking a step closer. "No. Get your ass up and get into bed, woman. I told you, you have the bed."

From her position lying on the couch, Sage had to look way up to meet his gaze.

"You're not sleeping here," Sage finally got out.

A soft growl tore from his chest as he pulled the blanket from her body. Then his arms slid below her knees and back and he lifted her against his chest.

Oh god, her body was touching his naked chest. Heartbeat tripling, she was almost too nervous to move.

Her eyes remained on his glorious chest, and she wanted to slide her hands across the ridges.

"If you don't stop looking at me like that, I can't be held responsible for what I do next."

"What you do next?"

When he reached the side of the bed, he didn't attempt to put her down like she expected. He just stood there, holding her to his warmth. "Sage..."

But she couldn't stop looking. It was impossible.

Rather than listen to the warning in his voice, she gave in to the craving to touch him. Lifting her hand, she placed it on his chest. His heart thumped below her hand. His skin was hot and smooth and hard all at once.

She wanted to touch him more. To run her hands over every inch of his skin. Her body craved more closeness.

When her gaze again lifted to Mason's, she saw in his eyes what she had no doubt was shining through her own. Need.

When he still didn't make a move, she finally keyed into what he was doing—letting her decide. Decide where this attraction would lead.

If Sage was smart, she'd remove her hands and look away. But she'd been smart her whole life. Just for tonight, she wanted to follow her heart rather than her mind. Give in to the all-consuming need to be touched. Kissed.

Reaching her hands up, Sage threaded her fingers through Mason's hair before pulling his head down. Then she pressed her lips to his.

Her heart began to gallop, and a moan escaped one of them. She wasn't even sure who. All she could focus on was his lips on hers.

Then Mason began kissing her back. It only took a moment for his tongue to push between her lips.

Lord almighty, the man tasted good. Heat pulsed from her lips right down to her core.

Sage was vaguely aware of Mason placing her on the bed and positioning himself above her. His body pressing hers to the mattress. The feel of his weight on top of her was tantalizing.

His mouth lowered from her lips to her neck. She sucked in a breath as his hand went to the bottom of her top, immediately sliding under.

She lay still as his hand made its slow journey up her stomach. She was scared to move in case he stopped. Then his hand encompassed her bare breast, and she immediately arched into him, breathing out a long sigh.

Her fingers slid through his hair as his mouth latched on to her neck. She felt the sharpness of his teeth on her skin. It sent waves of pleasure through her system.

"Mason..."

She didn't know exactly what she was wanting by saying his name. But it felt good on her lips.

In one swift move, Mason pulled her shirt over her head. Then his mouth lowered to her breast.

The moment Mason's tongue touched her nipple, a whimper escaped her lips. His tongue was hot and wet against her hard peak. She wanted more.

With torturous patience, Mason used his tongue to flick her nipple back and forth. Instinctively, Sage pushed her chest higher. He knew exactly what she needed. He took the nipple into his mouth and sucked.

Crying out at the force of the bliss, Sage scrunched her eyes shut, her hands latching on to Mason's shoulders.

She was vaguely aware of his hands lowering to her pants, but it was difficult to focus on anything but his mouth working her breast.

A moment later, Mason's body lifted, and Sage thought she might cry from disappointment.

Opening her eyes, she saw him remove the only scrap of clothing he'd been wearing. Then he came back to kneel above her. They were both now completely bare. At some point, he had removed both her pants and underwear.

Mason lowered over her body again until only an inch separated their faces. "You are so damn beautiful."

Sage couldn't drag her eyes from his. When he looked at her, he *really* looked. It was like he could see every little part of her.

Then his head dipped. He kissed her long and slow.

"Are you sure you want to do this?" he asked in between torturous kisses.

That was like asking a thirsty man if he wanted a glass of water.

"Yes." A whole bunch of yeses. She was too far gone to choose anything else. Her body yearned for his with an intensity she'd never experienced.

Mason smiled. "I'm glad, because it would have killed me to have to stop."

He eased her legs open. Her pulse jumped at the touch of Mason's thumb on her core.

Then, with excruciating slowness, Mason began to move his thumb in a circular motion.

Tipping her head back, Sage closed her eyes and took in the burning heat that built inside her.

Mason took advantage of her exposed neck and lowered his lips to a spot behind her ear.

As a finger entered her, Sage grabbed the sheets by her sides. She pulled them into bunches with her hands as he began to work inside her.

The pressure built like a hot flame in her core. The in-out motion of his finger combined with his thumb on her clit was both torture and pleasure.

Then Mason crooked his finger and hit a new spot inside her.

A cry escaped Sage's lips. She was close. But she wanted to feel *him*.

Reaching down, Sage wrapped her fingers around him. He was big in her hand.

A growl tore from Mason's chest. She could see his muscles bunch. Sage tightened her grip and began to explore his length, feeling the big man tense above her.

He hung his head and paused. His breaths deepened as he grew larger and harder in her palm.

Before she could anticipate his move, Mason grabbed her wrist and pushed her hand into the mattress.

His gaze flicked to his bag. She followed, realizing what he was about to do.

"I'm on the pill."

So please oh please don't move your body away from me.

Mason looked back to Sage. "Are you sure? I'm clean."

Wrapping her legs around his hips, she felt him at her entrance. "Me too. Make love to me."

She couldn't believe those words had left her lips. But then, there wasn't much she wouldn't do to have him inside her.

"You're too damn desirable," Mason muttered.

He positioned himself at her entrance. With excruciating slowness, he entered her. Seating himself completely inside her. She felt herself stretch to accommodate his thickness.

When he took a moment too long to move, Sage tightened her walls around him. Mason immediately tensed, then lifted his hips so just his tip was inside her, before pushing back in.

Sage blew out a long breath at the sheer pleasure that his movement brought.

"So beautiful," Mason murmured before beginning to move in and out of her body with slow thrusts.

She lifted her hips to meet his thrusts, unable to contain the moans escaping her lips.

Reaching down, Mason began playing with her bundle of nerves while increasing his pace. Sage cried out at his unrelenting torture.

Wrapping her fingers around his neck, Sage pulled his head down until his lips plastered to hers. Sage sucked and nibbled, every one of her senses consumed by the man above her.

The pressure in her core built, so powerful and overwhelming she knew it wouldn't be long until she hit her breaking point.

Almost like she'd said her thoughts out loud, Mason's hand moved to her breast and pinched. That was all it took.

Sage fell apart beneath Mason. Shattering, while his body continued to fill her. She shuddered violently, the ecstasy of her orgasm taking over her entire body.

Mason drove into her one last time before he growled out his own climax. His head lowered to hers as she felt him fill her.

After a few moments, he finally dropped to the side, pulling her body with him.

Mason held her tenderly.

Closing her eyes, she let the peacefulness of the moment capture her. The stresses of the outside world held no place here. It was just her and him.

CHAPTER 9

The sway of Sage's hips as she walked in front of him had Mason's jeans feeling uncomfortably tight.

Damn, she was sexy. All five and a half feet of her. He was glad she couldn't see him, because he was finding it hard to tear his eyes away from her behind.

Once they reached the reception desk, Mason lowered the bags and began the checkout process.

Last night had been beyond anything he ever could have imagined. It had been more than sex. At least it was for him. He'd felt like he'd *connected* with her in a way he'd never connected with anyone in his life.

Then waking up with her in his arms...he hadn't wanted to let go.

As far as he was concerned, Sage was his. He'd actually seen her as his for a long time, but last night had confirmed it. He just hoped Sage felt the same.

"Did you have a nice stay?"

Mason pushed the completed form back across the counter. "We did, thank you."

The lady smiled. "Have a lovely day."

Returning the smile, he lifted the bags and led Sage to the door. He subtly scanned the area as they moved. Just as he'd been doing since they'd left their room.

He hadn't noticed anything amiss yet. But that didn't mean they were safe. Last night, Sage had shared her location with Jason. Not their exact location down to the hotel, but Rockdale wasn't a large town. It wouldn't take much to find them.

And the last time Sage had shared important information with her brother, she'd been attacked.

Shifting his gaze to Sage, he noticed her small smile. She was quiet. *Had* been quiet all morning.

He understood. She was careful. She was the type of person who had to think about and process a situation. And that was fine with him. He could do slow. Hell, he could do snail pace as long as they were progressing.

Giving her a wink, Mason stepped outside. Again, he scanned the area. But just as inside, there didn't appear to be any threats.

Moving to the car, he had to wonder whether Sage was concerned about the timing of her last attack and her message to her brother. Although she was the most intelligent woman he knew, love could be blinding.

He knew she was desperate to help and save her brother. So it was possible that desperation was interfering with her ability to connect the dots.

Once they were settled in the car, Mason pulled out of the parking area. His hands itched to move across and touch her. He didn't. Instead, he firmed his grip on the wheel. If she wanted his touch, she would initiate it.

Christ, it would be hard to last the drive back to Marble Falls while keeping his hands to himself. Even just sitting next to Sage, he was intoxicated by her scent. It was some sort of citrus fruit blend and it damn well called to him.

Once they were on the long stretch of road, he checked the rearview mirror. Not a car in sight.

He looked at Sage, noticing her brow was furrowed. What he wouldn't give to know the thoughts that were running through her mind.

"You're quiet, sweetheart."

There was a beat of silence before she answered. "I know. I'm sorry."

She was wringing her hands like she was nervous.

Screw space and letting her initiate contact.

Reaching across, he placed his hand over hers. "You don't need to be sorry. I'm glad you're quiet."

"You are?"

"Hell, yes. I'm hoping it means last night meant something to you."

This time, she turned to look at him. "It did."

Happiness soared through Mason's chest. He'd thought it had but hearing the confirmation from her lips cemented it. "It meant something to me, too."

She turned her hand over and threaded her fingers through his. "I'm really glad to hear that."

The first genuine smile that morning stretched across her face. The tightness he hadn't realized he'd been holding released.

The next half hour passed with small talk and some comfortable silence.

The drive was actually quite beautiful. They'd entered the highway a while ago and had steadily made their way up a mountain. There was a steep drop beside the road that gave them views of the trees and bushes that scattered the mountainside. The top of the mountain was pretty barren but the farther down it went, the more forested it became.

If Mason wasn't so taken by the woman beside him, the scenic drive would have consumed his thoughts.

Even though Mason was calm on the outside, he was silently stressing out internally. Mostly, because he was tossing up in his head whether to tell Sage about what he'd done to her phone.

He didn't want there to be secrets between them. At the same time, he had no idea how she'd react. He only just found her and didn't want to lose her.

There was the possibility she could hate him for lying to her. For breaking her trust.

But at some point, he would need to tell her. Because he planned for their relationship to be forever.

Mason took a breath before speaking. "Sage, there's something I should tell—"

He stopped midsentence as a car came into view from his rearview mirror. It was the first car he'd seen in a while. A black car with tinted windows.

The car was coming at them fast. So fast that Mason had no choice but to press his foot to the accelerator.

He cursed under his breath as the car behind them did the same.

Reaching to the dash, he hit dial on the car Bluetooth. Kye answered on the first ring.

"What do you need?"

"We have a tail and they're not messing around. They're coming up behind us fast. I think they're trying to run us off the road."

Sage let out a small gasp from beside him and turned her head. Mason kept his gaze on the road. He couldn't afford a lapse in attention.

"I'm leaving now. I'll follow your tracker."

Just as Kye hung up, the car behind them hit their bumper and the car swerved. Spinning the wheel, Mason was able to straighten them, but he had a feeling more hits were coming.

The other car was faster. That meant he wouldn't be able to outdrive the guy.

Below the sound of the car engine was the pitter-patter of Sage's heart thumping. She was terrified.

But Mason pushed that to the back of his mind. He had to focus on getting them out of this.

His biggest concern at the moment was the drop-off beside them. If the car pushed them off the edge, it wouldn't end well for anyone.

A truck ahead of them came into view. The truck was going slowly up the hill. And in front of the truck, he could just make out a bend in the road.

Damn. That made everything harder. He couldn't overtake the truck because of the bend. But soon, the truck would force Mason to slow down, and there wasn't a doubt in his mind the asshole behind would hit them again.

An idea came to Mason. It wasn't ideal. Hell, it was fucking dangerous. But Mason was out of time and low on options.

"I want you to unclasp your seat belt and climb over to me."

For a moment she continued to sit, silent and unmoving. Mason hardened his voice.

"Sage, now!"

Jolting out of her stillness, she unbuckled her seat belt. He could hear her jagged breaths loud and fast. Fear was coming off her in waves. But, to her credit, she remained calm, and damn but he respected that.

Mason unclipped his own belt. But just as Sage began to kneel over the console, their car was hit again by the vehicle behind.

Letting out a string of curses, Mason struggled to keep them on the road. At the same time, Sage flew forward, her head smacking against the windshield hard.

When he'd gained control of the vehicle again, he looked across to see Sage pushing back. There was a smear of blood on the window.

He wanted to check that she was okay, but time was up. The truck was close. He had to act. Now.

Reaching across, Mason grabbed her arm and pulled her onto his lap.

Just before they got to the truck, he swerved the car over the cliff edge.

For a moment in time, there was quiet. Then, as the car flew through the air, Mason kicked his door open and jumped out with Sage in his arms.

He held her tightly to his body. Midair, he spun them both, angling himself so that he would take the brunt of the fall.

He hit the ground, hard. Sage remained against him but the impact of the hit would have been a heavy jolt for her regardless. Their bodies immediately began to tumble down the hill.

Holding Sage with one arm, Mason dug his fingers into the earth.

At first, the dirt moved with their bodies. Mason growled in frustration.

They were sliding toward the forested part of the mountain. He glanced down and noticed a tree below them to his left. Pulling his hand back, he waited until they were almost beside the tree before reaching out to grab it, anchoring them to the spot.

There was a bang that sounded from below. Mason didn't have to look to know it was the car colliding with trees.

Christ, he was glad he got them out. But they weren't safe. Not yet.

He knew they didn't have much time. Their pursuer would be out of his car, searching for them already.

The tracker on Mason's phone, which Kye would need to locate them, was likely destroyed along with the car. But Kye would have their last location. That meant Mason couldn't stray too far.

He estimated they were halfway down the hill. The hill was steep, but now that he wasn't falling, he could navigate it. Move them to the bottom and remain a step ahead of the other driver.

Mason lay Sage onto the ground and crouched beside her. She was awake and breathing, but her breaths were stilted.

"Hey. You with me, sweetheart?"

Sage watched Mason for a moment, but her eyes were glazed with shock. Rather than speaking, she nodded.

He wanted to check her for injuries. But he needed to get them away first.

"I'm going to carry you. I'm going to put some distance between us and them until the guys find us."

Not too much distance, but enough so that he was hidden from the enemy.

Without waiting for a response, he lifted Sage into his arms and began to trek down the hill. Along the way, he noticed a path but it would be too obvious, and he needed the shrubbery and trees for protection.

Mason had never been so grateful for the endurance that he'd gained from Project Arma. Without the enhanced abilities, he still would have been capable of moving them down the hill—as a SEAL, he was trained to be the best—but since his DNA had been altered, he didn't have an off switch.

That didn't necessarily give him an advantage, though. The person, or people, driving the other car were likely altered.

Mason tried to be careful with each step he took, not wanting to jolt Sage. He was worried about her and needed to find a safe place to properly check her over for any injuries.

Holding her a little tighter against his chest, Mason wanted to shield her from all of this. There was no doubt in his mind that whoever had trailed them was either sent by Jason, or the person pretending to *be* Jason.

The moment he got back with his team, he planned to step up his search for the missing brother. This was the second time Sage's life had been endangered after giving Jason information. It was two times too many.

Another thought came to Mason—was it possible someone *else* had bugged Sage's phone?

A small frown creased his brows. That was something he

needed to investigate when they returned to Marble Falls. He knew her phone probably hadn't been destroyed with the car; where his had been on the car's center console, hers was in her back pocket.

Mason took twists and turns as he trekked down the mountainside. At the same time, he ensured that he remained close to the crash site.

After about fifteen minutes, Mason got progressively more concerned for Sage's silence.

Spotting a cluster of trees, he moved to that area and placed her gently on the ground. Her eyes were now closed but he could tell she was conscious by her uneven breaths.

"Sage, honey, can you open your eyes?"

Slowly, her eyes slid open. "I think I have a concussion."

Mason studied her. Not just her eyes—her face, her body, everything. "I think you're right. How are you feeling?"

"Okay."

He growled softly. "This isn't a time for heroism. Be honest."

She swallowed before responding. "I'm really okay, Mason. I've got a bit of a headache and I feel slightly sick, but it's just a mixture of a concussion and shock."

He felt like she was still downplaying it. And it frustrated the hell out of him.

Moving his hands to her shoulder and hip, Mason spoke in an even tone. "I'm going to roll you to your side and check your head."

Her eyes begun to shutter again. "Okay."

Rolling her, he studied the back of her head. His body tensed. Blood matted her hair. The only reprieve was that the blood was no longer flowing. He needed to get her checked out, though.

Gritting his teeth, he prayed Kye was close. He'd called Kye and Oliver last night before he'd had a shower and warned them to stay close and expect trouble. And damn was he glad he had.

Even though Mason had been driving for half an hour before

being run off the road, he knew his friend would make it a lot quicker. He estimated it would take Kye half the time if he didn't get pulled over along the way. That meant he would find them soon.

The sound of rustling had Mason going still. Keeping his hands on Sage's body, he listened.

It sounded again. This time closer.

Lifting Sage, he placed her closer to a tree. It would protect one side and he would protect her other. Her eyes never opened.

Lowering his head, he spoke softly into her ear. "I'll be right back, sweetheart."

Then, Mason turned and positioned his body in front of hers.

He hoped that it was Kye and Oliver, but he knew better than to let his guard down.

His gun lay heavy in his IWB holster. He would use it if needed.

Mason didn't have to wait long. Carter, the leader of Project Arma's current SEAL team, stepped out from behind a tree. A smirk stretched across his face.

"Mason, old friend, we meet again."

"What the hell do you want?" Mason sneered.

Sounds emanated from the bushes to Mason's other side. Flicking his head around, he caught sight of John, another member of the corrupt team.

"Her, of course," John said, taking a step closer.

There wasn't a chance that was happening. "Then you've wasted your time, boys. You know I won't be letting her go."

Carter shrugged. "Fortunately for us, you don't have a choice. And I'm glad you're here, Mason. When Alistair didn't return, we connected the dots. You'll pay for what you did to him."

Both men stepped closer. Mason was outnumbered. All he could do was pray that Kye was close.

Quickly and without warning, John kicked at Mason's head. Mason ducked, narrowly missing the hit. The kick was quickly followed by Carter's fist, which landed hard against Mason's temple. A roar rang in his ears.

Ignoring the pain, Mason hunched down and kicked out at John, sending him to the ground.

As Carter aimed another punch, Mason used his lightning reflexes to dodge the hit and grab the arm. Twisting him, Mason shielded his body with Carter's as John jumped back to his feet and attempted to jab Mason.

Carter twisted and kicked Mason to the ground. Before he could land another kick, Mason jumped to his feet and punched the man's face.

The crunch of his nose breaking echoed through the trees, swiftly followed by his howl.

Good. Hopefully Kye was close enough to hear.

John came at him from the side and Mason swung two jabs at his throat, immediately cutting off John's air. The man hunched over and spluttered for oxygen while Carter wiped the blood from his face.

"This was a wasted trip because neither of you will be getting your hands on her."

Carter dodged the hit that Mason threw and grabbed his arms. Before Mason could break free, John was in front of him, throwing a quick, hard punch to his gut. Mason keeled over at the pain.

There was no time to recover as more punches landed, some to the gut. Some to the face.

Pain radiated through Mason's body, but he shut off the feeling. As fists continued to land, he refused to react.

John drew back a fist to throw another punch and Mason readied himself for the pain.

It never came. The big man's body was flung against a nearby tree.

"What the—" Carter's words were cut off as his body was torn away from Mason's.

Mason dropped to the ground and took a moment to recover.

Then his mind went to Sage. Looking behind him, he saw she was exactly where he'd left her, her eyes still shut.

Ignoring the violence around him, Mason moved toward her. The pain to his body was intense but he pushed through. His body healed fast. The pain was temporary.

Mason tried to listen to her heartbeat, but with his injuries, he didn't trust his advanced hearing. Placing his fingers at her pulse, he noticed it was steady.

"You okay, brother?"

Mason turned his head at Kye's voice. Scanning the area, he saw no sign of Carter or John. "I'm okay. Where are they?"

"Ax and Logan are chasing them. I'm getting you guys to safety."

And *Logan*? "Logan's here?"

Kye shrugged. "The guy jumped out the window and left without them noticing. We followed him. He said he was sick of being a prisoner. We offered to let him come with us. That way we can keep an eye on him. The CIA doesn't know he's with us yet. We'll deal with that soon."

Mason looked to the trees. They didn't know enough about Logan. He could easily be a plant sent to infiltrate their group.

"Ax and I have spoken to him at length and haven't been able to detect any insincerity," Kye said, obviously realizing what Mason was thinking.

Mason nodded and stood with Sage in his arms. If Logan really did escape Project Arma, then not only would the man need their help, but he may have important information they could use.

If he *wasn't* who he said he was, the team would be watching, ready to take him down.

But Mason couldn't focus on that right now. Sage needed his attention.

"We need to get her to a hospital."

CHAPTER 10

"No, thank you."

Sage spoke the words calmly, but firmly enough that the man knew it wasn't negotiable.

Mason cocked his head to the side. "It's been less than twenty-four hours since we were run off the road. The concussion alone means you shouldn't be left without someone by your side."

Sage held on to the doorframe that separated her hospital room from the connected bathroom. It was true that she wasn't so steady on her feet at the moment, but there was no way she was taking Mason in with her while she did her business.

"I won't take long and if anything happens to me, you'll hear and be able to come in. I can even leave the door unlocked so that you don't have to break it."

His jaw clenched but she could see that he was giving in.

"Fine. But I'm standing right here."

"I didn't think you'd go anywhere else."

Stepping into the small bathroom, Sage closed the door. It was sweet that he was so worried about her. He'd been like that for the last twenty-four hours.

When the nurses had told him he had to leave, he'd flat-out

refused. Phrases like "life and death," "protective detail," and "where she goes, I go" had been thrown around like confetti. Sage had kept quiet, knowing there wasn't a chance the nurses would win.

Mason had gone so far as to send someone to get her a clean set of clothing for this morning. It had both surprised and impressed her.

Once Sage was done, she glanced at herself in the mirror. Anyone looking at her would never have guessed what she'd been through. The hit to the back of the head had required stitches but was invisible when she looked at her reflection. Other than the stitches and concussion, she'd escaped unscathed.

Thanks to Mason.

She was lucky that he had been with her. She didn't want to think about what would have happened if he hadn't been in the car.

"Sage?"

Pulling her eyes away from her reflection, she turned and opened the door.

Mason stood exactly where she'd left him. Taking up all the space in the doorframe. Looking huge as per usual. Huge and sexy.

A smile curved his lips. "What's going through your mind, Doc?"

You. All six and a half sexy feet of you. Even though she'd been in a car chase and driven off the road, the man still consumed her thoughts. Did that make her crazy?

Mentally shaking her head, Sage returned the smile and moved to step around him. "Just thinking that I need to be getting home."

Her home being Mason's old apartment.

Midstep, an arm snaked around her waist and she found herself in Mason's embrace. "Wrong answer." His head dipped and his lips lowered to touch the skin on her neck. "You have no idea how glad I am you're okay. Yesterday was terrifying. And there's not much that scares me."

The combination of his words and touch was enough to steal her breath. "Thank you for saving me. Saving us."

Mason lifted his head, an intense look in his eyes. "The danger isn't over."

And just like that, she was sucked back into reality. The reality where people from Project Arma wanted her. Where each time she messaged her brother with important information, her life was put in danger.

Both thoughts were incomprehensible.

"And you still think they want me because I'm Fletcher's doctor?"

"I do. Like I said before, they realized how heavily protected he is. So, option B, take the doctor who's studied his DNA. They've been underestimating how heavily protected *you* are, because they don't know that you're one of us yet."

Sage's eyes widened. She almost thought she'd misheard him. "I'm one of you?"

"You sure are, Doc."

At the sound of Oliver's voice, she turned her head toward the door. Oliver walked in, followed by Kye, Bodie, Wyatt, and Luca.

Sage tried to push away from Mason; he didn't move an inch. The man was like a brick wall. Instead, he dropped one arm and moved the other around her waist, pulling her body into his side.

She had to admit, the feeling of being pressed against him wasn't terrible.

He led her to the bed and helped her sit before sitting on the edge himself.

"We came to check on you," Kye said once the door shut.

Oliver stepped forward. "How are you feeling?"

Sage tried not to feel intimidated, being surrounded by so many alpha males. It felt like they took up every inch of the small room. "I'm okay. Mason's been taking great care of me."

She had no doubt she would be a mess had he not been by her side the entire time. Distracting her from any and all looming danger.

Mason nudged her shoulder with his own. "I haven't done anything. You've been a powerhouse of strength."

Sage scoffed. "I clung to you after the crash and have mostly slept since we got here."

"You didn't give up. And you haven't fallen into a heap. Like I said, a powerhouse of strength."

Sage's cheeks heated at Mason's compliment. It wasn't that she thought she was weak. Her actions just weren't remarkable. But Mason made it *sound* like they were. He made her feel strong.

A cough pulled Sage's attention away. She looked up to see it was Bodie. "We also wanted to tell you that we're taking shifts looking after you. We'll keep our distance, so you won't feel our presence, but in reality, you won't be alone for a second."

Every man in the room grunted their agreement. An emotion Sage couldn't identify clogged her throat. Gratitude maybe?

It felt nice to have people looking after her. To want to protect her. Sage hadn't had that in a while.

"Thank you." Her voice was heavy with emotion as she said the two words. She instinctively leaned into Mason, and he placed a kiss on her head.

Wyatt indicated to the door with his head. "We're going to get out of here."

"If this guy gives you trouble"—Bodie pointed to Mason —"give us a call and we'll come sort him out."

Sage chuckled. And boy did it feel good. "Done."

Mason shook his head. "Get out, assholes."

Once the room was empty, Mason helped Sage under the sheets. She spent the next couple of hours resting while Mason alternated between phone calls and helping her as needed. Anytime she wanted anything, even if it was just water, he was there. The man was like her personal angel.

When it was time to check out, it couldn't have come soon enough for Sage. Even though her stay was restful, being a patient was completely different from being a doctor, and she would happily admit that she struggled with the positional swap.

Stepping outside, Sage grimaced as the sun hit her eyes. It sent a shot of pain through her skull.

"Are you okay?"

She turned her attention to Mason, who had an arm around her waist. "It's common to have light sensitivity after a concussion."

Mason cursed. "We should have waited until after dark to leave."

Sage couldn't help it, she laughed. After the events of the last few weeks, a bit of sun was nothing. "I'm okay."

Mason's tight features told Sage he didn't agree.

Once in the car and driving, she voiced the question she had been wondering since she woke up. "What happened to them? The guys who ran us off the road."

Although Mason's physical appearance didn't change, there was a new edge to his voice when he spoke. "They took off once Cage, Ax, and Logan arrived. Ax and Logan chased them but didn't catch them."

Sage tried to hide her disappointment. "I'm sure there'll be more opportunities to get them."

She just hoped those "opportunities" didn't involve her in any way.

Mason shrugged. "One way or another, we'll find them."

Sage had a feeling that when Mason said *them*, he wasn't just talking about the men who had run them off the road. He was talking about every person who had worked for the project.

She wanted to have a relationship with Mason. She knew that with absolute certainty. But two adults couldn't have a long-term relationship with secrets.

Wringing her hands, Sage took a moment before asking her

next question. "When you do find everyone who's been involved in the project, what will you do with them?"

Mason seemed to consider her question for a moment. "I'd like to think I would hand them over to the authorities."

Like to think?

Sage waited for Mason to elaborate, but he didn't. Because he was saying he'd likely kill them.

"What if they went into the project with good intentions?" And had no idea who they were working for.

Sage caught the small frown that marred his brow. "I don't want to lie to you. At the end of the day, my brothers are my priority. And they could have died. Those drugs could have killed them. A part of me wants to hear everyone's individual story." He paused. "Another part of me thinks that everyone who played a part in the project deserves some sort of retribution."

Everyone. Not just those who'd intended to hurt others.

Sage felt sick. There was no way she could tell him. Probably ever. And that made her heart hurt.

If he found out that Jason had worked on the drug that changed his DNA...the drug that changed his brothers' DNA...he was dangerous to Jason. And that made him dangerous to her.

The feel of Mason's hand atop hers had Sage swinging her gaze back to him. Mason was flicking his eyes between her and the road.

"I'm sorry if my answer wasn't what you were wanting to hear. What are you feeling right now?"

Fear. Doubt. Overwhelming despair that I can't have you.

But she didn't say that. Any of it. "I'm just looking forward to getting back to my bed."

Except she wasn't. Not even a bit.

She looked down at their hands but could feel Mason's eyes studying her. "I thought you could stay with me for a bit."

That had been her intention. To fall into bed with him each night. Be held in his arms.

"I think I just need a bit of time to process everything that's happened."

Mason didn't respond for a moment. She knew what he was doing. Watching and listening for signs that she was lying. He wouldn't find them. That last thing she'd said was the truth. Just not the whole truth.

When Mason did respond, he spoke gently. "I don't like it. But I understand. Like Cage said, one of us will be watching. Keeping you safe."

Sage nodded. For the remainder of the trip, she watched the trees pass by in silence.

After what felt like forever, they reached the apartment building. Mason helped her up to his unit. His touch made her sad. Sad that she couldn't keep him.

Each time she snuck a peek at his face, she saw the hard set of his jawline. Mason wasn't happy. But he was giving her what she'd asked for, and for that, she was grateful.

When it came time for him to leave, Sage had a moment of doubt. She wanted to take back what she'd said and ask him to stay. Or ask him to take her to his house. Whatever would keep them together. But she kept her mouth shut.

Mason did an apartment check, then stopped by the front door. Reaching his hand up, he placed it on the side of her cheek. His touch was both wonderful and agonizing.

"Before I go, I want to repeat what I said yesterday. Our night together meant something to me."

It had meant everything to Sage. More than it should have. "I know."

Then he dipped his head. Sage had ample time to move away. She knew he moved slowly to give her time to do just that.

But she didn't. Because she couldn't. The promise of Mason's mouth on hers was too enticing to refuse.

When his lips touched her, the kiss wasn't sexual. It was gentle and comforting.

Too soon, Mason broke away and took a step toward the hall. It took real strength to not reach out and pull him back.

"Goodbye, sweetheart."

Then he was gone. And she wished again that she could pull him back to her.

~

WHEN MASON REACHED the bottom step, he pulled his phone from his pocket. Bodie picked up on the second ring.

"What do you need?"

"Can you come watch Sage for an hour? Wyatt's not in his apartment, and I need to go home to feed the dogs and grab a shower. Then I'll be back."

Hunter had fed the dogs while he was away, but he hadn't asked his friend to feed them tonight. He'd assumed *he'd* be able to feel them once he returned with Sage.

"You didn't take her to your place?"

"No." Because he was too damn honest for his own good. He was still kicking himself for not lying.

Bodie didn't pry. "Be there in ten."

Pocketing his phone, Mason finished the walk to his car. He sat and waited for Bodie, all the while keeping an eye on Sage's apartment window.

The moment she'd asked the question, Mason had known she was asking about Jason. She was seeking clarity on what he might do with her brother once found.

Lying would have been easy. But there was a strong chance Jason was working with Arma. Trying to acquire information about Fletcher and putting his sister's life at risk. If that was the case, Mason couldn't let the man just walk free.

While Sage had been sleeping, Mason had checked out her phone. Other than the one he had inserted, there was no bug.

Jason was presumably using burner phones, so his phone wasn't bugged, either.

So, Sage's messages to her brother were putting her life in danger. The question was, why?

Was Jason working with Project Arma? Or was the person she was messaging someone else entirely?

At the sight of Bodie's car, Mason started the engine and headed to his place.

He needed to figure it all out, and soon, because Sage was important to him.

Sometimes people built things up in their heads of what might be. Then they were fundamentally disappointed when reality didn't meet the dream.

In this instance, that was not the case. Being with Sage the other night had felt right. Like he'd finally found what had been missing from his life.

He couldn't lose her.

If there was anything he'd learned in the last week, it was that Sage was his, whether she knew it or not.

CHAPTER 11

age sat in her car outside Lexie and Asher's home. They lived in a warehouse apartment above small businesses in the middle of Marble Falls.

Sage took a breath. She was here to do a health checkup on both Lexie and their son, Fletcher. But she was nervous. Because she hadn't seen Asher since that day at Marble Protection. The day after she'd broken in.

He had definitely been unhappy with her. The question was— was he *still* unhappy with her?

The call from him had been a surprise. He'd asked her to come over to check on Fletcher. He'd probably only called because no other doctor was as knowledgeable about their DNA.

Sage scrubbed her hands over her face.

Seven days. That's how long it had been since the car crash. And eight days since she'd slept with Mason.

The headaches from the concussion had lessened, but although she'd begun to feel better physically, her mental and emotional state was low. For one, she didn't feel safe. Even though one of the guys was always tailing her, and there was always a guy outside her apartment. She still felt the need to check her rearview mirror a dozen times each trip. Check and recheck that her doors and windows were locked at the apartment.

There was also Jason. The idea that her messages to him had contributed to her brushes with danger was soul-wrenching. She couldn't wrap her head around it. At the same time, she couldn't deny the timing of both attacks.

And then there was Mason. Beautiful but dangerous Mason. She'd messaged him and asked for space. Boy, had that been hard. Not that they'd been dating. But they'd slept together, so she owed him a message.

She wanted him. And she went back and forth over whether she could tell him about her brother. But each time she even considered it, his words echoed in her brain.

She just couldn't.

Grabbing the medical bag from the passenger seat, Sage slid out of the car. As she walked to the stairs leading to their home, she spotted the familiar car parked down the street. She could already see who was in it.

Mason.

The men were supposed to be sharing the job of watching her. But every time she looked over her shoulder, she saw him.

Climbing the stairs, Sage reached the top and raised her hand to knock. Before she made contact with the wood, the door swung open and Asher stood in front of her.

A nervous smile curved her lips. "Hi Asher, I'm here to see Lexie and Fletcher for their checkup."

"Hi, I wanted to catch you before you came in."

Oh crap. That couldn't be good, could it? A shot of nerves hit Sage. But she tried her best to mask the emotion.

Asher's brows pulled together. "Hey, it's nothing bad. I wanted to tell you that I'm sorry for how I treated you a couple weeks ago. I was a jerk. After everything that happened with Lexie, I was on edge and I took it out on you. You've been through a lot these last few weeks. It looks like it might be because of Fletcher. I'm sorry about that."

The knot loosened in Sage's stomach.

Even if the only reason for his sudden change toward her was due to feeling guilty, that perhaps he thought he was responsible for her brushes with danger, she didn't mind. Having the old Asher back was one less stress in her life.

"That's okay, I shouldn't have taken her key. That was wrong. And the attacks weren't your fault, so you don't need to apologize for that."

He took a step back and opened the door farther. "Come in. She's in our bedroom."

Feeling a bit lighter, Sage moved through the lounge and entered the main bedroom. She was greeted with the sight of Lexie sitting on the bed feeding Fletcher. It was picture perfect. She made mothering look easy.

Her head flicked up, a beaming smile on her face. "Sage, sorry, I know it's time for our appointment. This little man woke up hungry and now that he's the king of the house, I am his slave—albeit a very happy slave."

"Don't apologize for feeding your son. It's a beautiful thing to do and you look gorgeous doing it. You were born to be a mother."

A wave of emotion crossed Lexie's face. Sage knew bits and pieces about the self-doubt Lexie had suffered over her ability to be a good mother. But Sage had always known the strong, independent woman would take on the role with ease.

Sage sat on the edge of the bed, placing her bag on the floor. "I'm going to take your blood pressure. Once Fletcher is fed and happy, we can weigh him and do a quick check on him."

"Sounds great."

Sage got started taking the other woman's blood pressure, being careful that she didn't disturb Fletcher in the process.

"How have you been doing with everything?" Sage asked.

Becoming a mother was a huge step for any person. It was a completely new way of life, suddenly becoming responsible for another human being. There was also the fact that, on a physiological level, there were huge hormonal changes after giving birth.

"I feel amazing," Lexie said confidently. "And so lucky. To have Fletcher. To have Asher." The woman was glowing.

"They're lucky to have you, too."

"Thank you. I'm just glad Fletcher is healthy."

Sage nodded. "His DNA makeup is very similar to that of Asher's. I have a feeling he's going to be a very strong and speedy toddler."

Lexie chuckled. "I'll have my hands full, then, won't I. Especially if he inherits even a fraction of my attitude or Asher's stubbornness."

"If he gets your strength or resilience, he's a lucky kid."

Lexie's smile grew. "You're too kind to me, Sage. This is why I need you around more. As it is, I haven't seen you in weeks."

Sage tried not to cringe. No one had told Lexie about the trouble Sage had been having. No one wanted the new mother to be stressed with knowing that Project Arma was after Fletcher's medical information.

Sage recorded the blood pressure result. "Anytime you want to see me, just let me know. And your blood pressure is perfect, by the way."

"Actually, Evie asked me to mention that she and Shylah are heading to the bar tonight. She said she'd love for you to join."

Sage paused. A night out actually sounded good. She really liked both Shylah and Evie.

Shylah was a nurse who worked at the local hospital. Sage had been fortunate to have a couple of shifts with the other woman since coming into town. She was easy to like and get along with.

Sage had less contact with Evie, but from the few times they had spoken, Evie seemed lovely. She had a calm and gentle nature.

Both women were dating men from Marble Protection.

A few hours of girl time, with no thoughts of genetically altered assassins or her brother, actually sounded divine. Plus, the last week had been lonely.

"I'd love to join them." The moment the words left her mouth, she knew it was the right decision. Every other night for the last week she'd had to force her mind off her cocktail of problems.

"Great! They'll be so excited."

Just then, Fletcher made a gurgling sound and looked up at them with the same dazzling amber eyes as his mother's.

Lexie laughed. "Looks like someone's ready for their checkup."

∾

SAGE THREW her head back and laughed at Evie. The woman was attempting to skull a shot with no hands. Shylah had convinced her friend it was a fun idea. Sage wasn't entirely sure how.

Leaning forward, Sage felt compelled to try to stop the looming mess. "Evie, I wouldn't."

They had only been at the bar for an hour but already all three women had gotten themselves to the point of being tipsy. Not drunk, but if Sage didn't stop, it wasn't far off.

"If the woman wants to try something new, let her." Trouble sparkled in Shylah's eyes as she spoke.

Sage shrugged. If Evie wanted to end up wearing her vodka rather than drinking it, that was her choice. Besides, Luca sat only a table away. If Evie got herself into trouble, Sage had no doubt he would be beside her in moments.

At the table with Luca sat Eden, Bodie and, of course, Mason. The moment she had stepped foot inside the bar, she'd spotted him.

They hadn't spoken yet. Sage had been doing her best to keep her eyes off the irresistible man. Not that it was working. So far, she'd looked at him at least a dozen times. Each time she looked, his gaze was on her. There may as well have been a huge spotlight on the guy.

For the third time, Evie lowered her head and wrapped her lips around the rim of the shot glass. She lifted the glass, but before she could tip her head back, the drink was whipped from her mouth by a large, muscular arm.

Evie turned angry eyes on the man beside her. "Luca. I had it that time."

"That was never going to end well, darlin'." Luca placed the glass back on the table, a smile on his face.

Shylah shook her head, appearing less than impressed. "Well, now she'll never know."

Sage lifted her glass of vodka cranberry to her lips. "Sorry, ladies, I'm with Luca. He just saved a very nice shirt."

Evie looked down as if checking that she was in fact wearing a shirt. "I was going to drink it, not pour it on my clothes."

"That's what you think," Shylah muttered.

Everyone laughed. Everyone except Evie.

When Sage turned back to Evie, she caught Luca whispering into her ear, causing a light pink shade to tinge her cheeks.

They were cute. And Sage was staring like a crazy person.

A cough pulled her attention to the side. Shylah studied Sage with one eyebrow lifted.

Yep, definitely crazy.

Moving her attention back to her drink, Sage frowned when she realized it was empty.

"Time for a refill." Even as the words left Shylah's mouth, her hand wrapped around Sage's arm and she began pulling her in the direction of the bar.

Instead of heading to the side of the bar closest to them, she headed to the end opposite, farthest from where the guys were sitting.

If the other woman's goal was to have a private chat, Sage was pretty sure it wouldn't be happening in here. The guys could hear a conversation a block over.

"I know they'll probably still hear us, but why make it easy for them," Shylah said, reading Sage's thoughts.

When Shylah stopped at the end of the bar, Sage faced her friend. "I don't mind if they hear what we say."

Shylah raised a brow. "Not even Mason?"

Maybe Mason a little bit. Not that she would be admitting that out loud. "Nope. It's not like you're going to ask me if I love the guy."

Shylah leaned over the bar and signaled for the bartender. "Nah, I was just going to ask if you're screwing him."

When the young man behind the bar arrived, Shylah ordered them both another drink. Sage doubted it was a good idea for her to drink another so quickly. She'd nurse it.

"Screwed."

Shylah turned her gaze back to Sage. "What?"

"Screwed. Not screwing."

The other woman's eyes widened. "You had sex with Mason? Oh my lordy! When? Wait, it was when you went to Rockdale, wasn't it?"

"Eden told you about Rockdale?"

Rolling her eyes, Shylah paid for their drinks once they were placed in front of them, then turned back to Sage. "Was it amazing?"

"The sex? It was pretty good."

And by pretty good, what she really meant was absolutely incredible. It had been the best sex of her life. Not that she had much to compare it to. But she knew it was special.

Shylah's expression told Sage she knew she was downplaying

the sex. "So what happened? Why has the man been sitting there all night without making a move to talk to you?"

Because she'd pushed him away. Because she had a secret that she was scared to death the man would discover.

Squirming under Shylah's scrutiny, Sage looked away. She regretted it immediately. Her eyes went straight to Mason, now standing at the other end of the bar. Only he wasn't alone. A woman stood beside him. A tall blonde woman with legs for days. And she was giving Mason a look that said she was interested.

A sick feeling entered her stomach. The woman was stunning.

Just then, Mason's gaze found hers. Not wanting him to catch her staring, she quickly dropped her eyes to her drink.

She took a breath before turning her attention back to Shylah. "We just aren't a good match."

Not that her heart would accept that.

Shylah's brows knitted together. "Why not?"

For so many reasons.

The alcohol began to fade from her system and she was left feeling flat. "I just can't see it leading anywhere long term."

Shylah was quiet beside her for a beat, then she shrugged. "You're probably right."

Sage pulled back. That was not what she was expecting the other woman to say.

"I mean, just because the guy's infatuated with you, doesn't mean you need to pursue a relationship with him," Shylah continued. "You're clearly not into him. So best he goes after someone who *does* want him. Like that chick he's talking to. I'm sure she'll make him happy. Right?"

Sage knew what Shylah was doing. And it was working. "She's pretty."

"In an obvious kind of way, I guess. She's probably just trying to get him into bed, though."

The image of the woman in bed with Mason made her red with jealousy.

Sage didn't want him sleeping with another woman. Hell, she didn't want him *talking* to another woman. "Okay, I admit, I want him."

Shylah cocked her head to the side. "Then what the heck are you doing letting blondie take all his attention?"

Being cautious, as per usual.

Was it possible she could have Mason *and* keep her brother safe? Maybe remaining close to Mason *was* the best way to keep him safe. Eventually, she might gain the courage to tell him about her brother. And maybe by then, she could convince him that Jason was good. That he'd never intentionally harm anyone.

Suddenly, the idea that she could have both, a relationship with Mason and her brother's safety, seemed a very real possibility.

Her heart rate increased a notch.

Sage studied the man she'd been thinking about all week. She didn't want to watch Mason from across the room. Especially not with another woman. She wanted to *be* the woman with him.

She had been lonely for so long. Finally, there was a man in her life who made her happy. If she pushed him away, would she find that again?

Maybe, it was time to start trusting her heart.

Sage kept her gaze on Mason as she took a step back from the bar. "I'm getting my man."

"Yeah you are."

CHAPTER 12

 ason felt Sage's eyes on him, but he didn't look. He was trying to be respectful. Trying to give her the space she needed. But if she came to him, all bets were off.

The woman in front of him was still speaking. She'd approached him when he'd reached the bar and had been talking ever since. He hadn't heard a word she'd said. Not because he was trying to be rude, but because he couldn't get *Sage* out of his head.

From his peripheral vision, he caught Sage begin to head his way. His blood started pumping.

Mason interrupted the woman midsentence. "Excuse me, my girlfriend is coming."

Pushing off the bar, Mason met Sage partway.

"Where's the woman?"

There was an edge to her voice that he hadn't heard before, and it caused a smile to pull at his lips. "Not sure. Probably talking to some other guy."

She was clearly jealous. It was cute as hell. And it told him something important—she wanted him.

"She was pretty."

He lifted a shoulder. "Didn't really notice. I was too busy watching the beautiful woman at the end of the bar."

Beautiful didn't do her justice, though. Not really. Every room she walked into, she was all he saw. And he didn't know how to describe that in one word.

"You think I'm beautiful?"

It annoyed Mason that there was uncertainty in her voice. Did the woman not know how amazing she was both inside and out? How just about every man in the bar was watching her, hoping she would notice them?

"I don't think. I know."

She seemed pleased by his answer. "I think you're beautiful, too."

Mason couldn't help but chuckle. He'd been called many things in his life but beautiful was never one of them.

Without warning, she took his hand and began pulling him toward the door.

"Where are you taking me?"

Not that he would be opposed to this woman taking him anywhere. He would follow.

Sage turned her head but kept walking. Her smile hinted at mischief. It was a fun side of her that he hadn't really seen yet. The smile was fucking radiant. And he wanted to see more of it.

"Somewhere private."

Once they were outside the bar, Mason expected her to walk toward the parking lot. So he was surprised when she tugged him in the opposite direction. Toward the forest.

He was tempted to pull her back. Because although he had twenty-twenty vision no matter the light, Sage didn't. For her, there would just be the dim light from the moon.

But he didn't pull her back. He liked her sudden spontaneity. Not to mention the feel of her hand around his. He hadn't touched the woman in a week. He was a starving man. No way was he doing anything to stop her.

When Sage went to step through the cluster of trees, Mason felt compelled to mention the obvious. "You won't be able to see much in there."

She halted in front of him. Then she crept a step closer, her hands going to his shoulders. Reaching up, she snaked an arm around his neck and pulled his head down.

"So be my eyes."

The words were barely a whisper. But she may as well have shouted them, he heard her so clearly.

Her breath brushed across his neck and her chest pressed to his.

Damn, this woman was something else. And she was doing all sorts of things to his body.

Recapturing her hand, Mason took a step in front of her and began to lead them through the trees. He kept his eyes partly on the path but also on her steps, ensuring she didn't trip or walk into anything.

Mason had no idea where they were going. But she was safe with him. Always.

A few minutes in, Sage came to a stop. Looking back at her, he noticed excitement in her eyes.

"Do you hear that?" she whispered. "Water."

Mason *did* hear it. It was Marble Falls Lake. And it was close.

Sage took a step closer to him. "Take us to the water."

He would take her to the damn moon if she asked. Changing direction, he began to walk toward the sound of the lake.

It didn't take long for them to reach the embankment. Once they did, they stood watching the water. Actually, that wasn't true. Sage watched the water. Mason watched *her*. Transfixed. Moonlight bounced off her blonde hair and blue eyes.

Untangling their fingers, Sage reached for the hem of her top. Mason almost felt paralyzed to the spot as he watched her lift the floral material over her head. Her fair skin appeared almost white in the darkness. Her ample chest pushed against her frilly bra.

"What are you doing?"

Even though he asked the question, it was already damn obvious what she was doing. And it was wreaking all sorts of havoc on him.

Sage began toeing off her shoes and her hands unfastened her jeans. "It's a warm night. I want to go in the water."

Mason hesitated. Even though she'd only had two drinks, he didn't want her to do anything she'd regret in the morning. "I don't know if that's such a good idea, sweetheart. The water can be more dangerous than it looks."

Particularly when you threw alcohol into the mix.

Sage pushed her jeans down and stepped out of them. She looked desirable as all hell in her white bra and panties. There was a battle going on between his mind and his body.

"Guess you'd better join me and keep me safe then."

She reached behind her, and Mason immediately knew what she was about to do.

Stepping forward, he held her wrists lightly in his hands. "You've been drinking."

Sage tilted her head to the side. "I had two drinks. I am completely in my right mind. And I want to go for a swim."

He studied her face. He didn't see any glassiness in her eyes. Her features looked as set as he'd ever seen them.

When he dropped his hands, he heard the small sound as she unclasped her bra. Then her breasts spilled out.

Fuck. He was a dead man.

Swallowing, he watched her remove the last piece of clothing she'd been wearing. And then she stood there. Completely bare, looking like an angel sent down from Heaven.

Every inch of her was beautiful. Like a piece of art that you needed to admire, but equally itched to touch.

Sage took a step toward the water. "Join me."

It was like he couldn't not do what she asked. His body was moving on autopilot. Drawn to the woman in front of him.

He stripped off his clothes in record time and was by her side in an instant. Taking her hand, he led them into the lake.

The water wasn't warm. But it wasn't cold.

They walked until the water lapped at his waist and Sage's shoulders. She reached up and wrapped her hands around his neck, while he closed his arms around her waist. Her naked skin pressed against his, making him harden to a painful level.

He fixed his eyes on hers. "If we do this, I won't be letting you go."

She would be his. This would seal the deal.

Sage pulled herself up into his arms, wrapping her legs around his waist. "Good. I want you to hold me. Always."

Every inch of his heated body was aware of her. Ready for her.

When her mouth moved the short distance to his, he was lost. The only other person who existed in the world was Sage.

Mason wanted to kiss her slowly. Take his time and explore her.

Sage had other plans.

Her tongue invaded his mouth while she plastered her body tighter against his. Her pebbled nipples rubbed against his chest.

The water was calm around them. That was the *only* thing that was calm.

As their tongues danced, Mason reached between their bodies and engulfed her breast in his palm.

A sweet moan escaped Sage's lips.

He alternated between massaging her breast and flicking his thumb over her peak. More moans sounded from the glorious woman.

So damn responsive.

Switching to the other breast, he did the same. Sage hummed.

Mason had thought of nothing but her in the last week.

Flashes of their night together had been on repeat every damn day. Watching her without being able to touch her had been hell.

There had been some moments where he'd wondered if he had made it all up in his head. The passion. The fire.

Right now, under the moonlight, he knew he hadn't. Sage was made for him. It may as well be written in the stars.

Tearing his lips from hers, he lowered his mouth and captured one of her rock-hard nipples. He sucked and played.

Sage writhed in his arms.

Then he reached between their bodies and touched his thumb between her thighs. This time, it wasn't a soft moan that escaped her, it was a cry that echoed through the night.

Mason rubbed her, his lips trailing back up to again capture her mouth. But that only lasted moments.

When Mason inserted a finger inside Sage, she quickly tore her lips from his and flung her head back. Her breathing was heavy. Quick.

Mason watched the pleasure wash over her face as he rubbed and worked her. This was Sage in her natural state. This was Sage unbound. She was fucking glorious.

Mason intended for her to come apart like this.

As if sensing his intentions, Sage lowered her hand and wrapped her fingers around him. His entire body jolted at the touch. Mason closed his eyes and prayed for calm.

"Sage." Her name was torn from his chest. Pained.

He placed both hands on her hips and groaned as her hand firmly slid over his length. Sage used his moment of weakness to adjust herself, placing his tip at her entrance. Then, slowly, she slid her body down so that he entered her, inch by inch.

His breaths deepened. His body urged him to drive deep into her softness.

Sage lifted both hands and ran them through Mason's hair. Pressing her lips to his ear, she whispered, "Fuck me."

He was lost. The last thread of self-restraint that he'd barely had control over broke. He pushed all the way into her body. Without pause, Mason began to drive into Sage.

Her soft whimpers of pleasure cut through the night air. Their lovemaking was passionate and primitive and fiery all at once.

Tension built fast. Mason pressed his mouth to Sage's, swallowing her heated moans. The need he felt for the woman in his arms was ferocious.

Their bodies clashed in the water.

Sage ripped her mouth from Mason's and leaned her head back. Her body tightened around his as she came hard. Her cry so anguished and loud it would be heard for miles.

Mason kept thrusting until her pulsating body became too much. Growling deep in his chest, Mason pulled her head forward and pressed his forehead to hers as his body tightened.

He held her close as he hummed and vibrated.

He wouldn't be letting her go anytime soon. He couldn't.

CHAPTER 13

S age rested her forearms on the kitchen counter. She tried not to fidget as she watched Mason prepare breakfast.

His kitchen was huge, just like the rest of his house. Even his yard was massive. Sage had been there once before, for Lexie's baby shower, but seeing it a second time was still shocking.

Mason said he'd moved out of the unit and into the house for his two dogs. But Sage didn't have to be a dog owner to know that even they didn't require that much space.

Waking up that morning, the first thing she'd been aware of was the thick arm around her waist. The second thing was the heat against her back. The whole front of his body had been pressed against her.

Then every moment from the previous night flashed through her mind, right up to him carrying her to his bed.

And she didn't regret a moment of it. Because it had felt right. Being with him felt right. She was tired of fighting it.

"What's going through that brilliant mind of yours, sweetheart?"

Mason's voice jolted her out of her thoughts. She scrambled

to come up with a response that wouldn't leave her heart exposed.

"I'm just thinking that you should really let me help you with breakfast."

Lie. Big fat, I-don't-want-to-tell-you-the-truth lie. And, by the look on Mason's face, he knew it. But then, of course he did, he had training and a million superabilities, which allowed him to pick out the telltale signs of a lie.

"I'll pretend I believe you."

Mason flipped the bacon then turned his attention to the eggs. Delicious smells floated around the room, causing her stomach to growl loudly—and that was loud for normal hearing standards.

Heat rose to her cheeks just as the ringing of her phone sounded. Glancing down, she saw the word *home* flash across the screen.

Crap. It was her mom or dad. More likely Mom. Probably calling to check in. Sage loved her parents to death and missed them like crazy but the check-ins usually involved strong pressure to visit more and a dozen questions about Jason.

Questions she could only answer with more lies.

Sage considered letting it ring, but she knew it would just worry her mother. Kathryn Porter was a worrier. That, in combination with her age, meant the last thing Sage wanted to do was add stresses to her day.

"You can get that," Mason said over his shoulder.

Nibbling her lip, Sage hesitated for another half second before answering the call.

"Hey, Mom."

"Darling, I thought you weren't going to answer."

Every time she heard her mother's voice, the woman sounded a bit frailer. It ate at Sage.

"Sorry, I was just making breakfast." Watching and making were kind of the same, weren't they? "And remember, with my work commitments, there may be times that I miss your calls. How are you and Dad?"

"Oh, yes, I forgot about you working in the hospital." Her mother had been forgetting a few things lately, and it worried Sage to no end. "We're okay. Getting some gardening in. We've started ballroom dancing on Wednesday nights."

Sage smiled at the thought of her parents dancing. They weren't what most would consider coordinated, but she could imagine them enjoying themselves.

"That sounds like great fun."

"It is. It reminds me of our younger years." There was a pause down the line. "Your father and I miss you. When are you coming to visit?"

There it was. The question she got every call. Sage knew exactly what was coming next, and she felt a heavy dread.

Sage scrubbed a hand over her face. "Soon. Maybe in a month or so."

"Oh good. Your father will be happy. What about Jason? I haven't seen or heard from him in so long." A deep sadness echoed through the line. It was a sadness that resonated with Sage because she felt it every single day.

She took a breath before she told the next lie. "I know. I miss him, too. He's still working remotely. He's doing really long days."

This lie wasn't a spur-of-the-moment one. It was one that had continued for years. When Jason had gone into hiding, her parents had asked about him often. Sage hadn't known what to tell them. She'd seen the worry deepen, to the point where she was concerned about their health.

So, she'd told them that he got a job in rural Australia. There was terrible phone reception there, so he could text but not call. Seeing as her parents only had landlines, that meant they relied on Sage to pass on information about him.

Kathryn and Rod Porter hadn't questioned the validity of the story. Why would they? She'd never lied to them before.

Her mother sighed. "I miss him."

Swallowing the lump in her throat, Sage nodded even though her mom couldn't see her. "Me too."

Looking up, she caught Mason watching her.

Clearing her throat, she mentally shook herself out of the despair. "Sorry, I need to get going. I'll try to call in a few days, okay?"

"Okay, dear. I love you."

"I love you, too, Mom. Say hi to Dad for me."

Hanging up, Sage stared at her phone for a second before looking up at Mason. He wasn't looking at her; his attention seemed to be focused on plating the bacon and eggs. But she knew he'd heard every word. Even without the super hearing, he probably would have heard.

"My brother hasn't had a chance to see my parents in a while," Sage offered, feeling like she owed him an explanation. He would have been able to hear the lie clear as day.

"You don't have to explain."

But she felt like she did. "They worry. He'll be home soon, so I won't need to lie to them any longer."

At least she hoped he'd be home soon. Hoped and prayed.

Mason nodded. "I understand. Sometimes we lie to protect the people we love."

That's exactly what Sage was doing. But lying didn't come easily for her.

"I do miss him. That wasn't a lie."

Why the heck had she gone and said that? It probably had something to do with Mason staring into her eyes like he was staring into her soul. Making her want to bare every last secret.

He took a step closer. "How long has it been since you last saw him?"

Too long. Too long since seeing him, speaking to him, *everything*.

"A couple of years. He's been super busy."

Just not from work. He'd been busy running. Hiding. Keeping himself alive from people who wanted him dead. At least, that was what he *told* her he was doing. She wasn't so sure anymore. She wasn't so sure about anything.

"I'd love to meet him one day."

Luckily, Sage was saved from responding by loud scratching noises. They both turned to see two large greyhound faces pressed to the glass of the back door. She knew from previous visits that their names were Nunzie and Dizzie, and they were adorable creatures.

Sage couldn't hold back the laugh at the dribble that ran down the glass.

Mason rolled his eyes. "As you can probably tell, it's breakfast time." Opening the fridge, Mason pulled out what looked like a bag of mince.

"Fresh meat? Wow. Lucky pups."

Shaking his head, he headed toward the door. "They're spoiled." Pushing outside, he paused before he pulled the door shut. "I'll be right back."

Then, with a wink, he disappeared.

The smile remained on her lips after he left. She couldn't help it. The guy just made her happy.

She lifted her phone. It had become a habit that whenever her parents called, she sent the same message to her brother. And even though she had no idea what was going on with him, she still wanted to message. Just to remind the guy that he had family who loved him.

Mom just called. She misses you.

As Sage pressed send on the message, she heard the sound of a phone vibrate near where Mason had just been cooking. He'd received a message.

Just for a moment, she had an urge to go over there and see who the message was from.

Then she shook her head.

What the heck was she thinking? It was Mason's private phone.

She couldn't imagine how she would feel if someone invaded her privacy like that. Quickly dashing the thought away, she wasn't sure why she'd even considered it.

Maybe because you like the guy and want to know everything about him.

Mason reentered the kitchen, going straight to the sink to wash his hands. "Those mutts don't realize how good they have it. Ready to eat?"

Sage stood and helped Mason prepare the table. Once they were seated, she scanned the plate of food. It looked just as good as it smelled.

"Yet again you surprise me with your beyond-average culinary skills," Sage said as she dug into her eggs and bacon.

"There are many things that might surprise you about me. Give me some time and I'll share all my secrets."

Over breakfast, Mason and Sage talked about everything from politics to TV shows. It turned out they had more in common than she'd thought. Not only did they both think reality television was too scripted, Mason also admitted to refrigerating his chocolate.

Never in Sage's life had she met someone who agreed that chocolate belonged in the fridge.

She laughed as she helped Mason clear the table. "I've always refrigerated my chocolate and my family all think I'm nuts. Jason and I would have wars over the issue. The second he saw chocolate in the fridge, he would take it out. The moment I realized what he'd done, I'd chuck it back in. It was infuriating. It was the great Porter chocolate battle."

Mason shook his head. "Luckily for me, Quinn was on board with the cold chocolate."

Sage began to fill the dishwasher. She actually hadn't minded the chocolate feud. It had eventually turned into a bit of a game between them. And whenever Sage was sad or having a bad day, Jason would pop her chocolate straight back in the fridge and bring it to her an hour later.

The memory brought a heavy feeling to her stomach. Turning back to her phone, she noticed there was still no message from Jason. On impulse, she shot off another before she could talk herself out of it.

Jason?

Sage glanced up at the sound of Mason's phone vibrating against the counter again. A small frown furrowed her brow. Mason lifted his cell and pocketed it.

Her eyes remained on the phone in his pocket, even when he moved in front of her.

"That's probably one of the guys." Mason's arms wrapped around Sage. Pulling her body close, he pressed his face into her hair. "What do you want to do today?"

When his lips lowered behind Sage's ear and begun to nuzzle her skin, all other thoughts vanished. A trail of goose bumps fanned across her skin.

"I don't mind what we do."

"Hmm, leaving the ball in my court is a bit dangerous when the woman in my arms is so damn desirable."

Sage giggled as Mason's lips began to trail down her neck. Gosh, that felt good. *She* felt good. It was the first time in a long time, possibly ever, she had felt like this.

CHAPTER 14

Sage scanned the big house as she exited the car. It wasn't quite as large as Mason's home, but still a lot bigger than most.

Eden and Shylah had invited them over for dinner. Sage was excited but her anticipation was tinged with nerves. She and Mason had been on a handful of dates. So technically they were dating, although they hadn't said that word out loud.

That meant that tonight was a double date. A double date with the perfect couple, Eden and Shylah.

"You don't need to be nervous," Mason whispered once he was standing beside her. Taking her hand in his, he led them to the front door.

The couple lived a bit farther out of town. Sage had gotten the brief rundown from Mason. Basically, Shylah and Eden had been dating when the guys were at Project Arma, but when the program had been shut down, Shylah had gone missing. That had left Eden angry at the world and needing to be away from people.

Even if you weren't mad at the world, Sage understood the appeal of living a bit farther out. It was peaceful. There wasn't a neighbor in sight.

Mason raised his hand and knocked on the door. A few seconds passed before they were greeted by Shylah. "Sage, Mason, hello! Welcome! Come in."

Sage stepped forward and gave the other woman a hug. Then she took in the interior. Good lord, the house was amazing.

The ceilings were high with striking black pendant lighting and the entrance led to an open floor plan. A huge modern kitchen sat to the left of the room and opened to dining and living areas. And there was no way she could miss the big grand staircase in front of her against the wall.

It was nice. Very nice. Just like Mason's home. When she stopped to think about it, all the men had beautiful homes.

Mason left for the kitchen, but Sage remained, still taking it in.

Shylah took a step closer. "Gorgeous, isn't it?"

Gorgeous was an understatement.

Sage couldn't help but voice her thoughts. "They all have such beautiful homes."

Shylah was already nodding. "The guys got big payouts in compensation from the government after Project Arma shut down. You know, so they wouldn't sue and would keep quiet. More than enough for their business and to live comfortably."

That was news to Sage. Although, it wasn't a surprise. They deserved some form of compensation after what happened.

Shylah linked her arm through Sage's and led them to the kitchen. Eden and Mason stood by the counter, already holding beers.

Eden gave her a nod. "Hey, Sage. Drink?"

"Just a water would be wonderful."

Eden pushed off the counter and moved toward the fridge.

Sage wasn't a big drinker. Being a doctor, she liked to keep a clear head. The other night at the bar had been the exception. And even then, two had felt like too many.

Shylah went to the oven and when she pulled it open, the room filled with the most delicious aroma.

Sage eyed the contents of the oven. "My god, Shylah, that smells amazing."

Eden placed a glass of water in front of Sage. "If the woman wasn't a damn good nurse, she would be a chef. No question."

Shylah rolled her eyes from behind Eden. "It's just chicken mignon. Nothing special."

Sage laughed. "Sounds special to me." She shook her head at Mason. "Sorry, buddy, I'm a steak-and-veg kind of cook."

And even that was pushing it.

Mason wrapped an arm around her waist. It felt all kinds of good to have his body against hers. "I'd eat whatever you cooked."

Leaning his head down, he pressed his lips to her temple. Heat rose in her cheeks. When she looked back up, it was to see Eden and Shylah staring at them.

Shylah in particular had a smile from ear to ear on her face. "You guys look good together."

Eden shook his head. "Don't get Shylah started. Soon she'll be organizing a wedding followed by a nursery for you."

Mason's face dropped all humor. "No more kids until Project Arma is brought down. We don't have the manpower to protect them."

Eden's features hardened. "Agreed. It's unbelievable that Fletcher's DNA is just like ours."

Normally, a patient's information was confidential, but Sage knew that Asher and Lexie shared all of Fletcher's health information with the group. "It's quite extraordinary, actually. I predict he'll be just as strong and fast as you guys."

Mason and Eden shared a look. Sage could guess what they were thinking. That if the people behind Arma knew the DNA could be passed on in utero, they could create soldiers from the get-go. Bypass the drugs.

A child's mind was more easily manipulated than an adult's. If child soldiers were brought up and trained in a certain way, they would be the one thing Mason's team wasn't. Loyal.

The idea made Sage feel sick. She liked to think that no one would be capable of stooping to that level, but the reality was, no one had any idea what lengths the people behind Project Arma would go to.

"Right, enough of that. Time to eat," Shylah said, breaking through the silence.

Everyone pitched in, moving items to the table. As they began eating, the conversation remained light. No one watching would guess that the two men at the table were genetically enhanced warriors. No one would think danger loomed around the corner. It looked normal. It *felt* normal.

"You drank fermented horse milk?"

It had been Shylah who'd posed the question, but if she hadn't, Sage would have. The very thought made her feel ill.

Mason nodded. "Not intentionally."

"Nah, it was just stupidity," Eden laughed.

When it didn't look like Mason was going to say any more, Sage nudged him with her shoulder. "Now you have to tell us."

Shylah giggled. "Yeah, and we'll decide how stupid it was."

Mason shrugged. "We'd just completed a mission in central Asia. We weren't due to leave until the next morning, so we had a few drinks at the hotel bar. I couldn't read a damn thing on the menu, or understand the guy working there, so I just asked for something I couldn't get in the US."

"And he gave you fermented horse milk?"

Why the heck would someone be serving that at a bar?

"I found out later that it's popular there. It wasn't terrible. I've had worse."

Eden leaned back in his seat. "Don't worry, Sage. I have plenty of stories far worse than that one."

"Oh, I would love to hear them." She smiled, then frowned. "Do you guys miss it? Being SEALs?"

For a moment, she wondered if the question was too personal. She was relieved when neither man seemed annoyed.

Mason linked his hands behind his head. "There'll always be things that I miss. But the best parts of the job were working with the guys and helping people. I still get to do both." His lips tightened. "Besides, I wouldn't be able to go back."

Eden nodded. "Everything he said."

Shylah shrugged. "Their loss is our gain."

Pushing her chair back, she stood. "Should we clear the table?"

Sage helped Shylah, and the men also helped for a bit before going outside to do a perimeter check of the house.

Shylah began filling containers with leftovers. "I haven't seen you at the hospital lately."

Sage turned on the tap to rinse the dishes. "With everything going on, I extended my special leave. I'll still be looking after Lexie, Fletcher, and the guys, but that's it."

Shylah laughed. "Looking after all those people is already a full-time job."

To be honest, it didn't take up too much of her time. Although, that was a good thing. It meant everyone was healthy and uninjured. "It's a job I enjoy. Their DNA is so interesting to me. Everything about them is fascinating."

Even though the people who designed the drugs were terrible, they were terrible people with brilliant minds.

"I tell Eden every day that if he could fly, I would start calling him Clark Kent."

Boy, was that accurate. "Must feel good, bagging your own Superman."

Shylah walked to the sink and nudged her shoulder. "You too."

Had she? Glancing out the window, Sage saw Mason outside standing with Eden. Eden had his arms crossed, whereas Mason stood with his hands in his pockets. Both men looked tall and strong and fierce. But it was Mason she was drawn to. Mason who made her heart speed up. Her body feel things that she'd never felt before.

"I see the way he looks at you," Shylah said quietly from right beside Sage. As if on cue, Mason's gaze lifted and looked straight at her. His eyes were heated and intense. Flutters churned in Sage's stomach. "It's the same way Eden looks at me. Like they'd fight the world to protect you. Even when Eden was on Toved, and he was supposed to want to kill me, he still couldn't hurt a hair on my head."

Sage shifted her gaze from Mason. "Toved?"

The other woman appeared confused for a moment. "You don't know about Toved?"

Sage had never heard the word in her life.

Taking Sage's hand, Shylah walked them over to the couch. "Project Arma has been working on weapons to use against the guys. One of those weapons is a drug called Toved. We first discovered the drug when the guys raided a Project Arma warehouse and Asher was injected with it. He went crazy. Like, stark-raving mad. He attacked the guys. He basically saw everyone as an enemy. And enemy number one is the person you're most familiar with or close to. It's like a scent thing or something."

That sounded unbelievably scary and dangerous. "How frightening."

"Eden was also drugged. I drugged him."

Sage's eyes widened. For a moment, she thought she'd heard wrong.

Shylah lifted her hands. "Before you say anything, I did it to save his life. I was threatened and told that if I didn't give him the drug, they would kill him."

Sage sucked in a sharp breath. "Did he hurt you?"

Wetting her lips, Shylah shook her head. "He was angry. And scary. So, so scary. But he fought it. Me talking to him helped. Reminding him that I loved him."

"Oh my gosh, I'm glad you're both okay."

"Thank you. The doctor who created the drug is dead. But we worry that they may still be working on it. Trying to make it stronger so that no amount of willpower can fight it."

It seemed like a genuine concern.

"I hope that's not the case." Although, Sage didn't feel optimistic in the least. "If they find a way to make the men lose their humanity..."

"Yep. Danger times a million. Hence the urgency to find them."

Just then, Mason and Eden entered the room. Shylah stood and walked to Eden while Sage remained on the couch. Everything she'd just learned rolled around in her mind. There was so much danger. So much to fear.

And what if some of that danger touched Jason? Had *already* touched him? Mason had his team to protect him. Her brother had no one.

If Project Arma found him, there were a hundred different ways they could hurt him. Sometimes, death wasn't the worst outcome.

The couch dipped beside Sage, and she turned her head to find Mason watching her closely.

"Shylah told you about Toved."

She wasn't surprised he'd heard. "It's scary to think a drug like that exists."

"I know. But whatever they're hoping to achieve, they won't."

Reaching his arm out, Mason pulled her into his side.

But for once, his touch didn't comfort her. Fear for her brother sat at the forefront of her mind.

When Mason began talking to Eden, Sage used his moment of distraction to pull out her phone and send a quick message to Jason. Just to say that she hoped he was okay.

The moment she hit send, she felt a vibration against her hip bone. Looking down, she realized it had come from Mason's phone, which sat in his pocket.

Had he just received a message? At the same time that she'd sent one? *Again?*

When Mason's head lowered to kiss her temple, Sage tried to relax but couldn't.

There was something going on—and she didn't like where her thoughts were taking her.

CHAPTER 15

*M*ason lifted the sheet of paper from the table. On it were names. Lots of them.

Shaking his head, he closed his eyes. There were too many. But then, even a single name would be too many.

Opening his eyes, Mason drew his attention back to his team. They were in the Marble Protection office. Around the table sat Wyatt, Eden, Oliver, Kye, and Logan.

Although Mason hadn't spent a lot of time with Logan, his team had. They'd reported that, so far, he appeared trustworthy. But that didn't mean he was.

The team made sure at least one guy always had eyes on him. And to Logan's credit, he didn't seem to mind.

Over the last week, they'd helped Logan relocate his family somewhere safe. Somewhere Project Arma wouldn't be able to find them.

Wyatt had also spent a significant amount of time on the phone with Agent Sinclair. The guy wasn't happy Logan was with them. When Sinclair had threatened to take Logan back and arrest anyone who got in his way, Wyatt had reminded the guy of the agreement made after the closing of the project. That their team was to work *alongside* the CIA, and the agent had already breached the agreement numerous times.

When Wyatt threatened to go higher, Sinclair had quickly backed off.

Today, they were including Logan in the team meeting. There was a thick cloud of disbelief in the air. Disbelief tinged with anger.

"All of these men are missing?" Mason finally asked.

Wyatt nodded. "All of them disappeared at some point over the last two years. Every one of them were active in the military."

Kye leaned forward. "What branch?"

"All of them—Navy, Army, Air Force and Marines."

Another beat of silence.

"What a nightmare," Bodie muttered under his breath.

This was worse than Mason could have imagined. The team had found out months ago that Project Arma was recruiting soldiers who had been kicked out of the military. Now, it appeared they were also taking good men and holding them captive.

Eden turned to Logan. "So, once they took you, they put you on a team with seven other men, all of them also taken against their will?"

Logan nodded. The man looked pained. "All of us have military backgrounds but are from different branches of the military. They're all good men."

"Will you tell us about what it was like there?" It was Oliver who posed the question, but it was something they all wanted to hear.

Logan scrubbed a hand over his face. There was no fear or weariness in his eyes. Just anger and pain. "We were kept in a high-security property. It was surrounded by forest. Electrical fencing bordered the place. As I've mentioned already, it was twenty miles southeast of Rockdale. I gave the location to the

CIA but they said it was deserted by the time they searched the place."

It frustrated the hell out of Mason that nothing had come from that. "And it was just your team kept at the house?"

Logan nodded. "They have a main base where most of the operations occur. That was the first place we were taken before being relocated to the house. We were never taken to the main facility again so I wouldn't have any idea where it is."

It was smart of them to use smaller locations, because so far, that was all Mason and his team had found. If they could just locate the main base, the team would be able to shut down the heart of the operation.

"We were trained morning and afternoon, usually by the same group of former SEALs who were also genetically altered," Logan continued.

Mason and the guys shared knowing glances. They were all thinking the same thing. Likely Carter's team. It had to be. The men remained silent as Logan continued.

"We were given weekly injections. We did what we were told because if we didn't, they threatened our families." Logan shrugged. "We weren't tortured or beaten. For prisoners, our quality of life was good. The house we lived in was huge, we were fed well. We were taken care of. It took about a year for us to really start feeling the physical changes."

Logan paused. "It was a few months ago that we decided it was time."

He didn't need to be any more specific. Mason knew what he meant. It was time to escape. Reclaim his freedom. Return to loved ones.

"We didn't say it out loud because we were watched and listened to constantly. We figured out other ways to communicate important information over the years. One day, we were waiting until our trainers were due to leave. That's when we attacked. We'd never done anything like that before, so they weren't prepared. I was the only man to make it out. I ran as far and fast as I could. I can only assume that I got as far as I did because my team held off the guards and trainers. My team had become family. Now I need to get my brothers out."

A new emotion flicked across Logan's face. Guilt. He clearly hated that he'd left his team behind. Hell, if Mason had to leave his brothers in captivity, that would tear him apart, too.

The emotion looked genuine. It went some way toward confirming to Mason that the man was who he said he was.

"We'll get them out," Kye said, mirroring what everyone in the room was thinking.

Oliver nodded. "And then we'll destroy everyone who was involved."

Damn straight they would. Every single one of them.

Mason pushed the sheet of names across the table. "Do you recognize any names?"

Logan lifted the sheet and took a moment to scan the page. "Every guy on the team they gave me is on the list. Bar one." Dropping the sheet, Logan shrugged. "Makes sense. The missing guy only did a short stint in the Army before leaving."

Eden ran his hands through his hair. "We shouldn't have had to dig this up. We're supposed to be working with the government agencies to shut down the damn project. That was the deal when we got out."

Bodie nodded. "No shit. Soldiers started going missing the moment the project went underground, that's not a damn coincidence."

"They're trying to keep it quiet," Wyatt said calmly. "They didn't give this to me. They wouldn't give me a shred of information. Said they had nothing of importance. Evie hacked some confidential files and found the list."

Mason studied Logan. He was conflicted. He wanted to trust Logan, but trust didn't come easily to him.

If situations were reversed and Mason needed help freeing *his* team, he'd hope capable men would work with him.

"Thank you for sharing what you know," Mason said. "We'll do everything we can to get your brothers out."

Every other man in the room agreed.

Standing, the guys began heading out. Mason was having lunch with Sage and the thought of seeing her in a few minutes had him eager to get going. She never failed to make him calm, no matter the stresses he had on his mind.

Before Mason reached the door, Wyatt's voice stopped him. "Eagle."

He turned back to see his friend standing beside the table.

"I wanted to let you know that Evie and I have been working hard to trace Jason's current number, but we're not having any luck."

Figured. Why would anything be easy?

Mason took a step closer to his friend. "We need to figure this out, and fast. Twice now her life has been in danger after messaging him. From everything she's told me, they had a great relationship. So, either the guy has changed over the years, or it's not him at all."

He didn't know which he hoped was true. Sage spoke about her twin like he was her other half. Her best friend. There was also a deep pain and sadness in her eyes when she spoke about him. He knew it was because it was hurting her that he was missing.

"We've suspected from the start he may be working for them. And if he is, only he can tell us his motivation. If it's not him... then we know who it is."

Mason breathed out a pained breath. "I'm going to tell her about the bug I put on her phone."

The closer he grew to Sage, the more the guilt ate at him. It was time to end the secrets. Past time.

"I think that's a good idea."

Mason watched Wyatt exit the room. But his mind remained on Sage. It *was* a good idea. But it was also a sure way to test the foundation of their new relationship. Which was exactly why he had waited to tell her.

Fear sat heavy in Mason's gut. Fear that Sage would walk away from him. He didn't know how to deal with fear. It was an emotion he wasn't familiar with.

~

SAGE STEPPED out of her car. From her peripheral vision, she saw Asher exit his car, too. He was her guard today, although he did a good job of keeping his distance.

Sage glanced up at Marble Protection. She was meeting Mason there and they were walking to Joan's Diner for lunch.

A week had passed since their double date with Eden and Shylah. During that week, Mason and Sage had barely parted.

It had been nice. And she'd tried to tell herself that her sending and him receiving messages at the same time was just coincidence.

But then yesterday, Mason had left his phone on the bedside table when he'd gone to the bathroom. Sage had wanted to prove to herself that she had no reason to worry. So, she'd grabbed her own phone and sent a text message.

Mason's phone had lit up the moment she'd hit send. And it made her feel sick to her stomach.

When Mason had come out, Sage panicked. She'd given him some weak excuse of a stomachache to explain why she needed to go to the apartment. Alone.

She'd spent the rest of the day trying to figure out whether to straight out ask him about it. The problem was, if he was doing what she suspected, she didn't know if she could trust him. Would he even tell her the truth if she asked?

Pushing inside the doors of the building, Sage walked up to the front desk where Evie was standing.

The other woman's head immediately shot up and a wide smile curved her lips. "Sage, it's so good to see you. Are you here for Mason? He's in a meeting with the guys until midday, unfortunately."

Sage knew exactly what time Mason was finishing. He'd made their lunch date for twelve fifteen. That's why she had chosen to arrive at eleven forty-five.

She had also been well aware of the fact that Evie would be working at the front desk.

Behind her, she heard the sound of Asher entering the building but paid no attention. She knew he would head over to where Luca was and help out with the class.

"Sorry, I'm a bit early. Is it okay if I wait with you?"

Evie's brows rose. "Of course, come have a seat."

Sage walked around the desk. "I hope you don't mind. I don't want to interrupt your studies."

Evie was taking an online IT course. Not that she needed to. From what Sage had been told, the woman was a genius, particularly in the hacking department. That was why she worked on the team's IT needs alongside Wyatt.

"It's perfect actually, because I need a break."

At Evie's genuine smile, Sage almost smiled herself. Even though she felt like her world was about to crash down around her.

Taking a seat, Sage opened her bag and pulled out the box of Mrs. Potter's donuts. The older woman had a bakery down the road, and it was well known in town that she made the best baked goods. Sage knew that Evie in particular loved her donuts and rolls.

Evie's eyes widened as she saw the donuts. "Oh my gosh, they're not what I think they are, are they?"

Sage placed the box on the desk and nodded. "They are. I couldn't help but pop in on the way. Take one, please."

Leaning over, Evie took hold of Sage's shoulders. "I could kiss you." She took a donut and placed it in her mouth. The expression that crossed the other woman's face was one of pure bliss. "I forgot to eat breakfast and didn't realize how hungry I was until this very moment."

"I've never had that problem. Breakfast is the first thing I think about when I wake up."

Evie nodded. "That's usually me, too. Unless I get distracted by something. Usually some code I'm trying to crack or information I'm researching for the guys."

"How's that going?" Sage reached for her own donut. She wasn't hungry, so she resorted to picking at it.

"Working for the guys? I'm just glad I can be useful. Luca doesn't talk about it a lot, but every so often I see the stress on his face. Stress because the project hasn't been shut down yet."

Sage saw the same worry in Mason's eyes. He tried to hide it, but on rare occasions, the mask fell. "It must be so hard for them to deal with. But at least they have each other."

Evie nodded her head vigorously. "They keep each other alive. And not just physically."

"Do you ever wonder if Luca would betray you to save his brothers?"

Sage hadn't been planning to ask that question. But now that she had, she genuinely wanted to know the answer.

Evie raised her brows, clearly taken by surprise. "I guess at the start of our relationship, yes. But I like to think I'm his priority now, just as he's mine."

Unfortunately for Sage, she and Mason were at the start of their relationship. So it was unlikely the same applied.

"How are your studies going?"

Evie blew out a long breath before telling Sage about her latest assignment. Sage tried to listen, she really did. But her mind kept flicking back to Mason. To her phone. To the question she *really* wanted to ask Evie.

Ten minutes later, Evie took a break from speaking to take a bite of her donut. Sage shot a glance at her phone. Almost twelve.

She leaned forward. "Evie, there was actually something I wanted to ask you."

The other woman smiled. "Ask me anything."

Sage wet her lips before she spoke. "Is it possible...I mean, is there a device that you can put onto someone else's phone, that forwards copies of all that person's messages to you?"

Evie's eyes widened and she sucked in a quick breath. Her fingers visibly tightening on the donut in her hands.

There was real panic on the other woman's face. More than normal.

Oh, god. It was true. The device existed. And, by the look on Evie's face, it was on Sage's phone.

Her heart dropped. For a moment, she struggled to keep the devastation from showing. Not falling apart was consuming every shred of energy she had.

But she did. By the grace of God, she did.

In the next moment, Mason walked out.

Sage turned to watch him. In a minute, they would go to lunch. And Sage would confirm with the man that he was breaking her trust, and her heart.

CHAPTER 16

*M*ason shot a few side glances to Sage as they walked. Something was off with her. And it was more than the stomachache she'd mentioned yesterday. She didn't look sick, she looked distressed, and maybe a bit nervous. Her spine was unnaturally stiff and every step she took seemed stilted.

They were already halfway to the diner and he had spent the entire walk thus far racking his brain on what the problem could be.

"Are you feeling better today, sweetheart?"

She gave a tight smile. It was all wrong. "My stomach isn't feeling sick today."

Nodding, Mason looked ahead as he walked. Could it be something to do with Jason? Her brother hadn't written to her in weeks. Perhaps she was upset that she'd been contacting him more frequently but getting nothing in return.

Once they arrived at Joan's Diner, Mason pushed through the doors, only to stop at the sight of so many people. The place was packed. And loud.

Frustration hit him in the chest. He needed quiet. He needed to get to the bottom of whatever the issue was. There was no way that could happen in here. He'd have to raise his voice just to be heard.

Sage's hand on his shoulder pulled his attention down to her.

"Let's get takeaway and eat at the park."

Yes. That was the best idea he'd heard all day.

Taking her hand, he sidestepped the busy tables to reach the counter. Mason ordered a burger and fries. It was his regular order. When he turned to Sage, she ordered the same.

That right there was a cause for concern. The few times they had been out together, she'd studied the menu for a solid ten minutes before eventually deciding on what she was eating. Because she was pragmatic. Her decisions were almost always premeditated.

Pushing the concern to the back of his mind, Mason held Sage's hand as they waited, gently stroking the inside of her wrist.

Over the last couple of days, he had spent a lot of time with her. Her period of leave at the hospital had allowed Mason to remain by her side. There had only been a couple of rare occasions that he had needed one of the guys to watch her.

Mason's feelings for the woman grew more intense each day. She was brilliant, kind, and empathetic.

She was it for him. No woman had ever made Mason feel the things that she did.

He would fight tooth and nail to protect both her and her loved ones. That was why he intended to tell her about the phone bug. And to let her know that she could let him in. She was safe with him and so was her brother. Whatever was going on with Jason, they would tackle it together. As a team.

After a few more minutes, the waitress placed their bag of food onto the counter. Mason swiped it and led them both from the diner.

The park was a street away from Marble Protection. Mason

attempted to make conversation along the way, but Sage gave very little. One-word answers and the occasional nod.

When they arrived, he was glad to see that the park was empty.

Mason turned to Sage. "Table or grass?"

"Grass, please."

Sage dropped to the ground and Mason sat beside her, pulling out their lunch.

Sitting in nature, she looked peaceful. He just wished her expression matched.

Not able to stop himself, he reached over and pushed some hair behind her ear. To Mason's surprise, Sage flinched.

What the hell was going on?

When her gaze shot up, her eyes were conflicted.

Mason was done wondering. He wanted to know what was going on and he wanted to know now. "Tell me what's wrong."

Because he knew *something* was wrong.

Sage breathed in a long breath. He saw a dozen emotions flash through her eyes. Anger. Frustration. Sadness. But the overwhelming emotion he saw was hurt.

Suddenly, he had a feeling he knew what it was.

"I know, Mason."

A SMALL STRETCH of silence passed where Sage just watched Mason. Watched the guilt wash over his face.

He leaned forward and scrubbed his hands over his face. Like he was the one who was in pain.

Tears built at the backs of her eyes, but she blinked them away. She didn't want to fall apart. Not here. Not in front of him. She needed to be angry. Because anger would hide the pain.

"I'm sorry." When he finally looked up at her, she acknowledged that he did look sorry.

She had to swallow a few times before she could speak without her voice breaking. "How long?" When he took a moment too long to respond, Sage repeated herself. But this time there was an edge to her voice. "How long have you been receiving my messages, Mason?"

His jaw visibly tightened. "I put it in at Striker's house. The first time the guys and I met Fletcher."

A memory flashed through her mind. "You brought me my phone and said I dropped it. But I didn't, did I? You took it. You took it and put something in it."

"Yes. I did."

Dragging her eyes from his, she felt like she couldn't breathe.

He wasn't the man she'd thought he was. How could he be? That man was honest. Respectful. Caring. This man was none of those things.

Suddenly, she didn't want to be sitting with him anymore. She needed to get up. To move away.

The second she was on her feet, Mason was on his.

"This thing between us—is it just so you can watch me?"

"No."

He took a step forward. She took a step back. His closeness felt like a physical pain to her chest.

"Why? Why did you do this?"

The reason shouldn't matter. He'd done what he'd done and there was no going back. But she needed to know.

"Back when Lexie was pregnant and she was kidnapped by people who worked for Project Arma, we couldn't figure out how they knew about the pregnancy."

"And you thought it was me?" After she'd left her life behind in Woodway, relocated to *help* them. To help all of them. "I came here for Lexie. For the baby."

Mason's eyes softened. "Is that the only reason you came?"

Shaking her head, she refused to let Mason turn this around on her. "I don't have to answer any questions from you." She ran trembling hands through her hair. "So, you suspected I was the one who leaked the information, then you put a bug on my phone. Is that it?"

An expression crossed Mason's face. It gave Sage her answer before he spoke. That wasn't it.

"We searched your room while you were staying at the inn."

Her brows pulled together. "Who's 'we'?"

"Me, Striker, and Red."

"The open window..." The words came out in a whisper. The night she'd returned from the hospital and her window had been open. It had scared the heck out of her. That was why she checked and double-checked her windows when she left home now.

Mason shoved his hands in his pockets. "You returned home earlier than we thought. We didn't have time to close the window."

She nodded her head like she understood. But she really didn't. "Did you know I didn't sleep that night? I barely slept that week. But that's okay because you found what you wanted to find, didn't you. You found the bag I hid in the pillow. The one with my gun, money, burner phone, and picture."

The muscles in Mason's arms visibly tightened. "Yes. We found it."

Sage rubbed her eyes to push away the tears. She refused to break down in front of him. Even though her heart felt like it had been torn from her chest and stomped on.

She'd let the guy in. Developed feelings for him. Made love to him. And all the while, he'd been watching her. Reading every heartbreaking message she sent to her brother and saying nothing.

"What do you know about Jason?"

There was an edge of fear to her voice. She had no doubt that he heard the rise in her heart rate and saw the worry in her eyes.

"Just that he disappeared a few years ago. We haven't been able to locate him."

One small reprieve. They didn't know he'd spent the first year working for Project Arma.

So, they weren't hunting Jason. Not yet. Just searching for him. Searching for answers.

Again, Mason took a step forward, but this time, he placed a hand on her arm. "Sage—"

She yanked herself away from him like she'd been burned. The feel of him touching her right now was too painful.

A tear trailed down her cheek, but she quickly scrubbed it away. "I need to go."

She wasn't sure where. Just that she needed time to think. Space.

"Go where?"

Ignoring his question, she turned and began walking back to her car at Marble Protection. It was only a street away but felt like miles.

Every step felt heavy. She was moments away from breaking. Falling to the ground and sobbing.

"I'm sorry." Mason said the words quietly, but she heard.

She didn't want him to be sorry. She wanted to turn back time and have him never do what he did.

When she felt his hand on her arm, she spun around and pushed at his chest. His hand dropped but of course the man didn't move anywhere. "We made love!"

"I know."

"That meant something to me."

"It meant something to me, too."

She struggled to see how that was possible. "You bugged my phone. You've been reading my messages for months. When I told you about Jason, you acted like it was the first time you'd heard of him. How can anything genuine be built on that?"

It couldn't. At least it didn't feel like it could.

"You weren't exactly up front with me, Sage."

Her eyes widened in anger and disbelief. "That was *my* business. Do you tell me everything about you? Of course not. Maybe if you'd given me time. Let the trust develop, I would have let you in."

Not waiting for a response, Sage spun around and began walking again. She moved her legs quickly but for every two strides of hers, Mason only needed one.

He remained hot on her heels until she reached her car, but he didn't say a word.

When Sage was about to pull the door open, Mason reached over her and placed a hand on the door. Caging her to the car. Preventing the door from moving.

She wanted to turn and yell at the man. But she couldn't. She could barely speak. "I need you to let me go and give me space."

"I care about you." Even though she couldn't see his face, she could hear the pain his voice.

"You care about your team. Your brothers. It's okay because I get it. I care about my brother, too."

Out of the corner of her eye, Sage saw Bodie and Asher exit the building.

"I can't let you leave like this." Mason's voice was strained.

"You don't have a choice."

She felt like he was surrounding her. And she was suffocating.

Dropping her head, Sage lowered her voice. "Please. I need to go."

Mason remained. Then another voice sounded. Bodie's voice. "Eagle, let her go."

For a moment he didn't move. Then, finally, she watched his feet move away. Even though that was what she wanted, what she'd just asked for, it physically hurt to see him leave.

But she pushed that down. Opening her door, she climbed into her car. Then she drove away.

She knew one of the guys would be following, and for the

first time, their protection went from making her feel safe to making her feel watched.

The farther she drove from Marble Protection—from Mason —the more loneliness seeped into her soul.

After coming to Marble Falls, Sage had begun to feel like she had people who cared. It had been the first time since losing Jason. But could people care about you while also investigating you? Spying on you? She wasn't sure.

Tears began to fall down Sage's cheeks. This time she didn't attempt to wipe them away. They would just keep falling. Because she had begun to care about Mason. Maybe even love him.

CHAPTER 17

*M*ason watched her drive away and Bodie follow. Because *watch* was all he could do.

She shouldn't have found out on her own. He should have told her. Waiting as long as he had was a big damn mistake.

When the cars left his sight, he went back into Marble. He didn't stop at the desk. Or when he heard Asher call his name. He didn't want to be around people, dammit. Hell, he didn't even want his own company.

Walking into one of the workout rooms, Mason threw the door shut after him.

Christ, he was a fool.

For the first time in his life, he had no idea what to do. He might have just lost her. The only woman to ever penetrate his heart.

He wanted to throw his fist into the wall. Or beat the shit out of something—starting with himself.

He'd gotten distracted. Distracted by Project Arma, by keeping Sage safe, and he'd missed the signs. At some point she'd discovered what he'd done. And he'd missed it.

Fuck. Why had he underestimated her? He knew she had a brilliant mind and still he'd treated her otherwise.

Walking forward, Mason raised his fist and hit the wall. It did nothing to dim the anger that raged inside him.

He rested his head and hands against the wall. What the hell was he going to do? The idea of them being done forever had a fear racing through his veins that almost caused him to keel over.

Mason heard the door open behind him, but he didn't so much as open his eyes. He knew it was one of the guys.

"Well, that blew up in your face."

A muscle in Mason's jaw ticked at Asher's words. "Is this where you say you told me so?" It was the last damn thing he needed to hear.

Mason pushed off the wall and turned to see Asher leaning a shoulder against the doorframe.

All the guys had warned him against planting the device on her phone. He'd ignored them and gone ahead and done it anyway. Because he hadn't trusted the woman enough to ask her about her go bag. About her brother.

He'd done it to protect *his* brothers. To protect her. But intentions were inconsequential. Mason knew that. They all did.

"I don't need to do that."

Damn straight Asher didn't. Mason knew.

"Do you know what the worst part of it is? What makes me a real asshole? If I had to do it all over again, I don't know that I would do it any differently."

Maybe he would have told her earlier. But that was it.

Asher shrugged. "That's because Project Arma did a real number on you. On all of us. We lost the ability to trust. And we've all dealt with that in different ways."

Mason was a grown-ass man. He couldn't blame the damn project for all his problems. At some point, he needed to take responsibility.

"What the hell am I going to do?"

He needed to do something. Anything, to make this better.

Asher pushed off the wall and took a step closer. "What do you want from her?"

"Everything. I want all of Sage, and I want her to have all of me. She's supposed to be mine. I don't know how I know, but I do."

Asher didn't appear surprised by Mason's words. "Then here's my two cents. For now, give her the space she needs. We'll keep watching her, ensuring she's safe. With any luck, after some time, you can rebuild trust together."

It sounded simple. But there was always the chance that trust couldn't be rebuilt.

Looking back to Asher, Mason remembered when Lexie had wanted space. She had stayed with Luca and Evie, and Asher had camped right outside, refusing to leave.

"Like how you gave Lexie space when she was unhappy?"

A ghost of a smile pulled at Asher's lips. "Just because I know the right answer doesn't mean I can act on it. There isn't a thing on the planet that would keep my away from my woman."

That was exactly how Mason felt. It was an intrinsic need to be close to her.

"I hate that I didn't tell her." Mason ran his hands through his hair. "I hate that she found out herself."

Closing the distance between them, Asher clamped a hand on Mason's shoulder. "Everyone screws up. It's what we do after that seals our fate."

He hoped that was true. Because he would be doing everything he could to get her back.

"Thank you."

Asher gave a nod before leaving the room.

After taking a few breaths, Mason went to the office. And that's where he spent the rest of the afternoon. He went over any and all information they had on Project Arma, because he needed to be doing something. *Anything* to feel like he was being productive. To get his mind off how much he'd screwed up.

He studied and restudied the information until his eyes began to blur.

Pushing back in his chair, Mason stretched out his arms. Lifting his phone, he sent a quick message off to Bodie. He'd been bombarding the guy with messages all afternoon.

Bodie was alternating between watching her apartment window from his car and doing building walk-throughs.

The responses were all the same. She'd gone straight home and hadn't left her apartment.

Mason should head off soon and take the night shift. But he wouldn't wait in his car. He'd probably camp out by her door. Wyatt was across the hall and would likely offer, but Mason wanted to be close to her.

The closer he was, the better she was protected, and the better for his heart. He would leave the moment he heard her head toward the door.

He was lucky his body didn't need much rest. Not after Project Arma. A night of no rest was easier for him than most.

Bodie's response came through—no change.

Then another message popped up.

But this one was from Jason to Sage. His jaw clenched when he read it.

Can we meet tonight?

Mason watched his phone for the next five minutes. But she didn't respond. Probably because she now knew he was watching.

If his watching her messages stopped the woman from seeing her brother and kept her safe, then that was one small positive from the whole thing.

As Mason waited, the list of missing soldiers caught his attention. He lifted the page and studied it, noting Logan's name.

The team had planned for Logan to sit down with Wyatt and

Evie the next day and go through names and backgrounds of each man Logan had been teamed with. Hopefully something— anything—would be a clue as to where to find them.

It sure beat the pile of nothing they were working with at the moment.

About to stand, he stopped when Logan entered the office. The moment the man spotted Mason, he paused.

"Hey, Wyatt just sent me in here to wait for him. We're going to make a start now instead of tomorrow." Logan turned his head to look down the hall, then back at Mason. "I can wait in the hall…"

Shaking his head, Mason stood and walked around the desk. "I was just leaving."

Mason hadn't known Logan for long, but he liked the guy. All the guys had been watching him and couldn't detect an ounce of dishonesty. He seemed to be exactly who he claimed.

And what was more, he reminded Mason of his own brothers. He had the same determination and thirst for revenge in his eyes. And the same dangerous air about him.

Before Mason walked out, he stopped in front of Logan. The guy never showed much emotion, but he had to be struggling with everything.

"How are you holding up?"

Exhaustion flashed across Logan's features before he quickly masked it. "I haven't had freedom in years. It's strange. Good strange. What's hard is being away from the guys. I've spent every day for two years with them. Today's been tough. I want to be doing something to find them. I *need* to be doing something."

Mason got that. He would feel the same were situations reversed. "Tell me about them."

A small smile tugged at Logan's lips. "We don't have nicknames for each other like you guys. Callum is the big guy. He likes to crack a lot of jokes. He was good at keeping our spirits up when it felt like we would never get out. Flynn's pretty intense, but we need that. He keeps us focused. Aidan's the storyteller of the group as well as a damn good fighter. We tease Liam about being the pretty one. The man could probably be a Hollywood actor. I have no doubt the women would have flocked to him wherever he went."

Mason chuckled.

"Carter's the youngest in the group at only twenty-five, but you would never think so. He's serious and he's damn wise. Then there's Blake. He has a son, and it tears him apart he's missed years with him. The guy wears his heart on his sleeve. And Jason's the smart one. He studied science at an Ivy League university."

Mason started at the last name Logan mentioned. "There's a man on your team called Jason?"

Logan nodded. "He only did a short stint in the military. He was working as a scientist for Project Arma. It was when he discovered what was going on, and tried to run, that they took him."

A sick feeling churned in Mason's stomach. Moving to the computer, he went into the file they had on Sage and pulled up a picture of her with her brother. "Is this him?"

Logan walked around the desk, his brow furrowing immediately. "Yes, that's Jason. Is that the doctor with him?"

Mason straightened and linked his hands above his head.

Things began to fall into place.

He'd been right to be suspicious. It wasn't Jason. The person that Sage had been making contact with wasn't her brother. It was Project Arma.

Fuck.

The ringing of his phone pulled Mason back to the present. Noticing it was Bodie, he answered immediately. "Is she okay?"

"She tried to leave without me noticing." The sound of a running engine was muffled in the background. "I was doing a walk-around and caught her sneaking out the back. She didn't see me. I'm following her now."

Mason's legs were already moving. "Don't lose her. The person she's been messaging isn't Jason. It never was. It's them."

Bodie cursed through the line.

"I'll follow your location from your phone." Mason moved through the building. He could feel Logan hot on his trail but didn't stop.

He had to get to her. He had a bad feeling.

CHAPTER 18

"*I* love you. Hopefully it's over soon and I can come home."

Sage paused, midpacking, and let Jason's words wash over her. His voice calmed some of the storm inside her. She'd lost count of the number of times she'd replayed the recorded message since returning home.

If only his voice could fix things. Renew her hope and calm the turmoil like it had done so many times before. But it couldn't. It was like attempting to place a Band-Aid on a gaping hole in her chest.

Sage went back to her drawers and pulled out another shirt. She was being irrational, but she couldn't seem to stop. There was so much hurt inside her and it was driving her to do one thing. Leave. To get out of Marble Falls and put some distance between her and Mason.

To put some distance between her and *everyone*.

She didn't know if she actually would leave town. There was a great deal of danger for her. She didn't know *what* she would do. But telling herself she was leaving helped. Packing a bag helped.

She wanted to be angry. To throw things. To yell. But the

heartache was too raw. The loneliness and hurt were all she could feel. Like an ocean pulling her under. Drowning her.

When she felt the tears begin to build again, Sage stopped and closed her eyes. She didn't want to cry. Her eyes were already red and swollen from sobbing all afternoon.

A tear slid down her cheek anyway. Then another.

Sage turned around and leaned her back against the drawers. When her legs wouldn't hold her anymore, she slid to the ground. Her arms snaked around her legs and she hugged her knees to her chest. Almost like she was trying to hold herself together.

She'd fallen in love with Mason. It was an all-consuming type of love that had taken over her heart and soul. It seemed impossible in such a short amount of time, but it had happened.

That's why his deception hurt so much. That's why she physically ached at the thought of what he'd done.

The tears were unrelenting. They stole her breath and put a tremble through her limbs.

She couldn't help but question everything. Every beautiful memory of them together now felt heavy. Like they were shrouded in dark clouds.

He'd said that not everything was a lie, but her trust in him was fractured. She had no idea what was real and what wasn't.

Soon, sobs racked her chest. She didn't know how long she sat there and cried. Time held no relevance.

Just then, her phone vibrated, signaling a message. For a moment, she wondered if it was Mason. And she hated that she almost hoped it was.

She pulled the phone out of her pocket and sucked in a quick breath at what she saw.

Jason.

Can we meet tonight?

For a moment she sat there frozen, reading and rereading the words in front of her.

For so long she'd wanted to read this. Would have given anything for it.

She closed her eyes and leaned her head back. Her chest hurt. Everything hurt.

She couldn't go. There was a chance this wasn't Jason. A big chance.

But as soon as the decision to not go settled in her mind, a searing pain shot through her chest.

She'd already lost one man that she loved; losing another seemed insurmountable.

Her heart ached to see Jason. She had to go. For the small sliver of a chance that it was her twin brother, she had to.

When she pushed to her feet, Sage wiped the dampness from her face. For the first time all day, she could breathe. The internal despair dimmed.

She quickly moved to the kitchen. She couldn't respond to him on her phone. Mason would see the message and he would stop her.

Hell, he might be on his way to her already.

Luckily, she had another phone. The burner phone she kept in her go bag. She kept the bag in case she needed to get out of town in a hurry. Right now, she was beyond grateful she'd thought ahead.

Her heart hammered in her chest as she took quick steps to the pantry. Reaching to the back, she pulled out a big cereal box. First, she pulled out the bag of cereal.

There, in the bottom of the box, was the bag containing five thousand dollars in cash, a burner phone, a picture of her and Jason, and a loaded gun. Lifting the phone, Sage powered it on. She knew it was charged and ready to go. It was something she made sure of.

She quickly typed in Jason's current number before sending him a response.

This is Sage. Where do you want to meet?

Once she hit send, Sage placed the phone on the counter and waited.

As she waited, she lifted the photo. She remembered that day well. They were ten at the time, and their parents had wanted a picture before they went to the park.

Once they'd gotten to the park, some older kids had been harassing Sage. Even though Jason hadn't been much bigger than her, he'd marched up to the bullies and threatened to hurt them if they didn't leave her alone. He'd spoken with so much aggression that the boys hadn't so much as looked at her after that.

Sage traced the outline of his face with her finger. That was Jason. Her protector. It had always felt like it was the two of them against the world.

Nothing had changed.

Thinking about those moments dulled some of the hurt inside her.

When the phone screen lit up, Sage dropped the photo. Lifting the phone, Sage saw that Jason had sent her a pin for a location. The pin was a point in the national park near Mountain Canyon. At the end of the message, Jason asked Sage to ensure she wasn't followed.

That would be the challenge.

Pocketing the burner phone, she turned to leave but stopped. Spinning back, she grabbed the bag. There was a chance she wouldn't be returning to this apartment.

Grabbing the keys, she opened the door. Sticking her head into the hallway, she glanced both ways. No Bodie.

Creeping down the hallway, Sage headed toward the back stairs. She needed to remain unseen.

She had never been more grateful that the apartment had underground parking. There were two exits. She would take the back one.

Sage made it to her car without detection. Then, sitting

behind the wheel, she took a quick, calming breath before driving out.

Once on the road, she checked her rearview mirror. Nothing. No sign of Bodie.

On the drive, fear and doubt began to creep in.

She reminded herself that she believed this was Jason she was messaging. He'd done everything he'd told her he was going to do in the voice mail. Run, hide, use a burner phone and message rather than call.

Not only that, but over the years, he'd said things to her that no one else knew about. He'd reminded her of memories they'd shared. Granted, it was via text. But, still, they were memories that belonged to her and Jason. Memories that no one else knew about.

So, this was him. It had to be. That thought was the only thing keeping her from breaking.

She could still recall their last phone conversation. There'd been an edge to his voice. He'd spoken so fast, Sage had barely understood him. He'd said the drugs they were working on were like no other.

He'd also said he was worried. Worried about what the drugs would be used for. Worried about the entire organization.

Sage's hands clenched the steering wheel tighter. She'd begged her brother to leave the job and come home. But he hadn't. And then a few days later, he'd gone into hiding.

After what felt like forever, Sage pulled into the national park. She was about to step out of the car when she stopped. Making a snap decision, Sage rummaged through the go bag and pulled out the gun.

It was loaded, which meant it would be an extra layer of protection.

Sage climbed out and began to walk toward Mountain Canyon. The location Jason had shared wasn't too far.

After only a couple of minutes of walking, her steps slowed.

There was still plenty of light out, but an eerie silence surrounded her. She felt completely alone in the middle of nothing but trees.

Maybe it hadn't been such a great decision to leave in such haste. Had her desperation to dull the ache in her chest blinded her?

A trail of goose bumps covered Sage's skin. She had a loaded gun, but that in no way made her feel safe.

Shuffling sounded behind her, causing her to stop and turn.

No sign of anything. Not a person or animal. There wasn't even wind to rustle branches.

But just because there was no one in sight didn't mean she was alone.

Swallowing some of the rising fear, Sage was about to turn back toward the path when the shuffling sounded again. This time louder. Closer.

Acting on instinct, Sage lifted the gun and aimed toward the path. Her finger shook as she put it on the trigger. Every muscle in her body was tight with nerves.

"Who's there?"

Sage did a full circle, inspecting every inch of forest around her.

Still, she saw no one. The silence was deafening.

She had to decide her next move, and she had to decide fast. She wanted to go back to her car. Speed back to her apartment. Her *protected* apartment.

But she physically couldn't get her body to move in that direction. Because that would mean possibly walking away from her only chance to see Jason.

How long would it be before he agreed to meet again? It had already been three years since she'd seen him. And what if he *needed* her right now?

At the last thought, Sage's body moved before her brain could stop her. She took off in a run. Gun still in hand, she pumped her short legs as fast as they allowed.

Then, Sage stopped. She didn't think about how out of breath her lungs were. Or how her legs ached from pounding uneven ground. Because…in the distance stood a figure. The person was too far away for her to see their features. But just by the man's outline, it was possible that it could be him. It could be Jason.

Tears filled her eyes. It *had* to be Jason. The man had the same broad shoulders, he looked to be the right height. Even though her chest hurt from moving so fast, she started running again. This time moving faster.

Sage had made it another five steps when a heavy weight collided with her body, throwing her to the ground.

CHAPTER 19

Mason propelled his body forward, wrapping his arms around Sage and throwing them to the ground. He hit the ground first but quickly spun them around, covering her body with his own.

Sage lay still below him, his front to her back. Then she began to fight. First her arms punched out, then her legs kicked. Her body began to toss and turn below him uncontrollably.

Using both hands and legs, Mason immobilized her body. He could feel her attempts to push up, but she didn't achieve anything.

Sage's breaths became heavy pants. Then she sucked in a giant breath, and he knew she was moments away from letting out a scream.

He couldn't let that happen.

His hand came over her mouth before she could utter a sound. Apart from the soft, muffled whimpers, she was rendered silent.

He felt like an asshole. But he had to keep her safe.

In seconds, all hell would break loose. Five of his brothers hid within the trees, waiting for their enemies. Mason's job was to get her out. Keep her safe.

Dipping his head, Mason placed his lips by her ear. "It's me, Mason. You're safe. But we need to get out of here."

He felt some of the fight leave her body. When Mason's gaze darted around them, he caught glimpses of his team.

On the ride over, he'd suddenly remembered her burner phone. Fear had struck him hard. He knew immediately that she'd used it and was now about to step into a deadly trap.

Any normal day, and he had no doubt, Sage would have acted smarter. But high emotions can make even the smartest people do regrettable things. He had no doubt that's what this was.

"Can I remove my hand without you screaming?"

When she didn't attempt to speak or move, Mason slowly raised his hand. She remained still below him. He lifted his weight off her, while remaining crouched over her body.

He was about to stand when he heard the first sign of violence. Bodies colliding.

When Mason swung his line of sight toward the sound, he saw Eden atop a man. A gun sat in the dirt two feet away.

Then sound erupted from every direction.

Mason and Sage were in the middle of a damn war zone. He needed to get them out. Right the hell now.

Lifting Sage into his arms, Mason began to run.

What he didn't expect was the fists pummeling his chest.

There was desperation in her voice as she cried out, "Let me go! My brother's back there!"

Mason kept moving but the farther he ran, the more hysterical Sage became. In his efforts to prevent her from hurting herself or falling, he had to hold her so tightly, he was scared he was bruising her.

When he was a few miles from the commotion, Mason stopped and placed her on the ground beside a tree. He kneeled in front of her.

She immediately attempted to stand, but he'd predicted that. Grabbing her upper arms, Mason exerted enough force to keep her stationary, while using every effort to not hurt her.

"I need you to stop fighting me."

So much pain and turmoil colored her features. "I need to get to Jason! He needs my help!"

A piece of Mason's heart cracked. There was no way to shield her from the pain of the truth. "That's not Jason, sweetheart."

If anything, his words made her fight harder. Her body twisted and turned.

Mason spun her body and wrapped his arms around her. Her back was pulled tight against his chest.

He could see her muscles straining as she still attempted to move. "Please, Mason, let me go, it's Jason!"

"Have you ever actually spoken to him? Heard his voice?"

There was a moment of pause in her movements. "Yes. He left me a message before he ran. He told me what his plans were."

Mason closed his eyes for a moment before telling her, "Two years ago, Jason was captured by Project Arma. He's been a prisoner ever since. And he's one of Logan's team members."

Now her body stilled completely. "That's not true. We've been messaging for years. He knows things, he's *written* things that no one else knows. Facts. Memories."

"The project would have his old phone and laptop. They would have access to all his personal emails and texts. You can learn a lot about a person doing that." When she didn't respond, Mason lowered his voice. "You've been messaging someone from Project Arma."

A heavy silence hung in the air. Then he felt her body go limp.

Was she about to fall apart? If she didn't now, he had no doubt she would at some point. It was just a question of when.

Gathering Sage back into his arms, Mason sprinted to his car. Once there, he gently placed her in the passenger seat before moving to the driver's side, then speeding toward his place.

On the way, he threw numerous worried glances in her direction. She didn't move a muscle. Just continued to gaze out the window, her eyes devoid of emotion.

The longer she sat like that, the more Mason's worry grew. At the back of his mind, he knew he should be concerned for his brothers. For the battle they were fighting. But Sage's still form and empty eyes were his primary concern.

When they reached his home, Mason parked in his garage. Jumping out, he went around to her side before carrying her inside.

Her heart rate was slow. So too was her breathing.

Moving straight upstairs, Mason knew he needed to feed his dogs and make contact with his team, but first he needed to take care of Sage.

In the bathroom, he sat her on the edge of the bath. Dirt covered both of them.

Kneeling in front of her, Mason placed a hand on the side of her face. "I'm going to shower with you."

Sage remained silent. She looked at him, but it was almost like her gaze went right through him.

Stripping off his own clothes, then hers, he pulled her into the shower with him, grateful she was supporting her own body weight.

He had hoped the warm water might bring her back to him. Even if she cried or screamed or let out her frustration. But she remained silent.

Mason kissed her forehead. "Everything will be okay, sweetheart."

Washing his own body first, he then got to work on hers.

He knew that she was in shock. Shutting down was a way for her brain to protect her heart. When she was ready, she would feel everything.

Once they were done, Mason dried both their bodies and put one of his T-shirts on her. It went to her knees.

Gently, Mason placed her in bed before fetching some sleeping pills. She needed rest, and he doubted that she would be able to fall asleep on her own.

After he helped her take the pills, Sage's eyes fluttered shut. Mason spent the next ten minutes just watching her. Every part of him wished he could shield her from the pain of knowing her brother had been taken. But that wasn't possible. Instead, he would be right by her side. Helping her. Supporting. If she wanted him.

Eventually, her breaths evened out. Mason stood and went downstairs to feed the dogs and lock up. Fixing himself a meal, he ate quickly, not wanting to be away from her for long.

Less than ten minutes later, he was back in bed, pulling her back against his front. Some of the tension eased from his body.

Tomorrow would be hard. Tonight, he would be content with holding her.

～

SAGE SHOT INTO A SITTING POSITION. Her breathing was labored. Her heart raced.

Jason. He was in a cell. He had looked at her, on the other side of the bars. She was free. He wasn't. He'd asked why she hadn't known. Why she hadn't saved him.

The dream had felt real. Scarily so. But it couldn't be. Jason was on the run. He'd escaped the people who worked for Project Arma and was hiding.

Wasn't he?

The mattress shifted beside her, and she saw Mason push into a sitting position.

Sage glanced around the dim room. The furniture was covered in darkness. Mason's furniture. Because she was in Mason's room.

Slowly, bits and pieces from the previous night started

filtering back to her. Sage was in Mason's room because he'd taken her there. From the national park. The national park where she was meeting Jason. Only he hadn't been there. Because Jason was a prisoner. *Had* been a prisoner for years.

A sob rose in her chest. Turning to Mason, she needed him to tell her it wasn't real. "Is Jason really with them?"

The regret that flashed across Mason's face confirmed it before he spoke. "I'm sorry."

Another sob escaped Sage's lips, but this time louder. More pained.

Then came the tears. A long stream of tears that turned into heavy crying. Not soft, gentle tears. Sobs that racked her body and made her head hurt. Loud and ugly.

Sage was vaguely aware of Mason lifting her and placing her on his lap. His body surrounding her. Anchoring her as her heart broke.

She should have known. Shouldn't twins know when the other is hurting?

"How did I not know?" She spoke the words to Mason, but they were aimed at herself.

His large, warm hand rubbed her back. But a part of her hated it. Because she didn't feel deserving of comfort.

"Sometimes we see what we want to see. It's the mind's way of protecting the heart."

Guilt tore at her insides. Guilt for every moment of happiness she'd experienced over the last two years. Every smile. Every shred of joy. All while Jason was suffering.

She could hear Mason whispering soothing words in her ear, but it sounded distant.

Sage's fingers dug into Mason. She was probably bruising him, but she needed his strength. "He would have known had it been me. I should have done more."

The one time he needed saving, she was nowhere to be found.

"The moment Project Arma shut down, the moment your

brother went missing, you began working with us. Then you moved to Marble Falls. You've remained close to the project for him. So that you were the first to know when he was safe to come home."

She hadn't told Mason that. But it was true.

Mason's hand continued to rub her back and the tears began to slow. But the pain in her chest remained. "I feel guilty."

"None of this is your fault. You have helped in every way you know how. And that's gotten you here. You have me, my team, and Logan. And we're not going to stop until Jason is free."

At the mention of his team, another thought hit Sage. "You know that Jason worked for Project Arma?"

"I do. And I don't care in the least." His expression remained neutral. "Logan told me that the moment he worked out what was going on, they took him. But if Jason is anything like you, he would never have taken the job had he known."

She studied Mason's face. Everything he'd just said was true. Only she hadn't expected those words to leave his mouth.

For the first time in years, she didn't feel alone in everything. Some of the pain eased.

"I should have told you. I was scared. I know how strong your lust for revenge is. I didn't think you'd believe me when I told you he didn't know."

Mason gently pushed some hair behind her ear. "To be honest, if you'd told me a few months ago, I might not have listened. But now I know you. And I trust you."

She trusted him, too. Even if she didn't agree with all of his actions, he'd saved her tonight. Just like he'd saved her two previous times.

He'd said he would help her brother. And she believed him.

Laying her head on his chest, she closed her eyes. Suddenly feeling exhausted. "Do you really think we'll be able to save him?"

It seemed impossible.

"There isn't a doubt in my mind."

Mason lay back on the bed, pulling Sage down with him.

She hadn't forgotten about their earlier fight, but that seemed insignificant now in comparison to everything else.

She prayed that he was right. That they would find Jason and save him.

CHAPTER 20

"We can't trace the number. We've tried."

That was the third time Wyatt had said those words in the short hour they'd been sitting in Mason's living room. Sage wasn't sure why the guys kept asking. The answer wouldn't change.

Glancing down at her lap, she mindlessly pulled at a thread that had escaped her sweater. Wyatt, Kye, and Bodie had arrived that afternoon. And they'd brought Logan.

It was an effort for Sage to keep her eyes off the man. He had been living with her brother the last few years. He was the only man in the room who could tell her how he really was.

She felt Mason's arm tighten around her waist. She leaned into him. Absorbing his strength.

"We don't have anything else, Jobs," Kye said, clearly frustrated.

The guys had been going around in circles. No one had answers.

Sage scrubbed her hands over her eyes, the exhaustion from her fitful sleep beginning to wear on her. And sitting there was doing nothing to help. She knew everyone was doing the best they could. But so far, they didn't even have the beginnings of a plan.

Pushing to her feet, she noticed five pairs of deadly eyes fall on her.

"I'm just going to get some fresh air."

Mason stood beside her, but Sage placed her hand on his chest.

"I'll be right back. You stay here. Keep working on it. I just need a moment. I won't go far, and you'll be able to hear me."

Sage could tell by Mason's expression that he didn't like it. But she appreciated that he didn't push it.

She headed toward the back door and walked outside. Taking off her shoes, she moved to the grass. There was nothing more grounding than the feel of grass beneath bare feet. And boy did she need some grounding right now.

As the breeze brushed against her face, Sage closed her eyes and sucked in some deep breaths.

She'd only been standing there a few seconds when she felt soft fur brush across her legs. Smiling, she looked down to see Nunzie and Dizzie at her feet.

Dropping down, she cuddled the big pups. The dogs must have known she needed some extra loving, because they snuggled into her. "You guys are living the life, aren't you? No bad guys chasing you. No one trying to take your loved ones."

"He may have been taken. But he never forgot you."

Shooting to her feet, Sage spun around to find Logan less than a foot away.

"I didn't hear you come out here."

He shrugged. "I move quietly. It's a habit."

Now that he stood right in front of her, a million questions ran through her head.

"Ask me whatever you'd like, Sage."

She swallowed hard. "Does he hate me because I haven't found him?"

"Jason spoke about you a lot. Hate never came into it."

Emotion clogged her throat. "Jason spoke about me?"

Logan chuckled. "All the goddamn time. We were all sick of hearing about this perfect twin sister of his. If I hear the words *genius* or *brainiac* one more time..." A serious expression came over his face. "He was worried about you, though."

She wasn't surprised. Jason always put others first. "He's the one being held captive. Not me."

Logan shoved his hands into his pockets. "He was worried about the lengths you would go to...to find him."

His words only increased her guilt. "I haven't done nearly enough. I didn't even know he was taken."

"Something tells me you've done more than you think."

Sage didn't agree. But she wouldn't argue with him. "Do you think we'll be able to get him out?"

For some reason, she felt nervous for the answer. Maybe because only Logan knew how easy or difficult it would be to rescue him.

"Yes."

Logan sounded just as confident as Mason. It eased some of her fear.

One side of Logan's mouth pulled up. "You're exactly like he said you were."

Sage chucked. "You mean stubborn, demanding, and inflexible?"

"Driven."

She could picture Jason saying that. He'd always viewed her through a rosy lens. "Is he okay?"

"He's better than okay, Sage. Your brother is a damn warrior." A part of her heart healed at those words. "We were treated well, considering. We lived in a big-ass house. They fed us well. Trained us. I think they were hoping that once we saw what they'd turned us into, we would be loyal to them."

Sage scoffed. "Jason would never be loyal to them."

"Exactly." crouching, Logan scratched Dizzie's head. "They made two major errors. The first was assuming they could manipulate us into fighting their war. They chose strong-minded men. Good men. It was never going to happen."

He was right. If all the men had Jason's ethics, Project Arma didn't stand a chance.

"The second was placing us in a team. A team with like-minded individuals. They thought they were creating an army to fight with them. They weren't. They were creating an opposition with allies." Logan glanced up at Sage. He was all fire and rage. "They created teams of deadly enemies," Logan continued. "Your brother is my brother. And there isn't a thing I wouldn't do to save him or any of the others."

Some of the weight was lifted off Sage's chest. "You really care about Jason."

"I would die to protect him."

Logan stood. And without thought, Sage took a step forward and wrapped her arms around him. She hugged him tightly, wanting to be close to the man who cared about her brother.

"Thank you." She wasn't sure whether she was thanking him for easing some of the guilt or for loving Jason. Probably both. But she needed him to know that she was grateful.

Logan's arms came around her. "Your brother is a good man. And I'm not going to stop until he's free."

He was on her side. And it felt a little less lonely. Yes, Mason and his team were working on the same goal. But they didn't *know* Jason. They didn't love him like Sage did. Like Logan said he did. Would they go to the same lengths?

When Sage stepped back, she smiled up at the big man. "Let's go save our brother."

They headed inside. When they stepped into the living room, the four men turned their gaze on her and Logan.

She moved to sit beside Mason, and he immediately took her hand with his.

"Any ideas?" she asked the men softly.

It was Bodie who responded. "Not yet."

Sage wet her lips before she spoke. "I have an idea."

An idea that she knew would be met with resistance. But she needed to try.

"What is it, sweetheart?"

"They want me. We can use that to find them."

Mason's body stiffened.

"You want us to use you as bait?" Wyatt asked.

"Yes."

Mason's hand tightened around hers. "No."

"There are no other options—"

"I don't care." Mason didn't shout the words. He didn't even raise his voice. But they were unyielding. "There is no way in hell we're offering you up to those people."

"But Mason—"

"I said no."

His features were set. There was no sign of leeway.

Sitting back on the couch, Sage knew that if she continued, she would be fighting a losing battle. But if no one came up with a better plan, she would be bringing it up again.

CHAPTER 21

S age lifted a piece of popcorn to her lips, Mason's body pressed against her side. Heating her.

A movie played on the TV in front of them but she was barely watching. Heck, she couldn't even remember what the thing was called.

Sneaking a look at Mason, she saw his eyes were on the screen. But she wouldn't be surprised if he didn't know what was going on, either.

A few days had passed since discovering that Jason was a hostage.

The guys had done some research in that time. Apparently, Project Arma had stopped recording the majority of their new employees in the final year. That was why the government never discovered her brother was part of the project. Why Mason and his team never discovered it.

Sage had somewhat come to terms with the fact that Jason had been a prisoner for the last two years. At least, as much as she could. But no one had a plan yet.

She did. She just needed them to use her.

She wanted to broach the subject again. But she was nervous.

Nervous that she would get shut down before she finished speaking.

She had to try.

Blowing out an anxious breath, Sage opened her mouth to speak but quickly shut it.

Damn, why was she so scared? What did she think he would do?

Turning back to the bowl in her lap, she swished the popcorn around, trying to muster some courage.

"If you're planning to ask me again, the answer is still no."

Sage swung her gaze up. "You're not even considering the idea."

Mason's gaze darkened. "That's because there's nothing to consider. We're not doing it."

Now Sage was starting to feel angry at his blatant refusal. "We have no other options. None. My brother is god knows where, probably being punished for Logan's escape, and we're sitting here eating popcorn. They want me. Let's use that to draw them out."

"No."

No? Like his word was all there was to it?

"It's my body and my life. If I want to use myself to save my brother, then that's what I'm going to do."

Mason's eyes narrowed. Danger cascaded off him in waves.

If Sage didn't know for certain that he wouldn't hurt her, his expression would have sent a jolt of fear into her.

"Tell me then, how does this plan of yours work? Do you just text the number you have, pretending you don't know it's them? Send them your location and wait to be taken?"

She actually didn't have much of a plan at all yet. But she knew that if the team put their heads together, they could think of a way to keep her safe while drawing out the enemy.

Sage put a hand on Mason's arm. "Let's work together on this. All of us. Come up with a plan that's going to work."

The bowl was whipped out of Sage's fingers and placed on the table. Mason turned to look at her. Only he didn't seem annoyed or frustrated, like she'd expected. Instead, he looked...sympathetic?

"Even if we came up with what we thought was a bulletproof plan, nothing is certain. I'm not willing to risk you."

He wasn't going to change his mind. There wasn't an ounce of flexibility in his words. And it caused a wave of disappointment to crash through Sage. "I trust your team to keep me safe."

"And that's what we're doing. We're keeping you safe by keeping you protected."

She shook her head. She couldn't help but keep pushing. "I can't just sit here when I could be doing more." Sage bit her lip, hesitating a moment before saying the next words. "A week ago, I found out you were spying on me. That hurt. But I forgave you, I *still* forgive you, because I care about you. Because we're a team. And team members listen to each other. They consider each other's ideas, thoughts, and opinions."

There was remorse on Mason's face, but she already knew before he spoke that it wouldn't be affecting his decision. "I know. And nothing like that will ever happen again. It's *because* I care about you, because we're a team, that I can't let you do it. I need to keep you safe."

There wasn't a single part of him that seemed open to the idea. And it was frustrating.

"Well, you can do what you want to do, and I'll do what I want to."

The moment the words left her mouth, she knew how immature and reckless they were. Not to mention impossible. She hadn't even been able to sneak out of her apartment without being caught.

Mason's gaze hardened again. Knowing she'd annoyed him, she smoothed her hands down his chest. Getting the man angry wouldn't get her what she wanted.

"Please."

When Mason remained still and silent, Sage lifted her head and placed her lips next to his ear.

"Please, Mason. We need a plan."

Next, Sage lowered her hand to the hem of his shirt. Lifting it, she crept a hand underneath. Her fingers trailed across his firm, hard stomach.

At the same time, Sage lowered her mouth to his neck.

She didn't know exactly what she was doing. But now that she'd started, she couldn't stop.

Mason remained completely still as she began to climb onto his lap. Once she was nestled on top of him, she wrapped her legs around his waist. The evidence of his arousal pressed against her core, igniting a fire within her.

When Sage lifted her head, she saw need. Need and desire.

Lowering her head again, Sage nibbled his neck while grinding against him. When Mason still didn't make a move or say anything, she lowered her hand and cupped him.

Mason tensed. "This is a dangerous game you're playing, sweetheart. Sure you want to continue?"

At this point, she didn't know if she could stop.

To answer his question, Sage began to unbuckle his jeans. Then she dipped her hand inside his clothes and wrapped her fingers around him.

When she raised her head to meet his gaze, she saw a moment of fire in his eyes before he crashed his lips onto hers.

There was no slow seduction. It was hard and fast as his tongue entered her mouth and danced with hers.

A soft moan escaped Sage. Their lips were separated for a moment as Mason pulled her shirt over her head. Her skin cooled, but heated again when his big warm hands ran across her stomach.

Mason's lips were magic. The perfect combination of smooth and sure.

He tore off his own shirt, then reached behind her back and unclasped her bra. The moment her bare chest rubbed against his, the hunger inside her doubled.

Mason leaned her back onto the couch until she found herself beneath his large body. His lips began to trail down her cheek, then neck. Then they reached her breast.

The moment his lips closed around her nipple, all coherent thoughts left her mind. Arching, she clawed at his back.

Mason licked and sucked. Every so often she would feel the hard edge of his teeth brush against her sensitive peak almost playfully.

When Mason switched to the other breast, a new round of pleasure washed over her. The heat inside her rose. She responded to every little touch.

Mason's fingers lowered to the waistband of her pants and underwear, pushing them down her thighs until they were removed completely.

There was a moment of insecurity, when Sage was aware that she was naked while Mason wasn't. The anxiety didn't have time to set in, though, because Mason picked up a foot and kissed her ankle. His touch was gentle. Causing a tremor to course down her spine.

As he trailed his mouth up the inside of her leg, her breaths came out ragged. She ached for the man.

Once Mason finally reached the apex between her thighs, his mouth lowered to Sage's core. Pleasure hit her hard.

She was vaguely aware that *she* was supposed to be in control. But she wasn't. She probably hadn't had it to begin with. And she didn't care one bit.

Mason ran his tongue across her clit in long, slow strokes. He applied just enough pressure to make her feel desperate. She attempted to buck her hips, but he held her firm. His tongue unrelenting.

"Mason, please. I need you."

His mouth lifted and began to trail kisses back up her body, but the torture didn't stop. As soon as his face hovered above hers, his thumb began to rub circles on her nub.

Sage tried to writhe beneath him, but the weight of his body made any movement impossible.

"I'm not going to risk losing you."

Understanding his words was difficult and took more concentration than she felt capable of. He inserted a finger and a cry escaped her.

With his mouth now on her neck and his finger moving rhythmically inside her, she was close to release, but she wanted *him*.

"Tell me you won't ask me to risk you again."

Sage felt his hardness on her thigh.

At her silence, Mason placed himself at her entrance.

"I need to hear the words, sweetheart. Tell me you won't ask me again."

Sage had never found it so hard to understand words in her life.

Mason inched inside her a fraction. It just increased her desperation because it wasn't enough. She needed all of him. Every delicious inch.

"Mason—"

"Tell me, sweetheart, and I'm all yours."

Tell him. Tell him what?

"Tell me you won't ask me again."

She needed to tell him. Because she needed him.

Sage ground out the words she knew he wanted to hear. "I won't ask you. I won't ask you to risk my life."

Finally, Mason pushed inside her. Big and smooth and intoxicating. His mouth covered hers. Then he began to move, each thrust hard. In and out. The feeling of him filling her was like none other on Earth.

Sage cupped her hand to Mason's head, running her fingers through his hair.

This man was her everything. She needed him like she needed air.

Her breasts bounced and brushed against his chest. He slid a hand below her right thigh and lifted her leg higher. Her stomach clenched as he began hitting a new spot inside her.

"Mason—"

No sooner had she said his name than she shuddered violently. Her walls clenched around him as an orgasm tore through her body.

Her heart thudded hard inside her chest as she screamed his name.

Mason continued to thrust into her, then his body tensed. He growled deep in his chest at his release. She felt him throb inside her.

He continued to hover over her, his breaths just as deep as hers.

"You're mine, Sage Porter. And I'm yours. We keep each other safe." Mason's voice was deep and raspy. But Sage understood. They belonged together.

CHAPTER 22

*M*ason heard the curse from his position by the counter. Then came the clatter of the dropped pan.

Moving straight to the stove, he saw Sage holding her wrist. An angry burn was already covering her palm. Taking her hand in his, he led them to the tap and moved her hand under running water.

A frown marred Mason's brow. "How did you burn yourself?"

"I must have turned the wrong burner on and it heated the handle of the pot."

And then she'd grabbed it.

Inspecting her hand closer, he realized the burn didn't look too bad. Mason stood there for another few seconds before leaving to grab the first-aid kit.

"Time for the doctor to get some medical treatment from a rookie."

Sage turned off the tap then proceeded to inspect the items in the box. "For a rookie, you have a good kit."

"This is nothing. I have a much larger stash in the cupboard."

They both took a seat at the kitchen island and Mason got to work applying burn cream and a bandage.

"You must have been distracted." It was unlike Sage to make such a careless mistake.

A small smile touched her lips. "I was."

He'd felt her stress over the last few days. And he hated it. He wanted to take away her fear and anxiety. Replace it with anything and everything good.

When the bandage was in place, Mason stood. "Let's go out to dinner."

Sage's eyes widened. "Tonight? But we've taken everything out…"

Mason shrugged. "Who cares? My girlfriend's stressed and I want to take her on a date."

She leaned back at his words. "Girlfriend?"

Stepping forward, he pulled her to her feet and wrapped his arms around her waist. "You're right. I should ask, shouldn't I? Sage Porter, will you be my girlfriend?"

A slow smile curved her lips. "Mason Ross, I thought you'd never ask. Yes."

Even though he'd seen her as his girlfriend for a while, hearing it being made official made him want to fist-pump the air.

Lowering his head, Mason planted a kiss on her lips. "Now, I have a rule for this date."

She tilted her head to the side. "A rule?"

"Yes, ma'am. Just one. We don't think about the threats or the danger or Project Arma. Tonight, it's just you and me."

Her smile grew, and damn but did she look beautiful. "Deal."

"You're saying you don't think I'm spontaneous?"

Mason shrugged. "I think you're logical and you like to consider things before jumping into them."

Why did Mason's words make Sage feel boring? Didn't most people consider things before jumping into them?

She placed her fork down. Mason had taken her to a Chinese restaurant, and she'd eaten way too much. Not that she regretted it. The food had been amazing. "I can be spontaneous. Remember who initiated the evening in the lake?"

Her cheeks immediately heated. Had she really just brought that up?

Mason leaned back, a smile on his mouth. "We hadn't touched or spoken for days. It's understandable that you needed me right then and there."

Sage laughed out loud.

The smile slipped from his lips. "God, you're beautiful."

When Sage sobered, she bit her bottom lip. He made her *feel* beautiful. Along with a million other wonderful things.

Mason stood. "Let's get out of here so I can ravage you all night."

That was definitely something she could get on board with.

Once standing, Mason snaked his arm around Sage's waist. He kept it there while paying and during the short walk to the car. His touch was warm and intimate.

When they were driving home, Sage reached over and placed her hand on Mason's leg. It was like she *needed* to be touching the man. "Thank you for tonight. It was nice having an evening away from everything."

Mason had gone so far as to take her to a restaurant a town over. None of her worries had entered her mind. Not once.

"You're welcome."

Leaning her head back, Sage couldn't wipe the smile from her lips. For the first time in a long time, she felt content.

As she glanced out the window, she was struck by how clear the night was. It was like every star in the sky was shining.

Evenings like this were her favorite. Ever since she was young and she would watch the stars with her brother. "Can you stop?"

She expected Mason to ask her why. To at least give her a strange look. Something. But he didn't. He immediately pulled the car to the side of the road.

Sage didn't wait to explain. She jumped out and jogged toward the open field of grass.

She knew Mason was right behind her. She couldn't hear him, but she could *feel* him. It was like her body knew when he was close.

He was probably wondering what the heck she was doing. That was okay. He would find out in a moment.

When she was far enough from the road, Sage dropped to the ground and lay on her back. Mason hovered above her. It was impossible to read his expression in the darkness.

"Lie with me."

Mason didn't hesitate. He lay beside her, his left side touching her right.

"Are you trying to show me your spontaneous side?"

Sage shook her head. "I know I err more on the side of caution. I'm okay with that. I'm watching the stars."

And they were glorious. They scattered the sky. Little bursts of light in the darkness.

"You look like you've done this before."

Many times. "When we were little, Jason and I would sneak outside and watch the stars. Some nights we barely saw any. Other nights, like tonight, the sky would be covered in them, and we would just lie on the grass for hours."

Mason was silent for a moment. "What do you see in the stars?"

A million different things. The sky held secrets unknown that were so profound, it was unlikely anyone would ever discover all the truths.

"Beauty. Mystery. Wonder."

"I don't need to look at the stars to see all that."

Sage turned her head at Mason's words. He was looking right

at her. There was an intensity in his eyes that she hadn't seen before.

Wetting her lips, Sage shook her head. "I'm not that special."

Her whole life, she'd felt incredibly ordinary. Until Mason.

She wanted to look away from him. Turn back to the stars that scattered the night sky. But she couldn't. She was drawn to him.

"You're the only you on Earth, Sage. You're also the only person who makes me feel what I feel. That makes you pretty damn special, if you ask me."

She couldn't help but ask the next question. "What do I make you feel?"

"Like I can breathe. Like the cloud that follows me around, dimming my world, has lifted."

Suddenly, the stars seemed secondary to the beautiful man by her side. The man she hadn't meant to fall for but somehow had.

"I love you." The words tumbled from her lips.

She hadn't been able to keep them in any longer. She needed them out and heard and known. Because they were true. So damn true and real.

Mason's mouth stretched into a smile. "I love you, too, Sage."

She let his words sink in. The man loved her. And she loved him.

Happiness soared through her chest.

Mason rolled to his side and his face hovered over her own. Sage raised a hand to his cheek, needing to touch him. "You truly love me?"

He leaned his head down and touched his lips to hers. "There is nothing truer in this world than my love for you. There's no going back."

Sage didn't want to go back. She doubted she ever would.

Lost for words, she luckily didn't need to respond. Because his lips returned to hers and the world quieted. For a moment in time, they were the only ones who existed.

CHAPTER 23

*M*ason stood in his living room and studied the chip in Wyatt's hand. It was small. So small, most would likely miss it if they weren't looking for it.

Logan straightened from his position beside Mason. "So once this is inserted under my skin, you'll be able to track my location?"

Wyatt nodded. "Yes."

While the women chatted outside, the team met inside. The whole team. They could hear everything, so there was no danger. But they still had one man stand by the window, watching.

It was only a week and a half ago that Sage had first suggested using herself as bait to draw out Project Arma. That's what had given Logan the idea to use himself instead.

It was a good idea. Albeit a risk to Logan. But the man seemed willing to go to any lengths to save his team.

It had taken a week for the tracking chip to arrive.

The entire team was in agreeance that they trusted Logan. The man seemed to have one focus—find his team. Which was also their focus at the moment, too.

Logan nodded. "Let's do it."

"How do we get them to take Logan?" Bodie asked as he leaned against the wall.

"I'll distance myself from your team," Logan answered. "I have no doubt that they're lurking somewhere, waiting. Once they start seeing me on my own, with no backup, they'll take me."

"Won't that make it obvious that something's going on?" Eden asked.

Logan shrugged. "Maybe. Maybe not. They've profiled us. They know I like my own space. I'll start by moving out of Bodie's place and into somewhere by myself."

Kye blew out a long breath. "It could be hell for you when they get their hands on you again."

"They won't kill me. I can handle whatever they do if it's to save my brothers."

A beat of silence passed through the room. Mason had no doubt they were all thinking the same thing. Each of them would also go to great lengths to save their teammates.

"I haven't spoken to Sage about it." Mason scrubbed a hand over his face. "I don't think she'll have a problem inserting the chip."

What she might have a problem with was the team meeting and planning a rescue mission for Jason and not including her in the process. He hadn't wanted to tell her until the plan was solid. Particularly, because she was so eager to "help" by putting herself in danger.

Asher nudged Mason's shoulder with his own. "If she does have a problem, I'm sure you could find a way to get her to come around."

Mason shoved his friend.

"Ask her if she can insert it this afternoon," Wyatt said, pocketing the device.

That was the plan. The sooner the better. "Done."

A melodic laugh sounded from the backyard. He knew it was

Sage immediately. And damn if it didn't sound like the best thing he'd ever heard.

Mason headed out the back. The women were sitting on the grass in a circle. Lexie held baby Fletcher while Nunzie and Dizzie were lazing around getting pats.

The women looked happy and carefree. He just wished that they were as safe when the men weren't around.

He stopped as Sage lifted Fletcher into her arms. A smile spread across her face a mile long.

Just for a moment, Mason imagined that Sage was holding *their* baby. Hell, he would love to make a family with the woman.

"Dreaming up some babies of your own?"

Mason turned his head to find Wyatt beside him. The man was too smart for his own good. "Just thinking about the life we're going to make together."

And in Mason's mind, it was pretty damn special.

"You two are good together."

Mason wasn't about to disagree with that. "I have this churning in my gut telling me that something's coming. I'm so damn scared to lose her."

When Mason glanced over at Wyatt, his friend didn't look concerned. "Something will always be coming for us or our loved ones until we take care of our enemies. But those women have us looking out for them, and we're an army. Their lives are safe."

Some of the tension in his stomach eased. They *were* an army. And protecting their family wasn't a job they took lightly.

Clamping a hand on Wyatt's shoulder, Mason nodded. "This is why I need my brothers around. To remind me how fucking deadly we are."

"Damn straight."

Mason was about to walk ahead to Sage when his phone vibrated in his pocket. Pulling it out, he frowned at the screen. "It's Quinn."

She never called. The only time he heard from his sister was when he made contact himself. Quinn was always too engrossed in whatever story she was working on.

"Your sister from New York?" Wyatt asked.

"Yeah. I'll be a sec."

Stepping away, Mason put the phone to his ear.

"Quinn?"

The sound of car horns and people filtered through the phone line. "Mason, hey! How are you?"

Quinn was just about yelling through the line. But then, she always had spoken at higher decibels than most. "I'm good, sis, how are you?"

"I'm good." Quinn's response was quick. Almost too quick. "I'm actually calling because I wanted to ask you about something."

Mason's interest was piqued. He couldn't remember the last time she'd called to "ask him about something." It was likely it had never happened.

"Shoot."

"Do you still have that apartment in Marble Falls? The one you lived in for a while before you chose the dog life?"

He chuckled at Quinn's choice of words. "I do." And if he had his way, it would be vacant in the foreseeable future.

"Great! I was wondering if I could stay there for a while?"

Mason almost thought he'd misheard her. "You want to come and stay in Marble Falls?"

"I do. For a few months. Maybe a bit longer. I'm not sure yet."

Words failed Mason. Quinn was a big-city person at heart. He couldn't picture her here.

"You don't need to worry," Quinn hurried to add. "I won't bug you too much. Well, I'll try not to." She laughed across the line.

"Quinn, I'm gonna be honest with you, you would be bored out of your mind in Marble Falls. Why do you want to come here?"

There was a beat of silence. "I'm taking some leave from

work. Rent in New York is expensive and I'm a bit strapped for cash. I'm hoping my rent can be paid in sisterly love. I have some savings, of course I do, but not much. And I don't know when I'll be returning to work."

"You know you won't need to pay rent. Did something happen?" His head was spinning. Quinn's job as a journalist was her life.

"No. Don't be silly. I'm just a bit burned out. I need a break to look after myself. Some TLC. You always talk about how much you love Marble Falls, so I thought why not? Plus, I can spend some time with you."

Quinn was a damn hard worker so it would make sense if she was burned out. And he wanted to be there for her if she was going through a rough patch in her life.

"I'll be there in a few weeks," Quinn continued. "I'm looking forward to seeing you. I've missed you."

"I've missed you, too, Q." He used her childhood nickname. "I'll see you when you get here." And hopefully by then, some of the danger around Marble Falls would have decreased and Quinn wouldn't be landing smack bang in the middle of it.

SAGE SMILED at Fletcher's beautiful face. His chubby cheeks and gummy smile almost caused her ovaries to explode.

Lexie scooted closer. "Do you think his cheeks look a little rosy? I was worried he was getting a temperature."

His cheeks *were* slightly red. Placing her hand on his forehead, Sage shook her head. "He doesn't have a temperature that I can feel but maybe check his temperature in an hour or so."

Lexie nodded. "I'm sorry, I worry too much, don't I?"

"There's no such thing as too much worry for your baby. Worry is completely normal for all mothers." Sage handed Fletcher back to Lexie. "He's beautiful."

The worry eased from Lexie's face as she cradled her son in her arms. "Some days I just sit for minutes on end gazing at him."

Sage understood why. The little guy was gorgeous. She had no doubt that if she and Mason had a child, she would be no different.

As soon as Mason entered her thoughts, she couldn't help but turn and search him out. To her surprise, she saw him standing to the side of the yard, phone to his ear.

The conversation around her faded, her full focus turned to him.

Today, he wore a black shirt that pulled across his wide chest. The muscles in his biceps stretched the material. It was almost like his arms were going to break free.

But what she felt for him went deeper than looks. So much deeper. She loved his mind. His heart.

Who was she kidding, she loved everything about the guy.

Making the decision to trust Mason, to trust that his team would find Jason, had allowed her the time to focus on them as a couple. And boy, what a week it had been. Just about every moment had been spent with him, from waking in his arms to falling asleep curled into his chest.

"Woman, you are in loooove."

Sage whipped her head around to see Lexie looking at her with a knowing smile on her face.

Not just Lexie. Evie and Shylah were looking at her with the same expression.

Her cheeks heated. "I feel terrible finding happiness when my brother is in the situation he's in, but…"

But she couldn't stop loving the guy. Just like she couldn't prevent the overwhelming happiness that she felt when she was around him.

Shylah leaned forward. "Sage, we all met our men under hard circumstances. And it's better that some good comes out of everything rather than just bad."

Evie and Lexie nodded in agreement.

"It's good to have another woman in the gang." Evie smiled. "I mean, you've been with us since you came to Marble Falls, but now it's official."

She was grateful to have them, too. All of them, the women, Mason...the whole team. For the last few years, she'd been on her own, lying to her parents, trying to convince Jason to come out of hiding. Now she had friends. People ready to help and support her.

"I feel the same way."

Her eyes flicked back to Mason to find him still on the phone. But coming their way was Luca, Eden, and Asher, no doubt wanting to take their women home.

"Time to go, ladies," Asher called. Crouching down, he kissed Lexie's cheek before lifting Fletcher into his arms.

The women around Sage began to filter out. The rest of the guys also popped their heads out to wave goodbye.

Then it was just Sage. Waiting for Mason.

As she waited, she glanced over at his big house. Again, she wondered why he needed so much space when it was just him, Nunzie, and Dizzie. Most people with three kids had smaller homes with less land.

A minute later, Mason strolled over to where she sat. He dropped down behind Sage and pulled her back so she was leaning on him.

"Why did you buy such a big house?" Sage asked, blurting out her thoughts.

"Because I wanted fresh air. And space. And dogs." Mason paused before adding the last bit. "And a big-ass family."

Sage paused. "You want kids one day?"

"I do." There was no hesitation in the way he answered.

And that made Sage happy. Really happy. "I want kids, too."

She felt his lips press to her head. "Good."

Sage began to trace the veins on his arms. They popped out all over the place. "Who was that on the phone?"

"That was my sister, actually."

"Quinn?"

Mason's chest vibrated as he chuckled. "Why do you sound confused?"

She shrugged. "I looked over at you a few times. I thought you looked a bit...bewildered?"

"Oh, I was definitely bewildered. She told me she's coming to Marbles Falls. She's going to stay for a while. She'd like to stay in my apartment, actually." Her brows lifted, even though he wouldn't be able to see them. "I told her she could."

"You're kicking me out?"

"No. I'm asking you if you want to move in with me." Sage was silent, and Mason continued. "But if you don't, that's okay. I'll call Quinn back and get her to move in here."

Sage turned her head to look up at Mason. "I would love to move in with you, Mason."

She'd basically done so already. There was nowhere she'd rather be than with this man.

His head dipped and his lips pressed to hers.

When they parted, she leaned back into him again. "I'm excited to meet your sister."

"She'll love you."

She lay her head on his chest. Then they sat in silence. She didn't know how long they sat like that, but it would never be long enough. The peace of being held by the man she loved was everything.

Eventually, he moved. But it wasn't to get up. Instead, Mason reached down to lift her phone.

Sage pushed up to watch as he took something out of his pocket. Then, using the small device, he removed the back of the phone and pulled something out. Sage didn't need to ask to know what it was.

"We never really talked about the phone bug issue. Not properly." Mason put the back of the phone on before handing it to Sage. "What I did was an invasion of your privacy. And it was wrong. There were other ways I should have gone about the situation. I'm sorry."

Sage took the phone from Mason's fingers. "Thank you. It means a lot to me that you would say that."

After everything, the phone issue had pretty much slipped from her mind. But she was grateful that he would acknowledge it was wrong and that he could have handled it differently.

"I want you to know that the moment I got to know you, to know your heart, I knew you were a good person. The bug became about keeping you safe. Protecting you. Not watching you. But it was still wrong of me."

She could hear the sincerity in his voice. He meant the words he said.

Mason took Sage's hand in his. "There's something I need to talk to you about."

A sinking feeling came over her. Did the guy bug something else? Her car? Her *bedroom*?

Mason held her chin gently. "Calm, Sage."

Blowing out a slow breath, she waited for Mason to say whatever he was going to say.

"After you volunteered to use yourself to draw out Project Arma, Logan came to us. He wanted us to follow through with your plan, but to use him instead." Mason paused. He studied Sage's face. "We accepted."

Well, that wasn't nearly as bad as the thoughts that had been racing through her mind.

Sage nodded. She could tell there was more to come, so she waited for Mason to finish.

"We have a GPS tracking device and we would like you to insert it under Logan's skin. It needs to be inserted into his upper arm."

"You want me to implant a tracking chip into Logan's arm?" That was something she hadn't done before. But she couldn't imagine it would be too difficult.

"Yes."

As plans went, it wasn't terrible. "Okay."

Mason cocked his head to the side. "Okay? You're not going to try to convince me to use you?"

"No. I trust you. And I trust your team."

His lips spread into a smile. "I love you so damn much."

Her heart skipped a beat. She would never get tired of hearing those words. Not if she heard them on repeat for another fifty years.

"I love you, too, Mason."

He lowered his head and kissed her.

CHAPTER 24

*a*n hour later, Mason stood to the side and watched as Sage numbed Logan's arm.

She had managed to book a small patient room at Marble Falls Hospital. She said she could have inserted the device at Mason's home, but as it was a medical procedure she'd never done before, she preferred to have the resources of a hospital around as a safeguard.

Not that the hospital knew exactly what they were doing.

Evie and Wyatt sat to the side of the room. Evie had a laptop open on her lap. The moment the device was inserted, they would switch the GPS on and ensure it worked. Then, and only then, would Sage proceed to stitch up Logan. Not that many stitches would be required for the tiny incision.

Logan sat on the bed, shirtless. The man's anxious energy bounced around the room. Not anxious because something was being planted under his skin. The guy would have experienced a hell of a lot worse during his time in the special forces, and maybe even with Project Arma.

No. Mason knew that Logan was anxious because he wanted

the device inserted quickly. Every minute that passed was a minute his team was held by Project Arma.

Sage tapped his skin. "Do you feel that?"

"No, nothing." Logan's face remained impassive.

Sage nodded before making a small incision. Mason watched her as she worked. She was meticulous and efficient. Just like anyone would want their doctor to be. She took her time inserting the device, then lifted her gaze to Evie and Wyatt. "It's in."

Evie pressed keys on the laptop while Wyatt fiddled with his phone.

"Logan's location is reading accurately on the laptop," Evie said quietly without looking up.

"I've got it, too." Wyatt gave Sage a small nod. "You can stitch him up."

Sage went to work stitching the cut. As expected, only a couple of stitches were needed. The incision had been so small that it was extremely unlikely it would raise suspicions when he was caught. Once Logan had a shirt on, it would be out of sight anyway.

Sage applied a small bandage. "I used dissolvable stitches, so they won't need removal. Give it a few days, and with your fast healing, there should hardly be a mark."

Logan stood and pulled his shirt over his head. "Thanks, Doc."

Sage began cleaning while Mason, Logan, and Wyatt headed toward the door.

Once standing in the hall, Logan turned to look at them. "I'm gonna get out of here. Get a room at the inn here in town. In the next few days, I'll try to be as visible as possible and hope those assholes come after me."

There was an air of dangerous determination as he spoke.

Mason clamped a hand on his shoulder. "Look after yourself."

Logan nodded before walking down the hall. Mason hoped

like hell this plan worked and this wasn't the last time he saw the man.

Mason and Wyatt headed back inside and he immediately beelined for his woman. Standing behind her, he wrapped his arms around her middle. "You're sexy when you're in doctor mode."

A sweet giggle sounded from her chest. Mason nuzzled his mouth into her neck, wanting to hear it again.

Evie sighed from behind them. "You two are cute."

"As cute as me?"

At the sound of Luca's voice, Mason turned but kept one arm firmly around Sage. Evie stood next to Luca as he greeted her with a kiss.

"Rocket, you're not even in the same ballpark as me."

Luca straightened. "You're right. I have my own ballpark. And I must say, it's a bit bigger than yours."

Sage laughed. "Why don't we just agree that everyone in this room is cute."

"And Lexie and Shylah," Evie added with a sparkle in her eyes.

Sage nodded. "Yes, and Lexie and Shylah."

"Not sure about Kye and Oliver." Evie frowned.

"Maybe to some women. Bodie though—"

"Okay, you two, you've had your fun." Mason shook his head.

"Let's get out of here," Wyatt said.

Mason leaned his head down to her ear. "Yes, let's get home so I can have my way with you."

SAGE GIGGLED AGAIN. That was definitely a plan she could get on board with.

At the sound of her phone ringing, Sage stopped and pulled the cell out of her pocket. She could see it was Lexie before she put the phone to her ear. "Lex, is everything okay?"

"Fletcher has a fever."

Lexie's words were rushed. There was an underlying panic in her voice. In Sage's years as a doctor, she had heard mothers panic many times and it never got easier.

Speaking in a calm voice, Sage aimed to soothe her friend. "I'm at Marble Falls Hospital in room eight. Come by and I'll check him out."

The other woman confirmed that they were leaving immediately.

Once she was off the phone, she glanced up at Mason. There was a frown on his face. "I heard."

"I'm sure he's fine." She wasn't certain, but she knew that panicking wouldn't do anyone any good.

It was a short ten minutes later when Lexie and Asher walked through the door with Fletcher in Lexie's arms. They looked as anxious as ever.

Mason and the others left the room before Sage got to work.

The moment Sage felt Fletcher's skin, some of her worry lessened. He was warm, but not hot. As fevers went, his didn't feel too bad. But she wouldn't know for sure until she did a full health check.

Sage spent the next hour checking him over. His heart rate was normal and so was his breathing. He even seemed happy and relaxed throughout the appointment, gurgling away.

Sage took a blood sample and called Mason to escort her to the labs to study it herself. When she was done, she breathed a sigh of relief. She had good news for Lexie and Asher.

Mason returned to the hall as she returned to the family. Taking a seat on the edge of the bed, she smoothed her features. Fletcher lay in Lexie's arms, while Asher stood with a hand on her shoulder.

"Fletcher is going to be okay."

The sigh of relief that Lexie blew out was accompanied by tears in her eyes. "Are you sure? He's so hot."

"I've done a complete health check and tested the blood. Fletcher is healthy." Lexie appeared confused, so Sage quickly continued. "His temperature is only slightly above normal. There are a couple of things that could be responsible. The first is teething. Babies often get a temperature when they experience the pain of growing teeth. Although, Fletcher seems quite happy, which is not usually the case for a teething baby."

"What's your other idea?" Asher asked.

"That he takes after his dad and just runs warm. All the guys run slightly hotter than the average person. He has unique physiology, and we'll continue to learn about Fletcher as he grows."

"Are you sure it's nothing else?"

Sage placed her hand on Lexie's leg. "It's my professional opinion that your little man is healthy. The check I did was very comprehensive. If you're worried, we can monitor him and do another check tomorrow morning."

Lexie closed her eyes and put her mouth to Fletcher's head. When she spoke, relief was thick in her voice. "Thank you."

Sage squeezed her friend's leg before she stood. The moment she was up, Asher took a seat on the other side of the bed and placed his arm around his family.

Relief cascaded off the couple in waves. It was a precious moment for the family, and they deserved some privacy.

Sage exited the room expecting to see Mason in the corridor. But he wasn't there.

Pulling her phone out of her pocket, she noticed a message from Mason. He'd gone to the cafeteria with the team to give Asher and Lexie some privacy. She smiled at his stern instructions to not leave Asher's side.

She was just turning back toward the door when a sudden sting to her neck stopped her. Before she could move, an arm came around her waist and began propelling her forward.

When her brain caught up to what was happening, she tried to push the man away, but her limbs felt heavy. So heavy that the arm around her waist was the only thing keeping her upright. It continued to all but carry her forward.

She opened her mouth to protest but words didn't form. Only a whimper sounded.

It was like her body was entering a paralytic state. The man must have drugged her with a muscle relaxer.

Up ahead, she saw the parking lot exit. Panic began to bubble inside her. Once he got her outside, he would no doubt have a car ready to whisk her away.

She attempted to look for help, but her head felt heavy. She couldn't help but rest it on the man's shoulder.

Then, he pushed outside. And she was out of time.

CHAPTER 25

*M*ason lifted the disposable coffee cup to his lips. The hit of caffeine was good, but what he really needed was a shot of hard alcohol.

He was on edge. But then, so was everyone.

Mason darted his gaze around at Evie, Luca, and Wyatt. They sat in the hospital cafeteria. No one was smiling.

Worry was thick in the air. Worry for Fletcher's health was at the forefront of everyone's minds.

"I'm sure Fletcher will be okay," Evie said, breaking the silence. "Sage didn't seem overly concerned when she saw him. She wasn't running around. She was calm."

Luca lifted his arm and wrapped it around her. "You're right, darlin'. Everything will be okay."

Mason could only hope that would be the case. The uncertainty of it all was hard to sit through.

As well as worrying about Fletcher, there was the concern for Logan's safety. No one could ensure it. Plus, he was their only hope. If his tracker didn't lead them to Arma, they had nothing.

There was no way Mason wanted to look at Sage and tell her they'd failed. Failed to find her brother. Failed to save him.

He glanced across to Wyatt. "You haven't received any intel from the government on Project Arma activity?"

Like where the hell they were working from. Where their main facility was located.

Wyatt shook his head. "Nothing."

That didn't surprise Mason in the least. The assholes didn't want Mason or his team involved in bringing down the project. Whether it was because they thought they didn't need them or because they had something to hide was yet to be confirmed.

Luca leaned forward. "You still have a guy watching imports from the Congo?"

Wyatt had a guy at Customs and Border Protection ensuring there were no incoming packages of Agrilla. Agrilla being a newly discovered plant species used to create the drug Toved.

Wyatt's brows pulled together. "I haven't heard from him in the last month, actually. We'd been communicating via email. I've been meaning to look into other ways to get in contact with him."

That was news to Mason. A month was a long time. A lot could happen.

Mason opened his mouth to question Wyatt further when Luca's phone buzzed on the table.

"Striker?" Mason asked.

Luca nodded. "Yes. He just asked where we are. They're heading to us now."

That meant Sage would be down soon. And it couldn't be soon enough. With everything that was going on, he wanted eyes on her at all times. He'd only come down here because Striker deserved some privacy.

Evie sighed. "We'll find out if Fletcher's okay. That's good."

It was only a couple of minutes later when Asher stepped out of the elevator and into the cafeteria. He had an arm around Lexie, who held Fletcher to her chest. Only Sage wasn't with them. She was nowhere in sight.

A frown marred Mason's brow. Was she filling out paperwork? Picking up test results? Neither of those were safe things for her to be doing alone. Nothing was.

"Fletcher's okay," Lexie said as they reached the table. "He might be teething but it's more likely that he just runs hot like his dad."

Evie jumped up and moved around the table to embrace Lexie and Fletcher. "What a relief. I'm so glad."

Asher's gaze scanned the table at the same time as Mason pushed to his feet. A wild panic began to uncoil in his gut.

"Where's Sage?" Mason only had eyes for Asher as he spoke.

"I thought she was with you? She left the room after she told us Fletcher's test results. I thought you'd waited in the hall."

Mason pulled out his phone and called her number. Every second she didn't answer, his dread grew.

When the voice mail picked up, he tried again. Nothing.

Fear coursed through Mason's system. Something was wrong. There was no way Sage wouldn't answer. Not with everything going on.

When Mason turned to his friends, he noticed everyone was now standing. Alert and ready to move.

Mason didn't say anything. He turned, ready to run and find her. Wyatt's hand on his arm kept him stationary. "She could be anywhere. Running around the hospital searching will take too long."

"I need to find her." Mason was aware that the words had come out as a growl. But the fear inside him was all-consuming.

Evie raced back to her laptop and sat in front of it. Her fingers began flying over the keys. "There are security cameras in the corridors. It won't take me long to hack them."

Mason stood and waited. It was hell, and he thought he might combust from frustration, but he waited.

Luca walked around the table. He placed a hand on Mason's shoulder and squeezed. He didn't say anything. There was nothing anyone could say that would lessen the terror unless it entailed Sage's location.

"Got it." Evie turned the screen around and everyone watched.

Video surveillance began playing of Sage exiting the patient room. She looked around, then down at her phone. She seemed to be about to go back in when suddenly a man in a black sweater appeared beside her.

A raw anger coursed through his body as he watched the man stick a syringe into Sage's neck. Mason's breathing sped up and he had to clench his fists to remain still. He wanted to reach through the screen and tear the man's head off.

The man slid his arm around Sage's waist and they moved forward. Only she didn't move with her normal grace. Her body looked heavy. The man seemed to be almost dragging her.

There was a thick cloud of tension around them as the team could only watch what was happening, unable to do a damn thing to stop it.

As the couple walked out of camera view, Evie hit a few keys and switched to the end of the hall. They watched until Sage and her abductor pushed through an exit door.

Evie again attempted to switch cameras, but too soon her fingers stopped moving across the keys. "There should be a camera that covers the exterior of the building, but I can't find any footage."

Mason began to run. He knew it was too late. She'd be gone. But his feet didn't stop. He had to go to the last location she'd been seen. He had to find clues. *Anything.*

Footsteps sounded behind him. He knew he was moving too fast. But he didn't care. There was nothing he cared about more than getting to her.

Pushing open the back door to the hospital, the same door Sage had gone through, Mason stepped into the parking lot.

He was greeted by nothing but parked cars. No Sage. No enemies. Nothing.

"Fuck!" Mason shouted the word while grabbing at his hair.

She was gone. Taken by *them*.

Wyatt and Luca stood behind him. When Mason finally turned to look at them, he saw the same deadly anger that he was sure was on his own face. Because Sage was one of their own. And they all felt the loss.

Mason scanned the area, immediately spotting the smashed hospital camera lying on the ground.

He was living his own worst nightmare. And there wasn't a damn thing he could do about it.

All three men turned at the sound of the hospital door opening. Evie ran out, laptop in hand. Her eyes darted between the men, frantic, before landing on Luca. "I don't know if this is related to Sage, but when I clicked out of the hospital surveillance, I clicked into Logan's GPS." Evie paused before she continued. "He's moving—and he's moving fast. He's already out of town. I tried to call him but there was no answer."

Wyatt frowned. "Out of town? He told us he was going to the inn."

Luca moved to stand beside Evie. "Is it possible he took her?"

Ice shot through Mason's veins.

Wyatt shook his head. "It doesn't make sense that he would allow us to place a tracker in his arm moments before taking her."

"Unless he wants us to follow," Mason said quietly. "The whole thing could be a setup. He's been around us. He knows I'll follow if he has her."

He would follow her to the ends of the Earth.

Mason was already walking toward his car when Wyatt latched on to his arm. "We need a plan."

He wrenched his arm free and took a step closer to Wyatt. "We need to follow Logan. It's the only lead we have."

Mason turned again, but this time Luca stood in front of him. "You said yourself that it's likely a trap."

"Get the hell out of my way."

"No."

Mason took a step back and ran his hands through his hair. They were right. "Okay, we'll call the team. While we follow his tracker, they can stop at Marble Protection and get armed up. We'll assess what to do as we follow."

Wyatt and Luca both nodded and the three of them moved toward Mason's car. At the same time, they pulled out their phones.

There were many questions in Mason's head, but one thing he knew for damn sure—if Logan betrayed them, betrayed Sage, he would pay.

They had remained close to the guy since he'd come to town. Never dropping their guard around him until trust was built. Waiting for him to give them any sign he was working for the enemy.

It hadn't happened. He'd earned their trust slowly.

If he *was* the enemy, a lot of the blame lie on Mason. And he didn't know if he'd be able to forgive himself.

CHAPTER 26

*S*age focused on controlling her breaths. It was all she could do to stop from hyperventilating.

The moment the man had taken her outside, a blindfold had been placed over her eyes before she'd been lifted into some type of vehicle. Rough hands had been quick to tie her wrists and ankles.

Her entire body had flopped against what felt like a door the moment she'd been placed inside the vehicle.

Fortunately, the paralytic drug seemed to be mild. And although the drug had a rapid onset, most were fast-acting. In the time since they'd been driving, she'd already started to regain the ability to move some of her fingers and toes.

It was a relief that the muscles around her diaphragm that help the lungs fill with oxygen were able to move. She was sure that, had she been given a stronger dose, she wouldn't have been able to draw breath.

Sage didn't know how long they'd been on the move. Maybe twenty minutes? Maybe thirty? But so far, no one had spoken a single word.

The seat below her was hard and every time the vehicle went

over a bump or turned a corner, she hit a hard surface with her shoulder.

The jolts barely registered. Because fear overrode every other emotion inside her. Without the ability to move or see, she was close to a panic attack. But she attempted to breathe through it.

Whenever her mind drew to Mason, the fear increased. Fear for his well-being.

There was no way he wouldn't have noticed she was missing by now. He was probably going through hell.

But if anyone could save her, get her out of this tornado of mess, it was him.

Sage was pulled out of her internal thoughts by the sound of the engine switching off. The fear in her stomach crawled up her throat. It was so palpable she could almost taste it.

She heard the movement of people around her. Then, her body teetered sideways as the door beside her was opened. Before she hit the ground, the same rough hands grabbed her. This time, instead of being dragged, she was thrown over what had to be a shoulder. A hard shoulder.

Pain laced her stomach and moved right through to her own shoulders. As the person began to move, blood rushed to Sage's head.

One small positive was that she could now move her hands. Likely her legs, too, although she was too scared to test them.

Good. That was good. She had to focus on the good, because otherwise the bad would overwhelm her.

After what felt like forever, but was likely minutes, creaking noises sounded. Similar to heavy doors being opened and shut.

Then the air changed. Became heavy. Musky. It was a subtle change, and had Sage not had use of all her other senses, she may not even have noticed it.

After a few more minutes, and more of the same sounds, Sage was placed on a cold, hard surface.

A thud sounded across the room. Almost like something

heavy had been dropped. She heard a door close, followed by the click of a lock.

Then there was silence.

Sage lay on her back, too scared to attempt to move. She wanted to test exactly how many muscles were back to normal. But fear rendered her still.

Sage scrunched her eyes closed behind the cloth. She was using every bit of strength to not freak out. To remain calm. Panic would do nothing.

She pictured Mason's blue eyes in her mind. His warm hands as he touched her skin. His soothing voice as he told her he loved her.

Some of the panic receded. But it was quickly replaced with something else.

Regret. Regret that they hadn't had much time together. There were so many things she wanted to say to him. Do with him. Memories that would never be made.

No.

She mentally shook her head. This wasn't the end. There was a reason she was brought here. If they wanted her dead, they would have killed her on the spot. They didn't. That had to mean something.

A rustling came from close by, sending a jolt of fear through Sage. Then footsteps sounded. Footsteps that drew closer to her and made her heart pound.

A tangible fear rose inside her. When the footsteps stopped, she could almost feel the person standing by her body. They were close. Likely looming over her.

Suddenly, the cloth on her eyes was removed. Bright light blinded Sage, to the point where her eyes snapped shut.

Hands were then on her wrists. Gentle hands. Different from the previous hands that had touched her.

She blinked, taking a moment to adjust to the light. Everything remained blurry for a few seconds.

When she realized her hands were no longer bound, Sage attempted to push to her elbows, happy when she didn't drop back to the floor.

That was when she saw the big body kneeling by her feet.

Using a free hand, Sage scrubbed her eyes. Her arm felt impossibly heavy and her head dizzy.

Slowly, the figure in front of her came into focus.

Shock shot through her system. Shock and confusion.

"Logan?"

"Yeah, Doc, it's me."

Logan pulled the last of the rope from her ankles before extending his hands toward her. She hesitated, unsure her legs would hold her, before placing her hands in his.

Logan gently pulled her to her feet. At first, her knees caved. Logan caught her easily by releasing her hands and grabbing her waist. "You okay?"

Surprisingly, she did feel okay. Considering she'd been drugged not that long ago.

Once she was back on her feet, she moved from foot to foot, impressed that she was actually holding most of her body weight.

"They injected me with a muscle relaxer. I'm actually surprised by how much it's worn off already."

Logan slowly released his hold on her. Although Sage wouldn't say she felt steady, it was a far cry from the almost complete immobility she experienced a short while ago.

"The scientists are good at modifying drugs to suit their requirements."

Sage studied Logan's expression. "What are you doing here?"

For a millisecond, the possibility hit Sage that he could have played a part in her abduction. But as she took in their surroundings, she dismissed that idea.

They were in a concrete cell-like room. There were no windows, just a solid door. Sage was sure that if she tried the doorknob it would be locked.

"I didn't even make it out of the hospital before they took me."

Her eyes widened. "How did they take you?"

"Tranquilizer. It's specially designed for our kind."

Her gaze flicked to his arm, then back to his face. "But you've still got the—"

"They're watching," Logan interrupted. "And listening."

Sage shut her mouth, her gaze flying around the room. Sure enough, a camera sat in the top corner of the ceiling. They weren't even trying to hide it. Although, why would they need to? Sage and Logan were prisoners, and they knew it.

"They'll find us." Sage didn't know if she was telling Logan or trying to convince herself. But the words brought her comfort.

Logan frowned. "Usually, I can hear the wind through the trees. Car horns miles away."

"You can't hear them now?"

He shook his head. "Not really. The little I can hear is muffled."

Sage understood what he was saying. If they were far from cars and nature, it was possible the GPS signal could be lost.

Logan continued to study the room. "I think this is the main facility."

Before Sage could dwell on that, the click of the door opening echoed through the room.

Logan quickly took a protective stance in front of her. She had to crane her neck to the side to see who stood by the door.

What she saw was a man who stood well over six feet. He was older than Mason and his teammates, but that in no way took away from how capable he looked. A small scar ran across his right eye, adding to the air of danger he exuded.

"Logan, my son, I'm so glad that you've returned to us."

"I didn't really have a choice, did I, Hylar."

The man, Hylar, seemed unfazed by Logan's words. "Still, I'm glad you're back. Although, you know you have caused your brothers quite a lot of problems by running. It was the first time in years they actually felt like prisoners."

Sage drew back at that comment. She was sure that they'd felt like prisoners every single day, cage or not.

Logan didn't so much as flinch at Hylar's words. "Maybe you should take me to them."

A slow smile spread across Hylar's mouth, but the smile was wrong. Unkind. It made her skin crawl.

"Follow me." Without waiting to see if they would follow, Hylar turned and began to walk.

"Stay behind me." Logan whispered the words to Sage before he began to follow.

Sage trailed Logan, grateful that her legs were holding her. Her knees trembled, and she was somewhere between throwing up or passing out, but she forced her body to move.

They walked down a long corridor and again, the walls were concrete.

Every so often, they passed a closed door. Sage could only presume they were more rooms to hold prisoners.

A shudder ran through her body at what they would need so many cells for.

If this was the main facility, it was a far cry from what she was expecting. Wyatt and Evie had been searching for warehouse-type locations. This was no warehouse.

Sage stuck as close to Logan as possible without actually touching him. If it was Mason with her, she would have been grabbing on to him like a lifeline.

When Hylar reached the end of the hall, he opened a door and walked through. She could see that the room he entered was bright. A whole lot brighter than the dimly lit corridor.

She followed Logan through the doorway. When she took in the large space, a small gasp escaped her lips.

Gone was the old concrete. It was like she'd stepped into a completely different place. Some sort of high-tech laboratory.

In the center of the room were tables with computers and vials and test tubes. Half a dozen people stood at the tables wearing lab coats.

Her gaze darted to the side of the room, where she saw men. Huge, muscular men who stood with arms crossed. Guns were strapped to their legs and steely looks sat in their eyes. Like they were ready to move. Hurt. Kill.

She wanted to sink back at the sight of them.

Small goose bumps rose on her chilled skin but she avoided running her hands down her arms. She didn't want to breathe, let alone make any movements.

Then she saw what she'd missed thus far.

Cages. Huge glass cages that bordered the room. And inside each cage was a man. There looked to be seven, maybe eight in total.

She took a step forward, studying each one. She expected to see wounded men. Fear or anguish, maybe.

She didn't. She saw rage. Resentment.

It reminded Sage of the look she often caught on Mason's face when he thought she wasn't watching. When his mind was no doubt on Arma.

She studied each cage. It wasn't until she reached the last one that she noticed, where the other men were watching what was happening, this man was sitting on a seat, hunched over. It made it impossible for her to see what he looked like.

There was a familiarity about him. Something about him that made Sage want to draw closer. Moving on instinct, she took a small step forward.

"Sage."

She barely heard Logan's warning behind her; she was too focused on the man.

The man in the cage heard, though. At least, she assumed he did. Because he flinched. Then the muscles in his arms visibly tightened.

He was clearly big and muscular like all the others. He wore pants but no shirt. Bruises marred his body.

Finally, he raised his head. And her breath caught. Everything around her faded into insignificance when the same brown eyes that she'd been yearning to see for so long stared back at her.

"Jason."

She whispered the word so quietly that had normal people surrounded her, no one would have heard.

Then her body was moving. She'd taken three quick steps toward Jason when strong, unyielding arms wrapped around her.

Scuffling sounded behind her. So too did Logan's voice. But her entire focus was centered on her brother. He was so close. And yet she couldn't get to him.

The arms around her were like bands of steel. Preventing her from going where she so desperately needed to be.

A screeching filled the air. It took Sage a moment to realize the sound was coming from her.

Jason was now on his feet. So much bigger and stronger than she remembered, his face black and blue with bruises. His fists banged against the glass.

It was as if she had tunnel vision. All she could see was Jason. She needed to get to him.

"Sage! Stop!" Jason yelled.

And just like that, she stopped struggling. The shrieking sounds came to a halt. Her chaotic breaths were the only sounds in the room.

"Don't fight them."

She wanted to go against what he was telling her to do. But she couldn't.

As her breaths began to settle, reality seeped in. She had to focus on where she was. The company that surrounded her.

Jason's eyes moved to someone behind her. His eyes were black with anger. So much more anger than she'd ever seen in him before. The man was almost unrecognizable.

"Why have you brought her here?"

Hylar's voice sounded behind her. "She wanted to see you, Jason. And she has valuable information. It's a win-win all around."

If possible, Jason's eyes turned deadlier. "What information?"

This time, Sage forced her eyes away from her brother and turned to look at the man who seemed to be in charge.

"Come on, Jason. You know we watch your family. That's why you've been so scared, isn't it? You knew that she would search for you and land herself right in the middle of all of this."

Jason didn't say anything, but his gaze flicked to Sage. Questioning.

"She took a job caring for another team of mine," Hylar continued.

His team? Who was this man?

"So, naturally, we took it upon ourselves to get closer to her. We pretended to be *you*, Jason. We kept in contact with her. That was after we took your phone and laptop and used them to learn key information that would make your sister believe it was *you* she was messaging."

When Hylar said those words, Sage had to look away. She should have known it wasn't her brother. She hadn't.

"Why?" Jason growled.

Hylar took a small step closer to the cage. "Because, just like you, the men she's been looking after are valuable. And there was always the chance that one day, she would be needed." Hylar turned his attention to Sage, and she wanted to shrink back. "And we were right, weren't we, Dr. Porter?"

Swallowing, she forced her voice to work. "What do you need from me?"

"I think you know the answer to that. We want to know everything that you know about that baby's biological makeup. We could pursue the baby himself but he's very heavily protected. And it would start a war. We don't want to do that until we're ready. So we need you to tell us what the kid's DNA looks like. Are these men capable of fathering the next generation of soldiers?"

Nausea hit Sage like a tidal wave. He spoke about the men as if they were tools in his war. Objects that he could use as he wished, rather than living, breathing human beings.

"You've made the process quite difficult," Hylar continued. "But, you're here now. We will require you to provide us with all the information you have. Then you can join our team. You may be aware that we've lost a couple of our doctors. We're in the market for a new brilliant mind."

There was no way Sage would ever work for the man in front of her. For the organization he had built. But she knew that he wasn't asking. So where did that leave them?

"And if I refuse?"

That same sick smile pulled across Hylar's lips. Like he knew something bad was coming and he was almost excited about it. "There is no way out of this, Dr. Porter. If you refuse, it becomes a lot harder for you. But the result will be the same."

The room suddenly felt colder. Her heart rate pulsated wildly.

She tried to hide the fear as best she could. Surely, the worst they could do was kill her. They wouldn't kill her brother or Mason.

"Harder how?" She hated that her voice trembled.

"I'm glad you asked. You will be placed in a cage until you agree to give us the information we need."

A cage didn't sound so bad. Not compared to the terrifying forms of torture that had been racing through her mind.

Then Hylar continued. "Oh, but you won't be alone in this cage. You'll be with one of my men. And he'll be on Toved."

Sage swallowed hard as she heard Jason's fists begin to pound the glass. She even heard Logan fighting the guards behind her.

Hylar tilted his head to the side. "You've heard of it, haven't you? It's a drug that makes men so angry they want to tear apart anyone nearby. Bones may be broken. Shattered even. You'll be begging us to save you. And then, you'll share whatever information we request."

He took a step closer. She could feel that he hadn't told her the worst part yet.

"The man in the cage with you will hurt you, maybe even kill you, unless you tell us what we want to know. Destroying you will destroy *him*. Because that man will be your brother."

CHAPTER 27

*M*ason tried to relax, but it was damn hard when fury ran through his blood. Fury and fear. Fear that he would be too late. Fear that he would lose her.

Even thinking it made his heart hurt. He'd just found Sage. No way could he lose her now.

Luca shot a glance at Mason from the driver's seat. "We're not going to be too late. So get that thought out of your damn head."

Mason sat in the passenger seat while Wyatt was in the back. Fortunately, the rest of the team had made quick work of collecting what they needed from Marble Protection. They wouldn't be far behind.

Evie had called not long ago to say that the signal to Logan's GPS had cut out in Valley Spring. That meant one of two things. Either he'd entered a location with no signal, or the device had been destroyed.

He was hoping that once they got to Logan's last recorded location, there would be clues. Anything that might tell them where he had gone.

Then they just had to pray that Sage was with him.

A muscle ticked in Mason's jaw. "If they lay a fucking hand on her—"

"Then we make them pay."

Mason swung his gaze to Luca. His friend knew what it felt like to almost lose the woman he loved. He got it.

The car came to a stop on a side street. The moment Mason stepped outside, disappointment hit him. All he could see was grass and trees. There didn't seem to be a building for miles. They were in the middle of nowhere, dammit.

Wyatt had his phone in front of him and indicated away from the road with his head. "It's this way."

Mason and Luca jogged behind. As the three of them moved, Mason's unease just increased. There was nothing. Nothing but forested land.

When Wyatt came to a stop, frustration marred his expression. And Mason knew this was it. This was the last location.

"Is this it?" Luca asked.

Wyatt nodded. "Let's search the perimeter."

Five minutes later, they'd found nothing. Not even a footprint. If someone had been here, there would have been evidence. A snapped branch. Anything.

Mason wanted to punch something. Every minute that passed was another minute she was with *them*.

Footsteps behind them warned that people were coming. They turned to see Eden, Bodie, Kye, and Oliver step through the trees.

While the guys handed over some weapons, Wyatt hit dial on his phone.

Evie answered on the first ring. "Did you find anything?"

Wyatt scanned the area with his eyes. "Nothing. No signs that anyone's been here recently."

"No! That doesn't make sense. The signal definitely cut out there. If they were never there, then—" Evie cut off midsentence and there was a beat of silence.

Luca stepped forward. "Evie?"

"I just had an idea. Give me a second."

Mason had to clench his fists to stop from yanking the phone from Wyatt's fingers. They didn't have a second. They didn't have *any* time to spare.

A small gasp sounded through the line before Evie spoke. "There's an old tunnel system. It was used as a command center and raid shelter about fifty years ago by the Navy. It's directly below where you're standing."

Mason's gaze darted around. "Where's the entrance point?"

"I'm sending it to you now."

All seven men had their eyes glued on the phone as the location came through.

∾

CHAOS. It filled the room. Jason was yelling and hitting the glass of his cage. Logan was fighting the guards behind her. The room reeked of violence and rage.

But among it all, Hylar remained still. Watching her. Waiting for her to decide.

She couldn't speak. Her voice was gone. The moment she refused his request, her brother would be drugged, and she would be thrown into the cage with him.

Then Jason would likely turn into an enemy. A deadly enemy.

Hylar raised a brow. "Ticktock, Sage. What's it going to be? Give me the information I want, work with our organization, or force yourself and your brother into an impossible situation."

Hylar thought she was going to crack eventually. But the problem was, there was no way she could ever do what he was asking. If she didn't give in to their request, would they let Jason kill her?

"Imagine what it will do to Jason," Hylar said softly, "when he wakes up and realizes what he's done. You can save him. Tell me about the boy. Join my team."

It would destroy Jason. But for once, she didn't think she could save him. Because saving him meant danger for so many others.

When Sage remained silent, the smile slipped from Hylar's lips. "Very well." He turned to one of his guards. "Do it."

As soon as the words left his mouth, the energy in the room shifted. Jason stopped pounding and swung his head around. His eyes were black with rage as the door to his cage was opened.

Immediately, Sage knew what was about to happen. She lunged forward. Desperate to stop it.

Unbreakable arms wrapped around her once again. At the same time, Jason threw his body at the guard. Before he could make contact, the man shot what looked like a dart into Jason's midsection. Her brother fell to the floor with a thud.

Sage turned her attention back to Hylar. "What did you do to him?"

"It was just a little tranquilizer. What he's receiving *now* is what you should be concerned about."

Sage watched as the guard moved toward Jason and injected something into his arm. At the same time, the man holding her dragged her inside the cage.

When the guards left the cell, it was just her and Jason.

Out of instinct, she immediately took a step toward her brother's still form.

"Sage, don't!"

She halted at Logan's warning. Her gaze darted across the room to him. He was being held by three guards.

"Don't touch him. He's dangerous."

Every instinct screamed at her to get closer to her brother. She wanted to feel that he was really there. Check that he was okay.

It was hard for her brain to grasp that he would ever hurt her.

Logan spoke again. "The moment he wakes up, he won't be himself. All he'll feel is rage and he'll want to kill whoever gets close, regardless of who they are."

Blowing out a long breath, Sage took a step back.

Logan was right. She couldn't touch him. Not that a few feet of distance would save her.

When he woke, she'd need to do what she could to convince him that he didn't want to hurt her.

Sage leaned against the wall and slid down. Her eyes remained on Jason. She should be scared. She knew she should. But, while he slept at least, she wasn't.

She inspected his still form, noticing again how much bigger he was. He'd always been muscular. His muscles in combination with his height and intelligence had pulled women from all directions.

But now he was huge. Dangerous.

"Commander Hylar, we found something."

Sage tore her eyes from her brother to look over at the guard. One of the three who were holding Logan had pushed the sleeve of his shirt to his shoulder. The guard was holding a small bandage. The one Sage had applied earlier that day.

They'd found the tracking device.

Some of Hylar's earlier composure slipped as he studied Logan's arm. "What is this?" When Logan didn't immediately answer, Hylar took a step forward and shouted, "I said, what the fuck is this?"

A slow smiled pulled across Logan's lips. Still, he remained silent.

Suddenly, a loud alarm sounded. It was almost deafening.

A guard ran into the room, stopping in front of Hylar. "Commander, the facility has been breached. Explosives were used at the entrance."

Real fear crossed Hylar's face.

Another guard stepped forward. "What should we do, Commander?"

A wild look had come over Hylar's face. "They won't make it... We have too many men they'd have to get through."

Although she was sure Hylar's words were meant to be reassuring to his team, they didn't hold nearly enough confidence to make them effective.

He remained where he was for a moment before quickly moving to one of the computers. The screen was facing toward Sage, so she could see everything as he brought up what looked to be surveillance footage of a dozen areas.

Hylar zoomed into the footage of the hallway.

Sage couldn't hold back the gasp at seeing Mason shoot a man between the eyes. The dead guy hadn't stood a chance.

Beside Mason were Bodie and Eden. They moved down the hall, shooting anyone in sight without hesitation. Without emotion.

The guys moved like machines. With no remorse. Almost no humanity.

When Hylar skipped to other footage, Sage saw Luca, Wyatt, Oliver, and Kye moving in much the same way.

Dead bodies piled up in the men's wake. It wasn't just bullets they were using to kill. They occasionally broke rank, killing guards with knives or hand-to-hand combat.

Every person who tried to stop them ended up dead.

A guard had come to stand beside Hylar. "Fuck. They're good."

"No shit they're good! I trained them myself. And Carter's team is on a fucking mission. They're the only ones with the training to stop them." Hylar was no longer attempting to hide his fear. It was bleeding out of him.

Out of the corner of her eye, Sage caught movement. She turned her head to see Jason's entire body twitch.

Crap. He was waking.

"We have to stop them from getting in here. If they free these guys..." The guard indicated to the cages with his head. He seemed just as panicked as Hylar.

They clearly weren't expecting the location to be breached. Not today, anyway.

A loud explosion sounded, causing her ears to ring. The floor vibrated.

Sage looked back to the camera to see fire spread through one of the rooms. It was a room some of Hylar's men had just flocked to.

Hylar began moving. "We can't stop them. They're going to breach this room. We need to leave. *Now*. You three, stay and keep Logan secure."

She wasn't entirely sure where the man intended to go. He was walking in the opposite direction from where they'd entered the room. There were no other exits that she could see.

One of the guards restraining Logan stepped forward. "But sir—"

"That's an order!" Hylar paused to shout the words before continuing. Then he placed his hand on a rectangular screen on the wall. A door, which had been invisible a moment ago, slid open.

Of course. A biometric lock for a hidden door. A way out in case his facility was ever uncovered and infiltrated.

The scientists scrambled to fill boxes with materials. Then Hylar slipped through, trailed by most of his team and the scientists, the door sliding shut behind them.

She looked back to Logan to see him no longer fighting. Before Sage could feel any relief, a grunt came from Jason. Looking over, she saw his big body twitch again.

A pang of fear shot through her. He wasn't far off waking.

Jason twitched again, and a deep growl emanated from his chest. The growl reminded Sage of a wild animal. She'd never heard him make that sound in her life. She'd never heard *any* human make that sound.

It made her stomach churn. She pushed farther back against the wall.

"Sage!"

At the sound his voice, air whooshed from her body.

Mason.

Sage stood and was about to run to the glass when more movement across the room rendered her still.

Jason was now on his feet, facing away from her. Both his hands were pressed against the wall and his back was heaving. Almost like he was trying to control his breaths.

"Get. Her. Out!" Jason sounded like a stranger. The words seemed to have been torn from his chest.

Another explosion sounded, with more floor movement. At the same time, Mason began to bang on the glass, seemingly testing its strength.

She knew it would be no use. If Jason and his team were kept inside these cages, then they were unbreakable, even for Mason.

Jason swung his body around, then he straightened. His breaths remained deep. His entire face was pulled into a scowl. Everything about him looked furious and terrifying.

Her breath stopped and her heart galloped. There was a deafening alarm and explosions and gunshots all around her. A war being fought. Yet her sole focus was on the man opposite her.

Every instinct in her body screamed at her to go. Run. Escape the threat. But there was nowhere to go. The cage was locked. It was just her and Jason unless Mason figured out a way to get in.

Sage had never felt such terror in her life. It was all-consuming. And it made every coherent thought or action impossible.

Jason took a step toward her. He reminded her of a lion on the hunt, creeping toward his prey. Which was what Sage was—his prey.

"Someone bring over one of the guards. The door's code activated!"

She was sure that was Mason's voice from the other side of the glass. He sounded scared. Sage wished she had the courage to turn and look at him. But there was no way she could draw her eyes away from the threat in front of her.

Jason now stood less than two feet away. Reaching distance.

Before she could blink, he swung out and punched her in the shoulder.

Her body flew through the air and she hit the wall with a loud thud before dropping to the floor.

Her body hurt. Throbbed from each point of impact. But she didn't groan, didn't make a sound. She attempted to roll to her back.

Partway, a foot collided with her ribs.

Her breath was stolen. She bounced into the air before dropping back to the floor.

The doctor in her knew that something was broken. The crack had been loud enough for her to hear. Pain cascaded through her ribs.

"Talk to him, Sage!"

In the midst of her fear and pain, she heard the voice of someone in the background. Eden, maybe? He sounded out of breath. Like he was fighting someone.

"Sage. Sweetheart. Listen to my voice." Was that Mason? He wanted her to listen. Oh gosh, it was hard. But she'd try. "That's Jason in front of you. Your brother. You need to talk to him. Talk him down."

Talk to him. Mason wanted her to talk to Jason. Because it *was* Jason standing over her. Not some wild animal. Not an unknown threat.

Rough hands latched on to Sage's shoulders, lifted her body and throwing her against the far wall. Her head collided with the hard surface and she fell to the floor again.

A dizziness clouded her mind and wetness dripped onto the side of her face.

Blood. She was bleeding.

"Sage, please! Talk to him."

Mason sounded desperate. He wanted her to talk to her brother. She could do that. She'd been wanting to talk to him for years. And he was here now. In front of her.

"Jason." The voice didn't sound like it belonged to her. "I've missed you."

She saw the blurry outline of a boot in front of her, but it was unmoving.

"I've wanted to talk to you every single day. And hear you speak back. I just wanted to hear your voice for a moment. It wouldn't even have mattered what you said."

Jason grabbed her shoulders and lifted her. She was pushed against the wall hard. Her feet no longer touched the floor. His fingers bruised her with their punishing grip.

Tears began to fill Sage's eyes. Pain rippled through her body, both physical and emotional.

"But you were never there, Jason. Even when I needed you. I guess that's fair, though. You were here. In your own hell. And I wasn't there for you."

She watched Jason. Wanting to see his face as she spoke to him. Even if it wasn't the real Jason.

She saw the anger. The rage. But below that, there was just a hint of the old Jason.

She lowered her voice as a tear trickled down her cheek. "If you kill me...I forgive you."

Something changed in Jason's expression. His hands dropped and she hit the floor. Instead of moving forward, he quickly turned away. He walked to the opposite wall and threw a fist at it. Then another.

"Get her away from me!" Jason yelled the words so loudly that Sage's ears rang.

She struggled to hold up her body weight. The outside world was slipping.

Sage sagged back to the floor. When she opened her eyes, the room was a blur.

She thought she heard the glass door opening, but she couldn't be sure. There was movement in the room. New noises around her.

Maybe Mason would save her. Maybe he wouldn't. But at least, after years in captivity, her brother would finally be free.

CHAPTER 28

*M*ason watched the rise and fall of Sage's chest. She looked so small in the hospital bed. After witnessing her almost get beaten to death by her brother, he *needed* to watch her, to remind himself that she was alive.

Never in his life had he felt so damn helpless as when he'd watched her from the other side of that glass. It had taken too long to get to her.

Detaining the guards had been the easy part. Forcing one of them to key in the code had been harder. It had taken time. Too much damn time.

When they were finally in, Eden had taken Jason and he'd taken Sage. She'd been so still. He would never forget her still, slumped body lying on the floor.

The only thing that had saved Mason from losing his mind was the soft beating of her heart. She was alive. And he'd had to remain calm and get her medical attention.

Mason held her hand in his. He needed to touch her. Keep her close.

Two broken ribs, a lot of bruising, and a concussion with stitches at the back of the head. That was her list of injuries.

It was the concussion the doctors were most concerned about. She hadn't suffered her previous concussion that long ago, which made her at risk of brain swelling. Fortunately, after several scans, she seemed okay. But it was important that she was closely monitored.

A twitch of Sage's fingers had Mason drawing his eyes up to her face.

Was it possible she was waking? The medical staff had warned him that she could sleep for days.

A small frown marred Sage's brow. Then she lightly scrunched her eyes.

Mason firmed his hold on her hand.

That's it, sweetheart, open those beautiful eyes.

He'd been waiting almost twenty-four hours to see them. Twenty-four agonizing hours.

When her blue eyes finally slid open, Mason blew out a long breath.

Her gaze went to him and there was confusion on her face. Then recognition. Then panic.

Mason leaned close and spoke gently. "You're okay, sweetheart. We're at Marble Falls Hospital. You're safe."

Some of the panic lessened but didn't fade completely. "Jason?"

A small smile spread across Mason's lips. He knew his next words were the ones she'd been waiting to hear for so long. "He's safe. And he's here in Marble Falls."

Her eyes became misty, then closed. He watched as tears slid down her cheeks. "Thank you."

Reaching over, he caught one of her tears with his thumb. "Why are you thanking me?"

She opened her eyes to look at him with both relief and gratitude. "Because you saved us. If you hadn't come, I would be dead. And once Jason discovered what he did, it would have devastated him."

Mason didn't even want to think about the what-ifs of it all. There had been too much at stake.

"I'll always come for you, Sage. But you saved yourself just as much as I did. Jason's team told us what happened. You were strong and brave to go against what Hylar wanted. And even though you were terrified, you spoke to Jason. Talked him down."

Sage swallowed, a ghost of a smile tugging at her lips.

Lowering his head, he pressed a kiss to her lips. Damn, he loved this woman. And he never wanted to come close to losing her again.

When his head lifted, he saw her mind working before she spoke. "Did you catch that man Hylar?"

The muscles in his jaw tightened at the mention of his old commander. It was infuriating how close they always seemed to get to catching him, without ever getting close enough. "He was gone by the time we got there."

"He escaped along with everyone who had been in the room with him, except those guys holding down Logan. They went through a door that required his handprint for access."

It had been that damn door that had saved the commander. It only opened with *his* handprint. The asshole would have built it knowing it was his escape if the place was ever breached.

"Logan and his team told us. We were too late. We couldn't get through the door. But there'll be other opportunities."

While Mason had taken Sage to the hospital, his team had freed Logan's team. The men had then worked together to raid the rest of the facility. They'd either killed or secured every man who worked for the commander.

Unfortunately, during that time, Hylar had disappeared through the tunnels.

But there were a couple of positives to come out of it. The first was that they'd found prisoners. Men who'd been kept in cages and were now free. There could be other prisoners kept in homes around the country, like the one Logan was kept in, but at least some were free.

The second positive was that Hylar was now significantly disadvantaged. His main base was shut down. He'd had close to a hundred men working for him in that facility. Most of whom were now dead. Those who survived were behind bars.

Hylar's resources would be limited.

Asher had stayed behind to keep the women and Fletcher safe. He'd been the one to call the CIA once Mason and Logan's team had completed the raid.

Agent Sinclair hadn't been happy about not being notified earlier, but Wyatt explained how quickly everything had moved.

Turning her hand around, Sage weaved her fingers through his. "I heard them refer to him as Commander Hylar. Was he your commander?"

"Yes. He trained our team. Signed us up for the project. We found out a couple of months ago that he actually created Project Arma."

There was no way Sage would miss the resentment and anger in his voice. They were emotions his whole team struggled with.

She squeezed his hand. "I'm sorry. He won't be able to run and hide forever, though."

Was she trying to reassure him? After *she* was the one who'd almost died?

Mason shook his head. "You're incredible."

A full smile curved her lips. He'd been wanting to see that smile for too long. "Only because I have you by my side."

SAGE TRIED NOT to fidget as she sat on Mason's couch, but boy was it hard.

Her brother was due to arrive at any moment. She was

nervous. And excited. And her stomach felt like it was doing flips every two seconds.

A whole week had passed since the incident in Valley Spring. Since then, she had begged anyone who would listen to take her to see Jason. If she'd had his address, she would have gone on her own.

To Mason's credit, he had looked apologetic each time he'd said no. Well, not no. Just not yet. He would then go on about how she needed more time to recover from the concussion.

Sage was a doctor. She knew a head injury wasn't something to mess around with. Rest was important. And seeing Jason wouldn't be restful. It would be emotional and nerve-racking and momentous.

But just because she understood the reasoning behind something didn't mean her heart would just accept it.

The knock on the door had Sage almost jolting off the couch.

That was him. It had to be. Her nerves kicked up a notch.

Mason entered the room from the kitchen. She'd banished him there after the hundredth time he'd told her to relax.

Instead of going to the front door like she expected, Mason went to her. He took her hands in his and pulled her to her feet. Her unsteady, might-fall-out-from-under-her feet. Sage gripped his warm hands like they were a lifeline.

He squeezed her fingers. "Enjoy your time with your brother. I'll stay out back. Call if you need me."

Then, leaning down, he placed a light kiss to her temple before disappearing.

A few seconds passed while Sage took some calming breaths. She had to make her uncooperative feet work. Her feet that felt like they weighed a million tons and were glued to the floor.

Sage forced one foot to move forward. Then the other. Eventually, she stood in front of the door. The door with Jason standing on the other side.

With a trembling hand, she placed it on the knob and turned. The moment the door swung open, her breath caught.

Jason. Her twin brother. Her best friend and all-time protector.

Sage stood there and took him in. She took in his shoulders that had almost doubled in width. His thick arms that could probably lift a car.

She left his face for last. When she finally looked up into his eyes, they were harder, but they were Jason's.

He wasn't smiling. "I can wait in the car if my being here frightens you."

He thought she was frightened of him? Other than when she was with Mason, there was no one in the world she felt safer with.

Jason took a step back, causing Sage to pull herself out of her state of stillness. Propelling her body forward, she wrapped her arms around her brother's middle.

Pain shot through her broken ribs from lifting her arms, but she didn't care. Oh god, how she'd missed him. He smelled just like he used to. Like home.

"I missed you." Her words were muffled by his clothing.

Jason was slow to react. But when he did, he wrapped his big arms around her. The hug was everything she'd been missing. Warm. Protective. Familiar.

"You have no idea, sis."

They stood there for who knew how long, just grateful that the other person was really there. There was no part of Sage that wanted to separate.

But as much as she wanted to stay wrapped in the arms of her brother, she also wanted to look at him. Hear his voice. Listen to his laugh.

Slowly, Sage took a step back. They went into the living room and sat side by side on the sofa.

"Thank you."

She frowned at Jason's words. She had no idea why he was thanking her. She should be apologizing for not figuring out he'd been taken earlier. "I didn't do anything."

Jason cocked his head to the side. "So, you didn't spend the last two years worrying about me? Messaging and trying to convince me to return home? You haven't been lying to Mom and Dad to save their health while working with the survivors of Project Arma?"

Sage breathed out a shaky breath. She wasn't sure if it had been Mason or Logan who had told him all that, but she didn't care. "I thought you were safe. Hiding, but safe. I didn't know..."

Jason reached a hand across and wrapped it around hers. "You knew what they wanted you to know. And you did everything you could to help me. Thank you."

"Thank *you*. For surviving."

Jason smiled. But there were shadows on his face. He'd grown harder. "There wasn't a chance I was going to let them keep me."

"Are you okay?" Sage wanted to pull the words back as soon as they left her mouth. What a dumb question. Of course he wasn't okay.

"Contrary to the doom and gloom that I know is going through your mind right now, I'm okay. The only time I was placed in a cage was for the last couple of weeks. Don't get me wrong, though, I'm damn glad I'm free now."

"Do you know why they took you?"

His jaw clenched. "I made a mistake. I trusted my manager. Told him about my suspicions. I was taken that night."

One mistake, and his whole life had changed. "I'm sorry, Jase."

"It's a mistake I won't be making again."

She understood what he was saying. That trust had been costly and wouldn't be given again lightly. If at all.

"So, what now? Will you try to get another job in pharmaceutical research?"

He was already shaking his head. "I can't go back to that. For now, I'm just going to enjoy my freedom. One of the guys has a daughter a few towns over. He wants to go there, spend some time with her. We'll all go so we can watch each other's backs."

Jason was leaving Marble Falls. Just when she'd gotten him back.

She tried to smile but she knew it didn't reach her eyes.

"Sage, god, you look like you're going to cry. We're not going far. His daughter lives in Lockhart. That's less than a two-hour drive. Close enough so that we can help Mason's team bring down Hylar. Even though his main facility is gone, and he's lost most of his team and resources, the guy is a threat until he's dead." A small smile touched Jason's lips. "Also, Lockhart is close enough to keep an eye on Mason and make sure he treats you right."

Sage couldn't help but chuckle. The disappointment remained, but Jason was right. Lockhart wasn't that far. "You don't need to worry about Mason. He's a good guy."

Jason shrugged. "Seems that way so far. Never hurts to have a brother looking over his shoulder, though."

That was the old Jason she remembered.

"Have you called Mom and Dad?"

Jason ran his hands through his hair. "That's what I've got to do this afternoon. Thanks for covering for me."

"They'll be happy to hear from you."

She could just imagine their reactions. They'd go nuts. She anticipated tears and screaming.

Sage spent the next two hours on the couch with her brother, talking about everything and nothing. From the research she'd done on altered DNA, to the foods he'd been fed and his training over the last two years.

It was nice but over too quickly. Too soon, it was time for Jason to leave.

"I don't want you to go," she said quietly.

"Call anytime and I'll be here."

Well, his phone would be ringing constantly.

They both stood and walked out to his car.

"Nice rental."

She scanned his Nissan Versa, which looked nowhere near large enough for his long legs.

"I know. It was all they had. The government is coming up with a compensation package right now."

Money couldn't buy the last two years of Jason's life back. It couldn't buy back his old life or reverse the drugs he'd been given.

Jason bent down and gave Sage another hug before climbing into his rental. "I don't know when we're leaving yet, so I'll visit again tomorrow. But if you call before that, remember, I'll be here."

"Thanks, Jase. I should be able to wait. But if I don't see you tomorrow, I'm coming to find you." Sage meant every bit of that statement.

Jason laughed and then said a final goodbye. Instead of going back in, she stood and watched the empty street long after he'd driven out of sight.

She felt better than she thought she would. Because Jason had been better than she'd thought he'd be. He didn't seem "damaged" like she'd expected. Or bitter.

Sage knew that these things couldn't always be seen. But she was glad that, for the moment, he was doing okay.

When warm, muscular arms snaked around her waist, Sage smiled and leaned back.

Mason's mouth pressed into her hair before he spoke. "Everything go well?"

"Everything went perfectly."

"I'm glad. You deserve to be happy. Especially because you make me so damn happy."

Her smile widened, then she turned in Mason's arms. "I make you happy, do I?"

"The happiest man on the damn planet."

Without warning, he lowered his hands and lifted her body against his. He was gentle, so as not to jolt her ribs. Sage carefully wrapped her legs around his waist, crossing her feet. "I guess you make me happy, too."

A soft growl sounded from Mason's chest. "Is that so?"

She giggled. "Okay, maybe more than a little happy."

The humor faded from Mason's face. "I love you."

Her heart warmed at his words. "Good. Because I love you. And I don't see that changing. Ever."

Mason turned and walked them inside. Sage heard the door click shut behind them before Mason's lips were on hers.

It was the best kind of kiss. Because it held the promise of forever.

CHAPTER 29

a loud crash sounded from across the hall.

Wyatt's brows drew together as his gaze shifted to the closed door of his apartment.

The crash had been close. It almost sounded like it came from Mason's old apartment. Which was impossible, because Sage had moved out a week ago and the two of them were currently in Lockhart spending time with Jason.

Pushing away from his desk, Wyatt headed across the hall. Sure enough, the door to Mason's apartment stood open. Wide open.

Inspecting the door handle, he noticed it wasn't broken and didn't appear tampered with.

Not that it gave Wyatt any form of comfort. There were other ways to break into an apartment. But then why go through the effort if you were just going to leave the door open?

Shuffling noises sounded from inside. Wyatt could tell from the light steps that it was a woman. That by no means meant that he would drop his guard.

Edging to the door, Wyatt popped his head inside. The apartment was small, with a kitchen to the right and living area straight ahead. One bedroom was to the right of the living room, with another on the left.

What caught his attention were the drops of blood between the kitchen and the bathroom.

Stepping inside, he noticed boxes scattered around the living area. A Stanley knife sat near the boxes and that was clearly where the blood originated.

Either Mason and Sage had left the boxes and were currently being robbed, or someone was moving in.

Wyatt followed the trail of blood to the bathroom. Each step he took was as silent as the last.

When he glanced in, he saw a woman bent over the sink. At that moment, she began to mutter to herself, mostly a string of curse words.

Wyatt studied her. Wavy hair cascaded down her back. It was dark. In contrast to her bright red top, her hair looked almost midnight. And it was long. So long, it nearly reached the top of her butt.

That drew Wyatt's attention to her figure-hugging jeans. And blood rushed to his crotch.

Either this was the best-looking burglar he'd ever seen, or something was going on that he wasn't aware of.

Wyatt stepped inside the room and stood behind her.

When he looked in the mirror, he noticed her cheeks were a rosy pink. Her eyes were downcast, and suddenly, he needed to know what color they were. Were they as dark as midnight, like her hair?

He didn't need to wait long to find out. Suddenly, the woman raised her eyes.

Blue. Deep blue like the ocean.

When her eyes collided with his, she startled so badly, a shriek escaped her lips and she spun around.

Instead of being scared, like he'd expected, angry eyes landed on him. "Holy crap! Who the hell are you and what are you doing inside my apartment?"

"*Your* apartment?"

Her eyes narrowed as they scanned his face. "Look, I know I left the door open, but that wasn't an invitation for any Tom, Dick, or Harry to come in."

Wyatt wanted to chuckle but just stopped himself. "Which would I be?"

Some of the anger faded and her lips twitched. "You tell me."

Damn, she was cute.

He didn't know why the hell she wasn't scared of him. She *should* be. He was big at almost six and a half feet, and wide. He could be a real danger to her.

Instead, she looked like *she* was the one about to attack *him*. Verbally at least.

"You look familiar." The words slipped from Wyatt's mouth. Which was a rare mistake for him. Every word he spoke was usually premeditated. Measured.

This time, her lips didn't twitch, they pulled into a full-blown smile. Fuck, but she was stunning. "And you look both sexy and smart, a combination that is rarely paired together in a man."

She was sassy, too.

When a drip sounded, he glanced down at her hand. He could see she'd wrapped some cloth around it, but blood was seeping through.

"Want me to look at that?"

Her right brow lifted. "Are you a doctor?"

"No, but I've done some training on caring for wounds."

She seemed to consider his words for a moment, and he thought she'd say no. Most rational people *would* say no in her situation.

But then she began unwrapping the material and showed him the injury. The slice across her palm was decent, but he didn't think it looked bad enough to require stitches.

Wyatt took her hand in his, dwarfing it. She was tall for a woman, maybe five-ten. But nowhere near his height.

The moment he touched her, a zing ran through his arm. What the hell was going on? The woman was a stranger.

"I have a first-aid kit at my place across the hall if you want to pop over. I don't think this hand towel is going to cut it."

"Already inviting me to your place?" There was teasing behind her words before she shrugged. "Sure."

Wyatt almost wanted to growl at the woman. She clearly had no survival skills. She didn't know him from a bar of soap, and she was just going to follow him to his apartment?

But then, it wasn't his place to lecture her.

"This way."

When he walked through the living area, he subtly scanned the room. Not much had been unpacked except for a laptop, which sat on the counter. It was open and the screen displayed an email browser.

Interesting. So, one of the first things she'd done upon entering was jump on her computer.

When they got to his place, he held the door open and waited as she walked inside. "Do you always take offers to enter the homes of strangers? You don't even know my name."

A twinkle entered her eye as she looked over her shoulder. "Only strangers who look like you."

Wyatt chuckled as he headed down the hall to grab his first-aid kit. His apartment wasn't large. A bedroom, an office, and a bathroom were all to the left down the hall, while the front door opened directly to the kitchen and living area.

He didn't need much space. He wasn't home that often and when he was, he was on his computer.

When he returned to the living area, she studied the kit in his hands.

"That's a heck of a large first-aid kit for an average Joe."

This was actually only a small part of Wyatt's first-aid supplies. But he'd keep that tidbit to himself.

When she thought he wasn't watching, he caught her studying the space. Taking it all in. She had intelligent eyes. He could almost see her mind ticking.

That was probably why he was already drawn to the woman. Intelligence and confidence.

Sitting on the couch, he gestured for her to sit beside him. Then he took her hand again, enjoying the same zing that went through his system at the touch.

Wyatt swiped an antiseptic wipe across the wound. "Did you cut yourself with that Stanley knife that was lying on the floor?"

She tilted her head to the side. "You saw that? Alas, you're correct. I was rushing and got careless. Hence the cut."

Wyatt took his eyes off the wound for a moment to look at her face. "Why were you rushing? Got a job to get to?"

There was the tiniest jolt of her hand. So subtle most would have missed it. Wyatt didn't.

"Not that you need to know this, being a stranger and all, but I'm not working at the moment. I'm taking a break from my job."

There was a slight hitch in her breath as she spoke the last words. Her heart also accelerated.

Interesting. There was something that made her uneasy about her job.

"New in town with no job. You're quite a mystery."

"How do you know I'm new in town?"

"Because you are."

She didn't respond. Wyatt didn't know whether she was pleased by his comment or not. If he was being honest with himself, he was having trouble reading the woman. Which was unusual for him.

He began to wrap the wound with a bandage. "This should do. You might want to see a doctor, just in case."

"I'll keep an eye on it. Thanks for breaking into my place and offering to help a stranger."

Taping the end of the bandage, Wyatt reluctantly let go of her hand. "Technically it's not breaking in if the door is wide open. But how about we fix that whole stranger thing and you give me a name?"

A playful expression fell across her face. "How about instead of a name, I give you something else?"

What she did next surprised the hell out of him. The woman leaned forward and pressed her lips to his.

He was almost certain she'd intended to give him a quick peck. But the moment her lips touched his, he leaned into the kiss. As if his hand had a mind of its own, it went to the back of her head and swept through her black curls.

Her lips were soft and evoked sensations that were completely new to him. Rather than pull away, she sank into him. The soft pressure of her breasts against his chest had his blood pumping.

Then, just as quickly as the kiss had started, she stiffened and pulled away. Wyatt let go immediately.

When he searched her gaze, he saw shock. Likely, shock at their connection. It was damn electric.

Wyatt wasn't shocked. He'd felt something the moment he'd laid eyes on her. It sounded crazy, but he didn't care.

She tried to mask her emotions with a smile. "See, that was better than a name, wasn't it?"

Before he could respond, she stood and walked to the door. Then she disappeared across the hall without a backward glance.

Wyatt watched her leave, considering her words.

The thing was, he didn't need a name. He knew exactly who she was. He'd figured it out within the first five minutes of meeting her.

Quinn Ross. Mason's younger sister. The journalist from New York.

Even though he'd known who she was, he'd let her kiss him anyway. And he'd kissed her back.

There was the possibility that he was a dead man. At least, dead if Mason found out.

But for a kiss like that, he would die a happy man a hundred times over.

Order Wyatt today!

ALSO BY NYSSA KATHRYN

PROJECT ARMA SERIES
(Series Ongoing)

Uncovering Project Arma
Luca
Eden
Asher
Mason
Wyatt

JOIN my newsletter and be the first to find out about sales and
new releases!

ABOUT THE AUTHOR

Nyssa Kathryn is a romantic suspense author. She lives in South Australia with her daughter and hubby and takes every chance she can to be plotting and writing. Always an avid reader of romance novels, she considers alpha males and happily-ever-afters to be her jam.

Don't forget to follow Nyssa and never miss another release.

Facebook | Instagram | Amazon | Goodreads

CPSIA information can be obtained
at www.ICGtesting.com
Printed in the USA
LVHW032037110221
679036LV00001B/126

9 780648 946236